1

High winds howled and rattled the shutters of the coastal, two-story home nestled in the cul-de-sac. Large tree limbs surrendered to the gusts and snapped like twigs used for kindling. Oakview, Texas was poised on the edge of the Gulf and had been through this before, except that Hurricane Edward was stronger than anyone anticipated.

From inside the home, the child whose dark hair clung to tears on her cheeks, trembled. With watery brown eyes, she gazed up at her father. "Daddy, why can't we leave?"

The father returned her stare, noting the beads of sweat on her brow and the terror in her eyes. "I'm sorry, baby. It's too late to go now. I waited too long." He looked through the living room window at the rising waters filling the streets. Cars floated and crashed against each other like a strange version of bumper cars.

"Everyone's already gone." The girl's mother spoke as she pulled her daughter close. "We'll have to wait for rescue." She looked at her husband. "It's time to go upstairs."

With his hand extended, the man grasped his daughter and

wife as they hurried up the staircase to higher ground. There were no signs of the storm letting up. The last news report stated 45 inches had already fallen. It was almost as bad as Hurricane Harvey had been when some areas saw 50 inches fall. The worst part was that the eye hadn't reached land yet.

The young family entered the daughter's room which overlooked the street.

"I need to see how bad it is from up here." He rushed to the window. "Dear Lord in Heaven."

The live oak tree with its broad canopy that shaded the house for the past twenty years fought back against the relentless winds. It wasn't until the pop of splintering wood sounded that it became clear the tree was no match.

"No. No." The father's hands pressed against the window in disbelief as he watched the old tree whip and slash inside the storm.

"Get away from the window, Ron. Get away!" the mother shouted.

The ground split open. The roots broke free.

"Holy hell. It's coming down!" He pulled away and thrust himself in front of his family. With his back to the window, he wrapped his arms around them.

The girl screamed. The mother cried.

A booming crash erupted when the tree slammed into the house. Glass flew and branches pushed inside with such force that the entire home shuddered on the verge of collapse.

When the great live oak landed, there were no more screams.

Evacuation orders had been dispatched in the early morning hours on this October day. The mayor waited too long. Everyone with any authority waited too long and now countless Oakview residents were in danger. For some, it was already too late.

EDGE OF MERCY

A KATE REID NOVEL
BOOK 11

ROBIN MAHLE

HARP HOUSE PUBLISHING, LLC.

Published by HARP House Publishing
March 2020 (1st edition)

OAKVIEW HIGH SCHOOL, home of the Panthers, was now a makeshift command center and shelter for the residents. Inside the gymnasium, cots were set up, and folding tables were placed around the perimeter. Most of the tables had food and water waiting. Residents, those few who had enough time to leave, waited for the Sheriff to speak.

The stocky, middle-aged sheriff wore a brown uniform and hat, and approached the podium. Next to him stood a man in stark contrast. Slim, with pressed khaki pants, a red polo shirt, and a black FEMA windbreaker.

"Afternoon," the sheriff began. "This here's the assistant director for FEMA, Mr. Jake Landry, and we've just briefed him on the current situation. Now as y'all are aware, we still have lots of folks out there in the middle of this God-forsaken storm. Folks who are in some pretty dire straits right about now. So, with the help of our FEMA agents who have just arrived, along with my team and the rest of the first responders, it's time we ready our teams to get out there and find our people. Get them to safety." He looked at the assistant director. "Mr. Landry, I'll leave it to you to set up the teams headed by your Emergency Management Specialists. Let's get out there and find the good people of this community while there's still light."

"Thank you, Sheriff." Landry stepped up to the podium. "We'll have ten teams at first and once the storm subsides enough, we'll round up additional help. But the longer we wait, the worse the situation is going to get for those trapped in their homes. So, I'll shut up now and we'll gather up our resources and get moving."

FEMA's specialists were dotted around the room and recruited first responders and volunteers with similar experience.

"We need teams of five," the man in the windbreaker began.

"Any firefighters, officers, medical workers. These are the people we'll need."

A few men gathered near. Two were from the sheriff's department and one was a volunteer firefighter.

The specialist nodded. "Good. Thank you. Anyone else?" He looked around as others had gathered their teams. "I'll consider anyone with any relevant experience. Time's a wasting, people. We don't have much daylight out there and it's only going to get harder when the sun goes down."

"I'm an EMT." A man in his mid-thirties raised his hand and approached.

"An EMT? Perfect," the specialist replied. "What's your name?"

"Dr. Theodore Bishop."

"Doctor?"

"Yes, sir. Not currently practicing. Just a tech." Dr. Bishop shook his head to rearrange the jet-black hair from his face and pursed his thin lips. With his hands shoved in the pockets of his slim-fitting jeans, he moved in. "I can help with any medical situations and I stay pretty fit, so I can do some heavy lifting too, if necessary."

The specialist eyeballed him. "You're in. You'll be in charge of the medical kit. Can you handle that?"

Bishop nodded. "I can."

"Then let's roll out, folks." The FEMA specialist led the way outside the school gym and, in the downpour, turned to his team. "We'll be taking the southeast quadrant of the community. Lots of people still unaccounted for, so let's go help them." He stepped into the driver's side of a four-wheel drive, three-quarter ton pickup truck specially equipped with KC lights and a winch.

The others piled in, with Bishop as the last one to enter. He slid onto the leather-wrapped backseat and wiped the rain from his smooth face. Looking through the rear passenger window, his brown eyes narrowed, and he inhaled a deep breath through a pointed nose.

The truck's engine roared and the wipers were set on high but were barely able to keep up with the pounding rain.

"I gotta take it slow so we don't end up in trouble ourselves, but with fingers crossed, and butt-cheeks clenched, we should be there inside of thirty minutes." The FEMA specialist pressed lightly on the gas pedal and started onto the main road.

"Looks like a river out there," Bishop said.

The man next to him was an Oakview police officer and glanced out. "Sure as hell does. Cripes, I hope our efforts aren't in vain. So, you're a doctor working on the trucks?"

"What's that?" Bishop turned to him.

"You know, the ambulance trucks."

"Oh. Yeah," he replied.

"I'm with the Oakview P.D. Been on the force going on three years now. I'll tell you one thing, I never seen it this bad and I grew up around here. Not far from it, anyway. What about you? You from around here?" He offered his hand. "Dean Redmond. Sorry we couldn't meet under better circumstances."

Bishop took his hand. "Pleasure."

"So?" Redmond pressed on. "Where you from, man?"

"Louisiana. Call came in you all needed some help. A bunch of us came over to offer a hand."

"Well, we sure are glad you answered that call, Dr. Bishop. Is it still doctor? You know, since you don't have a practice or nothing."

Bishop revealed a close-lipped smile. "Still a doctor, but you can call me Theo."

The man from FEMA peered into the rearview. "This is it, fellas. We're stopping here and we'll take the boats out." He shoved the gear stick into park and cut the engine, leaving on the headlights. "Those clouds are dark as shit. Time to light it up around here." He switched on the KC lights at what lay ahead. "Jesus, would you look at that?"

Street signs were just above water in an area that looked like a lake. Only about two feet of the homes' front doors remained visible. Everything below had disappeared.

"What's the plan, sir?" Bishop asked.

"We'll divide up. Three in one boat, two in the other, and start searching the homes." He had parked on the highest point of a bridge above a creek that threatened to spill over. Eyeing the neighborhood below, he inhaled a deep breath. "I could use a hand over here, boys." He walked to the rear of the truck where a trailer had been hitched that hauled two small boats with outboard engines, both labeled "FEMA" on the sides.

The others assisted in unloading the boats and the teams were formed. Bishop rode with his new-found friend, Officer Dean Redmond from Oakview PD, and another man who had been a firefighter in the same small town. The other boat carried the FEMA specialist and another first responder.

Bishop sat in the front with the firefighter while Redmond took control. He peered up at the darkened sky as flashes of lightning scattered across it in attempt to rip apart the heavens. His hooded weatherproof jacket was helpless in shielding him from the wind-driven rains. He noticed the other rescue boat ahead of theirs slow down, and then the men jumped out.

"Here." The FEMA officer pointed to a house in front of him. "You go there." His voice carried above the winds and reached Bishop and his team.

"You heard him, fellas." Redmond cut the engine and hopped out into the rising waters. "Let's get inside and see what we can see."

Theo Bishop, who scarcely reached 5 feet 10, trailed the other two men with the medical kit under his arm, squeezing it for dear life.

They reached the home and swam below through a shattered window until their heads popped above the water again. A couch floated by, then a dining chair and several prescription bottles. Bishop looked at Redmond. "Who lives here?"

"Hell if I know. Best place to look is upstairs. Let's move." Redmond sloshed up the staircase. "Hello? It's the Oakview Police. Anyone here? Anyone hurt?" he shouted.

Bishop was close behind while the other man trailed farther down. "Hello? Anyone here?" His head whipped around to a bedroom at the end of the corridor. "Did you hear that?"

"I heard it." Redmond pushed the rest of the way up and reached the landing. "Oakview Police. We're here to help."

The voices sounded again. They were frail and barely audible. "In here." It was a woman's voice.

"This way!" Redmond rushed to the bedroom. "Oh no." He spotted an elderly couple tucked into a corner of the room. "Are you both okay? I'm Officer Redmond. We're going to get you out of here, all right?"

The woman nodded. "He needs his pills."

"Bishop!" Redmond yelled. "I need your help in here!"

Bishop ran toward them. "I'm here. I'm here."

"He needs some kind of medication..." Redmond was stopped short when another voice sounded. "Who else is in here?"

"Our granddaughter. Please, you have to help her," the woman said.

"Okay. Bishop, I'll take Nunes and go find the girl," Redmond began. "You see what this man needs. Then, I'll bring around the boat and we'll take them from the second-story roof. You got it?"

Bishop nodded. "Got it."

Redmond patted him on the back as he started toward the fire-fighter. "Nunes, there's a girl here. We need to find her. Bishop's taking care of them."

They disappeared while Bishop unzipped the medical bag. "What does your husband take, ma'am?"

"It's his kidneys. He's got high blood pressure because of it and needs his pills." She peered at her husband. "Gerald? Gerald, this man's going to help you. Now, you just hang on, okay?"

"Let me get you to the roof first, ma'am," Bishop said.

"No. No, you need to help my husband. Please."

"I don't know what I have in here and it's going to take me a minute to assess. We don't have much time and I need you out there for when my team is ready with the boat." Bishop helped the old woman off the floor.

Her clothes were torn and dirty and she stumbled to her feet. "Just help my Gerry, please."

"I will. I promise you, ma'am. I will. Now, come on." Bishop led her to the nearby window and peered out. "Okay, this looks all right. The shingles are in good shape on this overhang and it's mostly level." He took her hand and helped her through the window after stepping out on his own to test the surface. "It'll only be for a minute so I can help Gerry. I promise you. But I'm going to need you to hang on to this window frame, okay? You'll be seeing the boat any minute now."

"What about my granddaughter?" the woman asked.

"They'll get her. Don't you worry about that." Bishop made sure her footing was steady. "I'm going back inside now, and I need you to be very, very still, okay? When the boat comes, I'll be ready to get you loaded up. You and your husband." Bishop crawled back inside as he made his way back to Gerald. He placed his fingers on the man's wrist. "Okay, Gerry, can you tell me what it is you're taking?" After he checked the man's pulse, he began to rummage through the medical bag. "Are you taking beta-blockers?"

He nodded.

"Okay. That's good. Let me see in here." He scrounged through the bag and found a vial. "This should do the trick, Gerry."

Outside, the old woman squinted from the approaching spotlight. Redmond directed the boat toward the home and spotted the woman. "There she is." He smiled and turned back. "Your grandmother's right there and I'm sure your grandpa will be coming out soon."

The girl had been rescued and was now wrapped in a blanket. "Please help her." She was in her twenties and had tried to convince her grandparents to leave the house with her, but they refused, so she stayed with them.

"We're coming, ma'am. Just hang tight." Redmond slowed the boat and turned to Nunes. "I'll go get her."

"Where the hell is Bishop?" Nunes asked.

"Must be inside with the husband. After we get her loaded, I'll go in and see what's happening." Redmond climbed onto the roof with a harness at the ready. "Ma'am, as you can see, your granddaughter is waiting for you, so I'm going to need you to let me wrap this around your waist just so we don't get separated, okay?"

"My Gerry. I can't go without my Gerry." She looked back inside the house.

"I'm sure Dr. Bishop is doing everything he can for your husband. Right now, though, I need to stay focused on you. I need your help here, okay?"

She stepped forward and nodded.

"Okay, then." Redmond clipped the harness around her waist. "Just stay close to me, ma'am. You'll be just fine." He approached the rising floodwaters again as he reached the edge of the roof.

"Wrap your arms around my neck and I'll do the work." He shimmied down a front porch column and dropped into the water, nearly going under before paddling like hell to stay afloat. "Just a little more before we reach the boat."

Redmond paddled a few more feet when he felt Nunes' hand grasp his shoulder.

"I got you, man. I got you."

Redmond and the woman were pulled aboard, and Redmond quickly unlatched the woman's harness.

"Grandma!"

"Oh, my sweet girl." The woman fell into an embrace and was enveloped in her granddaughter's blanket. "I'm so sorry."

"It's okay, Grandma. They'll make sure Grandpa makes it out." She looked at Redmond. "Where is he?"

"I'm about to find out right now." Redmond turned to Nunes. "I'm going back in."

"You sure, boss? It's my turn."

"No, I got this." Redmond plunged back into the water and reached the roofline of the second floor. "Bishop? Bishop, you all right?" He stepped onto the shingles and headed toward the window. "Bishop? What's going on?"

Bishop stood. "I tried. I tried to save him."

"No." Redmond's shoulders sank as he turned to the boat. The light shone in his eyes and he couldn't see the granddaughter or grandmother, but they could see him—and the look on his face.

"Help me get him out of here," Bishop said. "We gotta at least do that."

THE HIGH SCHOOL gym was half empty while many still searched for victims. Children had fallen asleep on the cots and mothers and fathers prayed.

"What the hell happened out there?" The sheriff placed his hands on his hips and studied the team.

"I thought I could save him," Bishop began. "I tried. I just didn't have what I needed to treat him."

Officer Redmond placed a comforting hand on his shoulder. "You did everything you could, man. It was rough out there. I'm just grateful we managed to save a few. It's better than nothing."

"Once all the dust settles, the family will be able to bury their kin," the sheriff added. "Regardless, y'all did a hell of a job out there. Others are coming back with folks too. We're all doing the best we can." He nodded and walked away.

"Sheriff's right," Redmond began. "And once we get daylight, we'll get right back out there and find more. But for now, you should get some rest. I wouldn't mind closing my eyes either."

Bishop headed toward a chair against a back wall and slouched into it. He closed his eyes.

2

W hen the elevator doors opened into the parking garage, Special Agent Kate Reid felt the cold air nuzzle against her face. It was October in D.C. and autumn wasted no time kicking summer to the curb. Her grey peacoat flapped open for a moment until she pulled it around her and stepped over the threshold onto the concrete. As she headed to her car, Kate flicked back her long brunette hair while she hoisted the laptop bag onto her shoulder. The oversized bag looked even larger against her petite frame.

She slipped behind the wheel of her Ford Explorer and started the engine. It's six-cylinder motor rumbled, and the smell of exhaust seeped through the vents inside for a brief second. She pulled out of the garage and onto the road ahead, looking into the rearview mirror at the condo she shared with Nick Scarborough. It was difficult to tell from the growing distance, but she could have sworn Nick peered at her through the window of their bedroom that faced the road.

These past few months, since their return from Rio and Nick's demotion, the two had been walking on eggshells. Neither one was willing to admit the game had changed. Nick's dream had been to run the BAU team at Quantico and he had done amazing things since he was given the post. It was his no more and they both knew it was of his own doing. If anyone was going to destroy Nick's career, it was going to be Nick.

Kate could admit Agent Noah Quinn lit the fire, but Nick turned it into a five-alarm blaze that had been doused by the Unit Chief on their return from the international case. The new person in charge? Nick's subordinate, but longest-serving member of the team, Cameron Fisher. Today marked the day that it was to become official.

Her own part in the challenges she and Nick currently faced was all on her. It had been Kate's choice to put a tail on Agent Quinn to find out who he had been talking to. Quinn had done his best to uncover Nick's problem with alcohol, having gone so far as to question Nick's former girlfriend on the topic. It was a decision that was about to bring Kate before the Board to be issued a Letter of Censure for her actions. The impact on her own career was uncertain.

She had made some excuse as to why the two needed to drive to the office separately today. Something about her being behind on paperwork after wrapping up a consult in Philadelphia last week. It was bullshit. The idea of driving together, sitting in silence on what would be Nick's final day as Senior Unit Agent was like being a witness to an execution. Watching the death of a loved one's dreams and life-long ambitions might as well have been just that.

SCATTERED whispers filled the conference room as the team awaited Unit Chief Cole. It seemed the meeting between Nick, Cameron Fisher, and Cole was taking longer than expected.

Levi Walsh sat next to Kate. The two had grown close since she was given permanent status with the team on the recommendation of a man who was no longer a part of it. Much like her former colleague, Dwight Jameson, Levi had been an ally. Kate wondered why she leaned on men like them. They weren't old enough to serve as father figures, and she hadn't even had a relationship to speak of with her father until just a few years ago in any case. She smirked thinking, then again, maybe that was exactly what they had been—father figures, regardless of their ages.

Still, she was grateful to have Levi in Dwight's place, though she had stayed in close contact with Dwight, especially through the troubled waters of late.

Levi Walsh was the team's investigative analyst and worked closely with local law enforcement. He looked rougher than he was. In his early forties, his leathery features were more a result of years serving in the deserts of the Middle East, but his slight Alabama drawl and blue eyes could win over the heart of any woman. Although, he never saw himself as a ladies' man.

He never treated Kate differently or special, even though most people thought she was very special. Having survived a past like hers did make her different but Kate never used it as a crutch. In fact, she'd fought back on that very notion her entire career.

The new head honcho was slated to be Cameron Fisher. A rough around the edges ex-cop from New York, he merited the position. Some might say it should have gone to him in the first place. He'd been senior to the rest of the team and had earned the respect of everyone. Somehow though, Cole offered it to Nick. It had been well-deserved at the time, but the tensions between Cameron Fisher and Nick Scarborough didn't melt away for quite a while. Fisher was handling all of this like the pro he was. No grudges.

Although, with his new promotion, it could put a damper on his relationship with Agent Eva Duncan. Some could argue she was the conductor behind the scenes, guiding cases, sifting through leads. However, their still-newish relationship could be in jeopardy because the only reason it had been approved was that neither answered to the other in an official capacity. That was about to change. Eva had been hardened from the circumstances of her youth in Chicago which led her to take an all-business, no-nonsense approach to every case the team was assigned. She never let it get personal until she fell in love with Cameron Fisher.

As Kate continued to survey the room, there was a noticeable absence. Noah Quinn. The very man who had given Kate the opportunity to join this team was gone. Transferred. There had been a lot to learn from him, but Quinn used Kate for his own personal gain. It was too bad because he was the best profiler she'd ever met.

When Eva Duncan sat at attention, Kate, whose back was to the door, figured the three wise men were about to enter the conference room.

Unit Chief Cole led the way with Cameron Fisher and Nick Scarborough two steps behind. Interesting that they walked side-by-side, as though both were either reluctant to take the lead or reluctant to give it up.

"Good morning." Unit Chief Cole stood at the head of the table while Cameron Fisher and Nick Scarborough sat down across from one another. "I'm sorry for the delay. I realize we should've started this meeting twenty minutes ago and I know everyone is busy, so please accept my apology." Cole was in his late 50s and was a brilliant intelligence officer with a career that had spanned decades. "This period of transition has gone smoothly as far as I'm concerned and that is a testament to the leadership of this team, both current and former. Respect was never lost, and a dereliction of duties never considered. We've all had time to reflect on the past. Mistakes were made. While it is only human to make mistakes, in this line of work, there is little room for them or the damage they may cause. These mistakes have been owned and every attempt at rectification has been made. However, as a result, changes must also be made, and those changes will go into effect today. From here on out, this team will be headed up by your new Senior Unit Agent, Cameron Fisher. SSA Nick Scarborough will take on a new role. He is still a senior member of this team and as such, deserves the continued respect you all have shown him over the years." He surveyed the team again. "Any questions?"

"What about Quinn?" Kate had an inkling to what this answer might be, but it needed to be stated in front of everyone—for posterity if nothing else.

"He will not be returning. That isn't new information, but it is official. This makes you, Reid, our resident profiler. Under-standing that you were essentially Quinn's apprentice, you will still be required to consult with SSA Scarborough and/or Senior Unit Agent Fisher on any of your case findings. There is protocol and it takes time to learn this job. There are no shortcuts. Reid, you will be the one the team turns to for analysis and in-depth profiling. The only difference is, you won't have Quinn to bounce ideas off of, but you will still have the combined decades of experience both Fisher and Scarborough have to offer. I suggest you use them."

"Thank you, sir," Kate replied.

"So, if there are no further questions, we should all get back to the business of the day." With a wrap of his knuckles on the conference table, Cole excused himself.

Kate was the first to stand and offered her hand. "Congratulations, Fisher. I look forward to our new working relationship."

"It won't be any different than before, but thank you, Reid." Fisher returned the handshake.

Walsh and Duncan left the room with Fisher close behind. It was just Kate and Nick. Just like it had been since a time in her past she didn't like to recall.

"You okay? You left pretty early this morning." Nick smoothed back his dark hair that had turned just a little saltier and adjusted his dress pants that still fit perfectly against his trim waist.

He had a few years on the 34-year-old Kate and was now just on the other side of forty. As she looked at him, he appeared the same as he had that day in his car, back in California. Although now he was a little more jaded and suffered from demons that had finally caught up to him. She was all of 28 then. Still young and damaged after the awful events of that year. It was the day he said she would make a great FBI agent. It wasn't something she decided to tackle until a year later and solely a result of circumstances beyond her control, but he had seen in her then what she would become. Now, she could see that man. The one who had believed in her. The one who had loved her. Only now, he was also the one who had betrayed her. Not in the traditional sense one would think, but in the sense that he hadn't kept his end of the bargain. He let his demons get the better of him at the worst possible time. A split-second decision to walk inside a bar in the middle of a dangerous investigation in a foreign country, leaving everyone to fear for his safety and their own. His team needed him. She needed him. After spending a year in AA meetings, he fell. Rightly or wrongly, Kate hadn't yet forgiven him.

She considered his question if she was truly okay and figured it wasn't time for the truth. "I just needed some time to think and clear my head. A lot of things are changing, and I don't really know how to take on those changes just yet."

"You know what to do. You've always known what to do. It's only out of a responsibility to others that prevents you from doing it."

She formed a closed-lip smile. "Listen, I have to run out for a while. I'll catch up with you later?"

"Sure."

Kate walked away and for the first time in a long time, she didn't look back.

ON THE DRIVE into work this morning, Kate had received a text message from Noah Quinn. At first, she considered not responding but eventually thought better of it knowing that the FBI was a tight-knit community and she might one day need Quinn's help. She'd witnessed the burning of bridges Nick and Georgia Myers went through and while that was different, Kate wasn't going to burn down any relationship. That didn't mean, however, she was about to let Quinn get under her skin again. So, she agreed to meet him at a restaurant and had just arrived.

Dupont Circle was always a nightmare for driving and parking. Kate disliked venturing into the neighborhood, but it was just like Quinn to want to be seen, and it was nothing if not that. The long drive from Quantico had been annoying and the fifth attempt at finding a parking spot sent her nerves on end. As she parked and fed the meter, Kate inhaled a deep breath to calm herself. She hadn't seen Quinn in months and having her wits about her in his presence was paramount.

The restaurant was quaint, more of a café, which Kate appreciated. The larger, historic restaurants were overcrowded, loud and filled with politicians and lobbyists. Kate approached the host stand. "Hi, I'm here to see Noah Quinn. Has he arrived?"

"Agent Kate Reid?" The man asked.

"Yes."

"Right this way, please." The young man wearing all black led her to the rear of the café. "Here you are, ma'am."

"Thank you." Kate nodded before capturing Quinn's gaze. "Long time, no see."

He stood and extended a hand. "Reid, it's nice to see you. Thank you for agreeing to meet with me on short notice. Please, have a seat." Quinn gestured to the chair across from him. He had a boyish charm about him and was a couple of years younger than Kate. In fact, he had been the youngest profiler BAU had ever employed. Coupled with his handsome features, it was no surprise Quinn was full of himself.

Kate removed her grey peacoat and draped it over the back of the chair. She pushed her hair from her shoulders so that it would rest on her back. Upon taking her seat, she began, "So, I assume someone must've told you about the meeting today. Hence the text message."

Quinn cast his sights to his glass of water and took a sip. "I did hear that was happening today. How is Scarborough handling it?"

"He's a professional. He's handling it just fine," Kate replied sharply.

"Good. That's good to hear. And you?"

Kate shrugged. "Fine here. The only thing that's really changed for me is that you're no longer my boss."

Quinn smiled and nodded. "It was what you wanted from the beginning."

"Look, I'm here because you asked me to be and I realize there will probably come a time when you and I will have to work together again. Out of professional courtesy, I'm here. So, what is it that you wanted to talk about?"

"Good to know you're not up for small talk, Reid," Quinn began. "I thought you might like to know I'm being transferred to the New York field office."

"New York?"

"That's right. I'll be the resident BAU agent. It is a step down, obviously, but hey, I don't hold grudges."

Kate scoffed. "Well, you did try to blackmail a fellow agent. You also tried to manipulate me into trusting you with knowledge of my personal history. I'd say you got off easy."

"And what about you? What's your punishment for having me tailed?" Quinn raised his index finger as if an idea had dawned. "Oh, that's right. You got my old job. Someone with what, two years of experience?"

"I've been with the Bureau for five years now, Quinn."

"Sure, and that makes you an expert." It appeared as though Quinn was about to escalate the argument, but seemingly reconsidered. "In any case, I thought you'd want to know that I'm still just a phone call away, should you need anything from me. I'm offering you, as a professional courtesy, my wealth of knowledge, should you need it down the road."

"I do appreciate that, Quinn." Sarcasm laced her words. "Boy, I just don't think I could get along without knowing you were just a quick plane ride away."

Quinn appeared resigned. "Kate, please. Can we just stop this? Despite what you might think, I didn't ask to see you to fight. I truly wanted you to know that we can continue our professional relationship. In fact, I'd like to."

"Fine. Yeah, of course. I'm sorry."

Kate spent the next 30 minutes making small talk with Quinn. She ate a half-sandwich and a cup of soup and finished off her iced tea. They seemed to put aside their differences and instituted a policy of civility. From this point forward, Quinn would no longer be Kate's adversary. Was he going to be a friend? Not unless it was over her dead body. But she could agree to a professional arrangement. Time would tell how long that would last.

Eva stared at the television while it broadcast a mindless sitcom that she wasn't watching in the first place. Cameron was next to her, his eyes glued to the screen. Both were obviously thinking of what to say, neither sure of what those words should be. With Cameron in charge, the odds this relationship would go up in flames increased three-fold. Not because of their own doing, but because of the example they were setting.

Cameron had been reluctant to make it official to begin with, realizing that this could come to pass. Both had used Kate and Nick's relationship as a guideline and accepted that it was within the rules to date primarily because Kate answered to Quinn. Now things were different for all of them.

Cameron Fisher was the oldest member of the team, at forty-eight. Fine lines had deepened around his brown eyes. His beard, when it came in, was more gray than black. His hair was thick, greying and had begun to recede at the forehead. He reached for a toothpick from the side table as he sat on the sofa next to Eva and tucked it between his lips. It was a habit he picked up years earlier when he was with the NYPD.

Then there was Eva. She was 38 but didn't look a day over 30 in his eyes. Her caramel hair looked as though it had just caught the sun. Her olive skin was still smooth and soft. And her lips...her lips were full and beckoned him at his very moment. It was a shame there was a side of him that prevented him from letting go and loving her the way she deserved to be loved. He always held back, yet she never did. Until now. He sensed words were resting at the tip of her tongue that begged to be freed.

"Please tell me what you're thinking," he finally said. "We knew this was coming. Now it's here and we can't ignore it."

Eva turned her sights to him. The recessed lighting above cast a shadow on her head, giving her features a halo-like glow that made him want her even more.

"I don't think we have a choice, Cam. I think we have to end this." She turned back to face the television.

"We just need to talk to HR. This doesn't have to change anything. It could be considered a pre-existing condition."

She chuckled under her breath before returning her gaze to him. "I didn't realize our relationship was a condition."

"You know what I mean," he pleaded. "We should be grandfathered in. Do you think Scarborough and Reid are breaking up anytime soon?"

"Who knows right now," she replied. "I mean, their situation was different. Reid was hired on with the knowledge that they were already in a serious relationship."

"Exactly. They were grandfathered in and we should be too," he replied.

"Honestly, none of us should be dating. I mean, seriously, Levi is the only one who isn't sleeping with a member of the team."

"That is good to know," Fisher added. "All kidding aside, I don't want to end this. And I don't think you do either."

"I don't." She studied him. "But all of this has gotten so out of hand. So complicated. You and me. Scarborough and Reid. Quinn's gone for God's sake. It's all different now. Did you tell Kate her case was going before the board soon?"

"Cole was supposed to mention it, but I think he'd prefer it come from me since I'm..."

"The boss," she said. "He's right. It should come from you. It'll shape the rest of her career."

"It doesn't have to. Scarborough was censured a few years ago and look at him now?"

"Right. He's been demoted," she replied. "Look, can we just put a pin in this for a little while? We both need time to process everything and figure out where we stand and where we want to be."

Fisher nodded. "I can agree to that. Does that mean we can't have sex?" He smiled.

She laughed again. "Really?"

He turned up the palms of his hands. "What? What'd I say?"

3

The front passenger tire of the ambulance truck plunged into a pothole as it drove along a crowded Baltimore road, jarring the occupants inside.

Pete Fryer was driving and quickly swerved to the left to avoid the rear tire suffering the same fate. Medical supplies rattled in their cabinets. He looked to his partner. "Oh man, sorry about that. Thing came out of nowhere."

Dr. Theodore Bishop grabbed the bar above the window. "I didn't see it either. Don't worry about it."

Pete nodded. "You know, it was a good thing what you did for those people in Texas. Taking your vacation days to go there and help out."

"I hope I didn't leave anyone here in a lurch," Bishop replied. "They needed a lot more help than what I alone could offer. It looked like a third-world country. But there were a lot of good people doing their best."

"Your being gone was no skin off my teeth," Pete added. "It's good to see someone with your skills putting them to good use. I would've gone if it hadn't been for my family."

Bishop looked through the passenger window and rolled his eyes. "Sure, man. You have to be there for your own family. I get that."

"This is it." Pete gazed through the windshield. "The brownstone up here on the left. Third one in."

"The seizure?" Bishop asked.

"Yep. 55-year-old female. Her son made the call." Pete pulled the keys from the ignition and jumped out of the truck. "Let's get the bags and see what we're up against."

Bishop jumped out of his side and jogged around to the back where Pete had already grabbed his kit. Bishop reached for his and followed his partner to the door.

A young man stood in the doorway wearing a look of panic. "Thank God you're here. Come in. Mom's in the kitchen."

"Has her condition worsened?" Pete asked.

"I don't think so."

Pete waved Bishop to follow into the kitchen and spotted the 55-year-old slouched in a dining chair. "Ma'am, how are you feeling? Are you experiencing any chest pains?"

She appeared weak and only nodded. Her skin was ashen and her curly blonde hair with streaks of grey was disheveled.

Pete checked her pulse and turned to Bishop. "It's weak. Let's get her into the truck." He looked to her son. "What happened when she started to have the seizure?"

"I don't know. I was in my room. I heard a crash and ran downstairs. That's when I saw her on the floor. I rolled up the dish towel and put it in her mouth. You know, like they say you should put something in their mouths?"

"Well, that's um... it doesn't matter. You called us," Pete added.

Bishop ran outside to retrieve the stretcher. On his return to the kitchen, Pete had prepared the woman. "Sir, can you give us a hand?"

The woman's son, a kid not more than 25, trembled and his eyes watered.

"Hey, it's okay. We're going to take care of your mom, but we could use an extra hand to get her onto the stretcher."

"Yeah, okay." He approached them. "They're going to take care of you, Ma."

She smiled faintly.

"On the count of three," Pete said. "One, two, three."

The men carefully placed her onto the board.

"We can take it from here. Do you want to ride in the truck with her?" Pete asked him.

"I'll follow so I can have a car."

"Okay. We're going to take her to St. Michael's. Stay behind us and we'll run the sirens."

"Thank you." The son grabbed his coat and his keys and followed them outside.

Pete and Bishop loaded up the woman in the back before Pete jumped into the driver's seat once again. "Theo, keep a close eye. We'll be there in 7 minutes." He fired up the truck and switched on the sirens.

Bishop monitored the woman's vital signs. "It's okay, ma'am. Your son is right behind us and he'll see you at the hospital. Has this happened to you before?"

She shook her head.

"Okay. The doctors at St. Michael's are excellent and will take great care of you." He reached inside his medical bag.

"How she doing back there, Bishop?" Pete asked, still driving full-bore.

"Stable for the moment." He held a needle and pushed the

plunger to clear out any air trapped inside. "I'm going to put this into your IV, okay?" Bishop glanced to Pete before injecting the needle into the woman's IV line. He held her gaze with a tender smile.

Her eyes widened and she gasped for breath while wearing an oxygen mask.

Bishop's brow creased for a moment before he peered at her vital signs and noticed the spike in her heart rate. "How much longer, Pete? She's in distress."

"Shit. Three minutes. Don't let her go, man." Pete pressed harder on the gas pedal and a noticeable lurch in the truck propelled them.

The woman tried to claw at her chest and her eyes remained fixed on Bishop. She tried to speak under the oxygen mask, but only muffled words emerged.

"We're almost there, ma'am." Bishop's tone was remarkably cool. He reached for the defibrillator behind him and readied it for use. "You'll be fine." He looked back to Pete. "Gotta use the paddles. We're losing her." This time, his tone was imbued with urgency.

"Shit. Hang on, ma'am. We're almost there." Pete gripped onto the steering wheel and weaved in and out of traffic as best he could in the bulky truck. "Come on. Come on. Get out the way!" he shouted.

"She's going into cardiac arrest." Bishop stared at her while she expressed panic and fear. He turned on the machine and opened her blouse, placing the pads on her chest. "Clear."

Her chest heaved as if someone reached a hand into it and yanked on her heart. Bishop peered at the monitor. The brief shock appeared to stabilize her. He continued to observe the monitor when her pulse grew erratic once again. "I'm going again."

Pete glanced back. "Come on, man. Don't let her go. Don't let her go, Theo." He returned his eyes to the road. "We're almost there."

Bishop readied the paddles again. "Clear."

The woman, who continued to gasp, looked at him with confusion and worry. Her head shook wildly. "Help me." Her words were barely audible beneath the mask.

"It's not working." Bishop looked at the machine. The light was on, but nothing happened.

Pete roared into the emergency entrance of the hospital where nurses and doctors were standing at the ready. The call of their arrival was made as soon as Pete started the truck. He cut the engine and crawled into the back. His eyes darted between Bishop and the woman. Then he gazed at the monitor. "What the hell?"

"I'm sorry," Bishop dropped his head. "I tried. She wasn't responding. She's gone, man. She's gone."

"Fuck!" Pete slammed the cabinet mounted on the side.

The back doors swung open to reveal two nurses and a doctor standing outside.

"She didn't make it." Bishop looked at them. "I did what I could."

Senior Supervisory Agent Nick Scarborough had everything he'd ever wanted. The transfer to Quantico. The promotion to Senior Unit Agent. Kate. Yet he'd let it slip through his fingers. His grasp on Kate was tenuous as well. How much longer he could hang onto her was up to her. Nick had risked it all and for what? Something he thought he had a handle on. After all, he'd struggled with alcohol before and came out on top. But it seemed this might have been one time too many. One risk too great.

Unit Chief Cole had ordered Nick to talk to the Bureau's

psychiatrist. His AA meetings, which he had been attending, were still a requirement. Now, Nick sat on the modular cream-colored sofa in the shrink's office while the doctor jotted down notes from her chair across from him. He rested his right leg over his left with his hand on his ankle and twitched his foot.

"I know you think this is a waste of your time, Agent Scarborough, but trust me when I say that it isn't," the doctor said. "You and I have been at this for a couple of months now and frankly, I still believe you're holding back."

He scoffed. "I'm not holding anything back. Look, I'm here because Cole ordered me to be. I don't know what you want from me. I'm going to my AA meetings. I haven't had a drink since Rio."

"That's all well and good, Nick, but you also haven't come to terms with the idea that you, the head of your team, put your own people in potential danger as a result of your actions."

"So that's what this is about?" He peered at her. Her brown eyes judged him and her downturned lips with the lines of a smoker pursed. "You think I don't feel remorse over what I've done?" Nick looked away. "You have no idea how I feel, Doc."

"You're right. That's why it's time you tell me because you're not getting out of here until you do. We can keep meeting twice a week for the next year for all I care. Somehow, I don't think that's what you want. So why don't you share what it is you're going through. Then we can both move on."

"It was a weak moment for me, okay? I slipped up. I did what I had to do to get close to the man who could tell me what I needed to know. Oh, and by the way, that man happened to be the head of a ruthless gang. It wasn't like I had a choice."

"I know you didn't." The doctor tucked her blonde hair behind her left ear. "In that moment, you faced an impossible situation. But that's not the moment in question, is it? It's what happened after that when you did have a choice. That's the heart of the problem."

FISHER HAD REQUESTED a meeting with Kate and as she started into the hall, heading for his office, she was stopped by Eva Duncan. "Morning."

"Morning," Duncan said. "I was hoping you had a minute to talk?"

"I'm supposed to meet with Fisher now. But after?" Kate asked.

"Sure. I'll be in my office."

Kate noticed the mild disappointment at the delay. "Is everything okay?"

"Yeah. Of course. Go on. I wouldn't want you to be late. We'll catch up later." Duncan continued along.

Kate peered back at her with an unsettled feeling. There had been a lot of unsettled feelings lately and she looked forward to moving on from these troubles.

She stood in Fisher's doorway of the office that used to be Nick's. "Hey, there. You wanted to see me?"

"Yes, come on in. Close the door behind you, would you?"

Kate closed the door and walked inside, taking a seat across from Fisher's desk.

"Listen, I know we haven't had a chance to talk much since all this became official. I guess I wanted to take your temperature, so to speak."

"I'm good. Really. Look, just because Nick and I are in a relationship doesn't mean I can't be objective when it comes to our team."

"Are you sure about that?" He asked. "It would be tough for anyone; I can promise you."

"I just want to move forward. I'm here on my own now and I refuse to let you or any member of this team down."

"I'm sure that would never happen," Fisher added. "But there was something else I needed to mention and that is, well, I am looking to bring in a senior profiler."

"Another Quinn," Kate said.

"Yes." He held up his hands. "Please don't take this as a slight on you. It's just that you simply don't have enough..."

"Experience. I know that. I can accept that. Can you tell me who's at the top of your list?"

"I don't have a list yet. That's something I'm working on, but I thought it only fair to bring you into the fold, so you aren't caught blindsided like we were."

Kate nodded. "Ah. I see. This goes back to when I was brought in."

"That's not what I meant. Well, I guess it is, but I don't hold anything against you," Fisher said. "Hell, I don't hold anything against Scarborough or Cole either. I just handle things differently. And believe me, I know what Quinn was. I also know he was damn good at his job. Now I need to find someone who can fill his shoes and continue to mentor you until the time comes for you to take the lead."

"And you expect that to happen?" Kate asked.

"Of course I do. I've worked with you long enough to see what an incredible talent you are, Reid. No doubt about that. But this is BAU. This is Quantico. There are a whole lot of agents who would kill to be in your shoes right now."

"Agents with a lot more experience than me."

"Yes. So, I need to do what's best for this team, and I hope you can accept that."

Kate nodded. "I can. I do. For now, will I be able to run consults on my own?"

"Absolutely. Until I find a suitable candidate, it's your show. I know you can handle it." He inhaled a breath. "That's all I've got for now. Unless there's something else you'd like to talk about?"

"I'm good." Kate pushed up from the chair. "I'd better clear my boxes from Quinn's office." She smiled. "I like mine better anyway."

"If I thought you were serious, I might take offense that you decided to move in," Fisher added. "There is something else, your hearing. It's in three weeks."

Kate stopped and turned back. "Okay. I'll be ready. By the way, I'm glad it's you here, Fisher."

"Thank you."

THEO BISHOP STOOD before his boss with his hands clasped at his front. "I realize I asked this very thing just a few weeks ago, but I feel compelled to help. It'll just be a few days; a week tops."

The Maryland EMS system was an independently run state operation. Bishop was employed at the city center location in Baltimore. It was one of the busiest operations in the state. He knew this was a big favor to ask and especially considering he'd only just asked this very question a short while ago. How far he could push his boss's generosity remained to be seen.

"I'll tell you, Bishop, things have been brutal around here lately. We're short staffed as it is."

"I know, sir, and I wouldn't ask if I didn't believe they truly needed the help. It could make for a nice news story. Maybe give the department some good PR," Bishop added.

"I suppose it could. I'll tell you what. I'll give you three days.

Mind you, it'll come from your sick pay and/or vacation. Whatever you have left at this point. You understand?"

"I do, sir. Thank you. You have no idea how much this means to me and the people of Riverside."

"Go on then. See what you can do to help those people. God knows how many more will be evacuated before it's all said and done. The whole damn state is ablaze."

"California's suffered a lot of wildfires, no doubt. Thank you, sir, and I'll keep in close contact." Bishop turned away with a smile.

THE TRIAGE CLINIC was one of three stationed at the perimeter of the fire. Hundreds of people had already been evacuated but some chose to remain to protect their homes. However, garden hoses weren't going to do much to contain this beast. It had been burning for a week and the Santa Ana winds combined with the parched lands made for near-impossible conditions.

"We have another one, Doctor." Bishop pushed a gurney toward the doctor in charge of the station. "Looks like 3rd degree burns on the hands and lower arms."

"I'll take it from here, thanks." The doctor ripped the patient's long-sleeved shirt and began to examine him.

Bishop started outside the makeshift building and approached another volunteer. "Any idea where they want us to go next?" His face was sooty and sweat poured off of him.

"You should take a breather while you can. I'm sure it won't be long." He studied Bishop. "Where you from?"

"Back east."

"Long way to come to volunteer. I admire you for that. I'm from the area myself. Been an EMT for about 5 years. This is some crazy shit. It's getting harder to breathe. They might have to push farther out."

"Could be," Bishop added.

"What's your story? You a tech too?"

"Doctor, actually. It's a long story. I'm just here to help."

"You two." A firefighter approached them. "We need some help over here now!"

"Break's over," Bishop started toward the firefighter. "I'm a doctor. What do you need?" He peered back and noticed the man he had been speaking with was diverted to help another.

"Get him bandaged up. I'll leave it up to you but looks to me like it's not that severe. You got this?" the firefighter asked.

"I got it." Bishop smiled while the firefighter left. "He's right, sir. I think you'll be just fine. Looks like some second-degree burns." He continued to examine him. "Maybe some first-degree too. Nothing that you can't go to your local hospital and have checked out. I'll get you in good enough shape that you can leave here. Does that sound like a plan?"

The man nodded. "I just wanted to protect my house. But the heat..."

"I know, sir. You did what you could." Bishop cleaned and disinfected the man's burns before applying a topical treatment. "You know what, I'm going to give you direct-injection antibiotics. They're the strongest we have and will fight off any infection you might get as a result of these burns." He opened his medical kit and retrieved a needle. "You'll feel a slight pinch here."

"I doubt it, Doc. I don't feel nothing but the burn." He held out his arm.

Bishop inserted the needle and pushed the contents into his arm before placing a cotton ball on the site. "Put some pressure on this for just a moment and I'll get the bandages."

The man began to writhe on the gurney. He gasped for breath

while foam erupted from his mouth. With his hand, he clutched onto Bishop's arm.

Bishop swung around and noticed the man in distress. He surveyed the area. Doctors, EMTs, and others were busy treating patients. He looked down at the man again who still had a death grip on his arm. "You'll be okay. It'll pass in a minute." With his free hand, he pushed down on the man's shoulders so he wouldn't draw attention. "Shhhh. It's almost over."

4

As much as Kate wanted things to return to normal, both personally and professionally, it seemed like the more she wished for that to happen, the longer it was taking.

Kate needed something to sink her teeth into to take her mind off all the upheaval that had happened lately. It had been a mistake to meet with Quinn yesterday. She should've known better but had truly wanted to keep the relationship from burning to the ground. Quinn would have to reconcile his behavior as she would hers. Maybe when they both did that, they could move on and work together in some small capacity someday.

For now, however, she would settle for an opportunity to work on something on her own before Fisher had a chance to bring in another supervisor. And it looked like her wish was about to be granted.

"Reid, you have a minute?" Fisher walked into her office.

"Of course," she replied with anticipation on her breath.

"I got a call a few minutes ago from the Denver field office.

They could use some guidance on a case that dropped into their laps last week."

"Okay. Is this something for the team?"

"No. We don't need to commit our full resources to this. Not at this time, anyway. But I thought it would present an opportunity for you to showcase your talents without being under the thumb of Noah Quinn, or anyone for that matter."

"When should I leave?"

"Based on what I know from the agent in charge, my best guess is that this should take a couple of days for you to get up to speed and be able to draft a profile for them. It's a fairly straight-forward case. You've handled worse. So, I can count on you?"

"Absolutely. I'm ready at your say."

"Good. I'll send over the details and the contact for the field office. You should get yourself booked on the next flight to Denver." Fisher started to leave. "I know what you're capable of, Reid. I've seen you in action and frankly, I've been in awe on occasion. I want to see what you can do all on your own."

"I won't let you down."

Fisher smiled. "I know you won't." He continued into the corridor.

This wasn't the first opportunity to act on her own. Nick had given her something similar when they worked at the Washington field office and she'd been allowed to spread her wings and work on the case in Los Angeles. But here, this was a different story. Fisher had been reluctant to accept her at their first meeting. He'd also been reluctant to accept Nick as his boss, but that was an entirely different situation. Now, he was giving her a chance to see what she could do without being under Quinn's watchful eye, or Nick's.

She picked up the phone and booked the next flight from D.C. which was due to leave in four hours. "Plenty of time."

The next call was to the agent in charge. "Agent Surrey? I'm Kate Reid with BAU Quantico. I understand you all have an interesting case on your hands?"

The agent filled Kate in on the details of the multiple murders and where they currently stood.

"I'm booked on the next flight and should arrive this evening. We can meet up tonight if you'd like?" She smiled and nodded. "Great. I'll call you when I arrive. I look forward to meeting you." Kate ended the call.

THE MEDICAL EXAMINER's office in Oakview, Texas was nothing more than an old house in the center of town. It was only a satellite office to the main location in Galveston, and the population of Oakview scarcely required anything larger. In fact, most of the cases involved drownings or on a rare occasion, murder. But something drew the attention of the doctor as he read the newly released toxicology reports on two victims of the hurricane earlier this month.

He picked up the phone. "Dr. Ruiz, this is Dr. Levitan in Oakview, do you have a moment to discuss a case with me?" He nodded. "Great, thank you. I just received the tox screen back on two victims who died during the hurricane rescue efforts." He paused. "Yes, it has taken some time to get the office opened again after the damage, but we are recovering, thank you. Anyway, this one I'm looking at now, a 63-year-old male with Stage 4 renal disease. He apparently died while being rescued, but what I'm seeing here on this report, well, it concerns me, to say the least." He flipped through the pages. "The report indicates severe hyperkalemia. Yes, that is associated with his kidney disease, however, his medication list, as submitted by his wife, shows his disease was being well managed. I think the hyperkalemia was brought on by an injection of potassium chloride. The level of potassium was well outside the normal range." He listened again. "I guess what I'm saying, Dr. Ruiz, is that it looks like this man was given a lethal dose of potassium chloride, which induced the hyperkalemia and caused his death."

The young doctor listened to the more experienced one and nodded his agreement. "The other patient I was concerned about died from a lack of oxygen. It raised concern only in the sense that this victim did not drown and was on no medication, according to her family. The woman was 35 and in good health. I'd like to send both of these reports to you for review. And if there are any signs of asphyxiation I might have overlooked in the female victim." He waited again. "Thank you, Dr. Ruiz. I'll await your call."

Being the younger, less experienced examiner, Dr. Levitan wondered if Dr. Ruiz would give his full attention to the concerns of the two victims. All told, 35 people had died as a result of Hurricane Edward. It devastated the small community of Oakview. What Levitan refused to let happen was to overlook a potential murderer in their midst.

He stood from his desk and retrieved his cell phone, pressing one of his contact buttons.

The line answered. "Oakview Police. How may I direct your call?"

"Can I speak with Detective Castillo, please? This is Dr. Levitan from the M.E.'s office."

"One moment please."

Levitan listened while he was put on hold before his call was again answered.

"Dr. Levitan. How are you?"

"Detective Castillo. Doing all right, all things considered. And you?" Levitan asked.

"Still cleaning up the mess Edward left behind. What can I help you with Doc?"

He flipped through the reports again. "Do you have time to meet for lunch today?"

"Sure. Is that all I get to know right now?"

"I'd prefer to speak in person. Say noon at Rosita's?"

"Sounds good. See you then, Doc."

"See you then."

THE PLANE LANDED and Kate retrieved her laptop bag along with an overnight bag. As she made her way to the curb-side pick-up, a man who looked like he was FBI stood in front of a black SUV. Definitely FBI. He held a sign with her name on it and she approached him. "I'm Agent Kate Reid."

"Ah, good. You're right on time." He offered his hand. "Brighton. Neil Brighton. Nice to meet you. I know you spoke with SSA Surrey, but he asked that I make the trip to bring you in. We should get going. It's already late and I'd really like to get you up to speed just as quickly as possible. Jump in."

Kate stepped inside and closed the passenger door while Brighton sat behind the wheel.

He pressed the ignition. "We sure are glad one of you Quantico folks made time in your busy schedules to pay us a visit."

"That's our job," she replied.

"I suppose so." He tossed a brief look her way. "You hungry? Did you manage to get any dinner? We could stop somewhere and take it to the office if you'd like. I wouldn't mind a bite. It's been a long day."

Kate noticed that Brighton was a talker. Nothing wrong with that, it just wasn't who she was. He looked to be around her age, give or take. Average looking but fit. Short dark hair and a slightly rounded face with big blue eyes. And when he smiled, his teeth filled every inch inside that mouth. "I could eat. Thanks. How long have you been with the Denver office?"

"Six years now, I suppose. Something like that. You? How long have you been at Quantico? That's the big-time, right? Must be something to work with the brainiacs over there. I bet you're never bored. You must see some crazy stuff."

Kate was beginning to get the sense that she wasn't likely to get a word in edgewise with this guy. But she was nothing if not cordial.

PETE FRYER HAD BEEN an Emergency Medical Technician going on ten years. He'd started right after high school, received his certification and off he went. The only place he'd ever worked was right here in Baltimore. When he opted to bring up a matter of concern to his supervisor, he didn't hesitate because everyone who worked here with him was considered family. Everyone except for the new guy, Theo Bishop, his partner and the guy who ran off to volunteer every chance he got.

"Evening, Chief." Pete walked into his supervisor's office with his hands in his jacket pockets.

"Hey, Pete. What's going on? It's a little late for you to still be here, isn't it?"

Everyone called him "Chief," but Ray Zimmerman was the lead paramedic. In the hierarchy of EMTs, Pete was at the intermediate level. Zimmerman was at the highest level; he was a paramedic and in charge of the team.

"Yeah, I should be getting home, but I was trying to catch up on my reports. Listen, um, you got a minute?"

"Sure. Take a seat. What's on your mind?" Zimmerman leaned back in his chair. He was a tall, ball-headed man who looked intimidating, but to those who knew him, he was a softy.

"Theo is still volunteering at the wildfire over in California, right?" He pulled out the metal chair and dropped into it.

"Yep. I actually just heard from him today. Says he'll be back the day after tomorrow. Why? You miss him or something?" He chuckled.

"Not really. He's not the type of guy to buddy-up to people, I don't think."

"All right. What's got you concerned then? That woman you lost? Pete, you know it's part of the job. It happens. You and Theo did everything you could."

"See, that's where I'm not so sure, Chief."

Zimmerman's brow creased and he folded his arms over his chest. "What do you mean?"

"I don't know." Pete stared at the floor for a moment. "I just. I just don't know what happened. I mean, the woman was stable, then she wasn't. Just like that." He snapped his fingers.

"Are you saying Theo screwed up something?"

"Maybe. I'm probably way off base here, but he just doesn't seem right to me, you know?"

"Not seeming right and making a mistake on the job are two very different things, Pete. Stop dancing around what it is you want to say and just say it. It won't leave this room. I can promise you that."

Pete captured Zimmerman's gaze once again. "I guess what I'm trying to say is, what if Theo did something on purpose?"

The chief's expression fell blank. "Pete, now I think you

should be really careful what you say here because I want to be sure I'm understanding you as clearly as I can."

"I think you know what I'm saying, Chief. Theo's been here, what, less than a year?"

"Something like that."

"I wonder how many patients we've lost since that time. He's only been my partner since this summer. What about before that?"

"He was partnered with Hopkins."

"And she's gone. She quit," Pete added. "I'm just saying, I'm starting to get a bad feeling about Theo. I mean, how does a guy who used to be a doctor end up working as an EMT?"

"I asked him that very question. He said he couldn't afford the malpractice insurance anymore. I didn't think anything of it after that."

Pete grunted. "Okay. Say that's true. How the hell does he afford to keep taking time off and flying around the country to play hero every time some natural disaster strikes?"

"Come on now. You can't fault a man for wanting to help others in need. With his medical training, I'm sure he's an invaluable resource to those people." Zimmerman pulled up in his chair. "Look, I get where you're coming from. You just lost a patient. It hurts like hell and you start looking for any explanation for how it could've happened. You do bring up some valid points, so here's what I'm going to do. I'll review Theo's report on the DOA and I'll look for any inconsistencies. Then, I'll reach out to the ME and see what she thinks. If you want to know the cause of death, she'll have it by now or very shortly. Will that settle your concerns for the time being?"

He nodded. "Yeah. Thanks, Chief. I appreciate you listening to me." Pete stood. "I'm going to head out now."

"Good idea. I'll let you know what I find out." Zimmerman waited for Pete to leave before peering through his office window.

He rubbed his smooth chin and shook his head. "Malpractice insurance, huh?" He turned back to his computer and typed in a command. "Probably something I should've done sooner, but better late than never."

The screen populated with the file of Dr. Theodore Bishop. The 33-year-old graduated Fieldbrook Medical School in Rhode Island five years prior. He received his EMT certification last year and worked for EMS in Pittsburg for a brief time before moving to Baltimore where he was hired on.

Zimmerman studied the information on the screen and considered the timing of it all. "Where did you do your residency?" He'd known that it took something like three years in residency before one could become a doctor. There had been a time when he considered med school before opting to become a paramedic instead. The amount of schooling and the cost alone was enough to dissuade him. But he recalled something about the programs.

He pulled up the medical licensing board in Rhode Island to find out where Bishop served his residency. "Our Lady of Mercy. Providence." He jotted down the details. Everything seemed legitimate and it was too early in the morning to make any calls.

Zimmerman shut down his computer and pulled on his coat from the back of his chair. "I'll have to take a fresh look later." He walked outside and reached his car, then slipped into the driver's seat when an idea struck. With his phone in hand, there was one person who he wondered if she had the same concerns as Pete.

"Hopkins. Hey, it's Zimmerman."

"Chief?"

"Yeah. How you doing? How you liking your new post in Manhattan?" He pulled out of the parking lot and onto the main road.

"It's great. Wow. I'm surprised to hear from you. What's up?"

"I hope I didn't catch you at a bad time, but I wanted to ask you something."

"Not a bad time at all. I'm off today, so I'm catching up on my Netflix shows. Ask away."

"You were partnered up with Theo Bishop, you remember?"

"Oh yeah. I remember."

He noted the shift in her tone. "What can you tell me, if anything, about your thoughts on the good doctor?"

She scoffed. "You really want to know?"

"I do indeed."

"Well, he and I never really bonded, you know? He was kind of standoffish. Not a friendly guy."

"Okay. What else?" He pulled onto the turnpike.

"I don't know, Chief. I guess...Well, I guess he was kind of weird."

"Did you, at any time, suspect something was off with him? Not necessarily his personality, but I don't know, his handling of patients." He noted the long pause. "Hopkins? You still there?"

"I'm here. You want the truth, Chief?"

"Please."

"There were a few times when I didn't know if it was me, or the circumstance, or what, but I didn't think certain situations turned out the way they should have."

"I see. And you never came to me with your concerns?"

"No. I guess not. Like I said, I didn't want to think. I could never be sure, and I didn't want to accuse someone of something they didn't do." She paused again. "Why are you asking about him now, Chief? What's going on?"

"Honestly? I don't know if anything's going on. Just that I had my own concerns and I wanted to see what your thoughts were."

"I think if you're concerned, then there's probably a reason to be."

"You might be right. I won't keep you. It sure was nice to talk to you, Hopkins and I wish you continued success in your new life."

"Hey, Chief, if you need to talk again, I'm here."

"I appreciate that. Goodbye."

"Goodbye, Chief."

Zimmerman set down his phone and pulled onto his driveway. "Well, hell."

5

The high-strung Agent Brighton knocked on the door of Kate's hotel room. A briefing took place after her arrival last night, and this morning Brighton was slated to take her to the crime scenes. She'd been up until the early hours studying the case file to cover the bases and was ready to get started.

Kate opened the door and wore a pleasant smile. "Morning, Brighton."

"Morning, Reid." He stood at attention and looked as though he could hardly contain his excitement to show her around. "Should we get going?"

Kate stepped through the door and before she could say a word, Brighton continued. "You want to grab a coffee on the way? I've had two cups this morning already, but it's cold and I wouldn't mind another. You know, I'm an early riser and tend to start my days just before dawn. The wife hates it except when I get the kids ready for her to take to school in the morning. Then I'm not such a pain in the butt. But you know, I love being a dad. It's the best thing in the world. You have any kids, Reid?"

Kate could do nothing to stop this train and simply nodded and smiled when appropriate, answering with the occasional "yes" or "no." There was no room for anything else. It was going to be a very long day.

"Brighton," she finally interrupted. "Where's our first stop?"

"Oh, right. It's in the Highland Hills neighborhood in the suburbs of Denver. Did you get a chance to review the files? I have no doubt you'll take the ball and run with it. I've heard a lot about you, Reid, and after our briefing last night with SSA Surrey, you showed the team it was the right call to bring you in."

"Thanks." Kate stepped into Brighton's car. "I'll take that coffee if you don't mind."

THE MARYLAND BOARD OF PHYSICIAN'S office had just opened. Ray Zimmerman had waited in his car for 30 minutes and now was the time to get some answers. He stepped out and pulled on a heavy coat as the day was off to a cold start. Zimmerman took in a deep breath and peered at the building, second-guessing his decision to pick at this scab. Nevertheless, in the event there was something rancid beneath it, the burden rested on his shoulders to bring it to light and let it heal.

He continued toward the building and walked inside. "Good morning. I wanted to get information on a formerly licensed physician. Who would I speak to about that?"

The woman behind the front desk cast up her gaze. "Is this doctor licensed in Maryland?"

"No, actually. He is a certified EMT here, though. Does that make a difference?"

"Not really. We only have access to records of doctors licensed to practice in this state. I suggest you make a call or visit where the physician was originally licensed."

Another woman who sat kiddy-corner behind the same front counter cleared her throat. "That's not entirely true, Carla." She looked at Zimmerman. "We do have access to databases from other states. It's how we verify previous employment details. But I'm afraid the only people who can request such a search would be prospective employers. A hospital here in the state. Do you work for one of the hospitals?"

Zimmerman shook his head. "No, I don't. But thank you so much." He started to leave when the woman called Carla spoke again.

"If you're in contact with one of the state hospitals, or have worked with anyone there, I suggest you have them give us a call. They could authorize a records search."

He smiled. "Thank you. I'll do that. I appreciate your help. Have a good day." Zimmerman reached his car and knew exactly what to do next. With his phone in his hand, he made the call. Having been a paramedic in Baltimore for going on 20 years, he knew a lot of doctors. This one, in particular, happened to be the Chief of Surgery at St. Michael's. If he couldn't pull records on Bishop, no one could.

"Dr. Caldwell, it's Ray Zimmerman. I didn't interrupt a game of golf, I hope?"

"Not this morning. How are you, Ray? Haven't heard from you in a while."

"Doing well, Doc. Thanks. Listen, I wanted to ask a bit of a favor."

"Shoot."

Zimmerman started his car. "I was wondering if you could put in a records request on a doctor who works for me."

"You have a doctor working as an EMT?" he asked.

"Odd as that sounds, yes, I do. His name is Theodore Bishop. From what I understand, he was licensed in Rhode Island."

"Are you looking to dig up something on this guy, Ray? Is there a reason you're asking for this?"

"We've known each other for a long time, Doc. I think you know I wouldn't ask something like this without good reason. Will you help me?"

"I'll see what I can find and shoot it over to you just as soon as I can."

"Thank you. It's important, Doc."

FOR THE FIRST time in a long while, Nick felt as though he could breathe. That he had been freed from the elephant on his chest. He knew the reason was that Kate was in Denver consulting on an investigation. The odd sensation that he felt better without her around meant their relationship was in worse shape than he thought. Maybe this break was necessary for the both of them.

As he sat in his office, coming to terms with his new role on the team, he wanted to dive back into his work. That was how he chose to handle things. He pushed down the problem and refused to let it consume him. The phone on his desk rang. "Scarborough here."

"Nick Scarborough. How the hell are you, man?"

Nick creased his brow. "Good, man. What's going on?"

"You don't know who I am, do you?"

"It's been a long week. I apologize, but no."

"It's Mitch Palmero, man."

Nick pushed back in his chair and wore a smile. "Palmero?

Wow. It's good to hear from you, brother. Where the hell you been?"

"Still riding it out in Houston. But you. You're in with the big boys now. Quantico. That's crazy. Senior unit agent. Never thought I'd see the day."

Nick closed his eyes for a moment. "I'm not in the role anymore. But I am still here with the BAU team. Cameron Fisher is the senior unit agent now."

"Oh."

The pause was long enough that Nick thought he'd lost the call. "You still there?"

"I'm here, man. Look, it doesn't matter anyway. You're the one I need to talk to."

"You have something cooking?" Nick asked in an effort to push past the awkward admission.

"As a matter of fact, I just might. I got a call from our satellite office in Corpus Christi. You remember that hurricane a few weeks back over in Oakview, near Galveston?"

"Yeah, of course. It was all over the news."

"It was, yeah. The media split just as soon as the worst of it was over, forgetting all about the cleanup efforts. But anyway, that's not why I'm calling you. There's this detective in Oakview who got involved with a couple of suspected murder cases that took place during the rescue efforts."

"Holy shit," Nick replied.

"Holy shit is right. People out there needing help and hell, I don't know. It's messed up. Anyway, it's too late to make this long story short, but I'll do my best to sum it up. I think we could be dealing with a serial-type killer. What makes this shit scarier is this person appears to have had medical training of some sort. I don't know for sure if that's the case, but I can say with almost certainty that the individual last seen with these two victims was an out-of-state EMT volunteering his services."

"Don't suppose you were lucky enough to get a name?" Nick asked.

"Well now, wouldn't that make things nice and tidy? We're in the process of hunting down registries for the volunteers as well as trying to find any other volunteers who might've come across this person."

"Have you considered looking at ViCAP to see if you get a hit? Out of state means this guy could live anywhere and be doing the same thing," Nick added.

"We did, in fact, check out the database. And that's the reason why I'm reaching out to you now. I don't have final confirmation just yet, but it's looking like there's a coroner in Riverside, California who had a similar situation with three victims. He took it to the cops and the detective entered the cases. I'm still working on making a more solid connection to see if this is real. Can you and your team lend us a hand?"

"I'll have to run it by Fisher. Let me do that and I'll get back with you."

"Thanks, man. It'll be good to do some work together. Been way too long. I'll wait for your call."

Nick hung up the phone and pushed up from his desk. He made his way to Fisher's office and stood just outside. "Hey. Can I talk to you for a minute?"

"Yeah, sure. What's going on?"

Nick walked inside and sat down. "I got a call from an old acquaintance at the field office in Houston. I'm waiting on additional details, but he thinks there's an unsub out there killing off people he's supposed to be rescuing."

"What?" Fisher creased his brow.

"That's what I said. Look, I can't say this is in line with our typical case, but it does seem interesting. And might be worth a look."

Fisher laced his fingers behind his head. "Tell me more."

Zimmerman clocked in for the second shift. He still awaited word from his friend and chief of surgery on the records for Theodore Bishop. He didn't know what he was going to do with them, but maybe they would shed some light.

"Evening, Boss." Bishop strolled into his office. "I'm back. Just like I said I would be."

Zimmerman's jaw dropped for a split second before he recovered. "I forgot that was today. Welcome back. How was it out there? Sounded like they lost a lot of homes and animals."

"Oh, yeah. It was pretty devastating, that's for sure. I was just glad to be able to lend a helping hand. They were in desperate need of medical assistance. They still are, but I couldn't stay there forever. I need to keep this job." He smiled.

"Well, I'm sure everyone will be glad to see you've returned safely."

"I didn't miss anything, did I, Chief?"

"Nope. Not a thing." Zimmerman returned a smile until Bishop left, then his face fell sullen once again. He wanted to tell him to just go home and take a day or two to recover. Pete was going to have a conniption, but what else could he do? He had no proof Bishop had done anything wrong. Pete, though, he would struggle to sit in a truck with him tonight, given what he suspected.

Zimmerman picked up his cell phone. "Hey, Pete. It's the Chief. Listen, um, maybe you should take the night off?"

"Why would I do that?" Pete asked.

"I need some time, Pete. I'm working on stuff we talked about and Bishop's back and..."

"He's back?"

"Yes. Which is why I need to figure this out."

"Chief, that's all the more reason why I should come in tonight. It's not a good idea to let Bishop out there alone. I mean, are you kidding me? No. I'm coming in and that's all there is to it. See you in an hour."

Zimmerman dropped his head into his hands when the line went dead. Maybe Pete was right. If what he believed turned out to be true, it was the best way to protect the patients. "Good God. What the hell am I supposed to do?"

He didn't have long to contemplate an answer because his cell phone buzzed on his desk and it was the one person who might hold the answer.

"Dr. Caldwell. You have no idea how good it is to hear from you," Zimmerman said.

"Well, I'm not sure you'll feel the same after what I managed to get my hands on regarding this Theodore Bishop. I'm going to send this to you via email, but to sum it up, this Bishop character has been in and out of trouble with various medical boards since the beginning. Even going as far back as medical school where he graduated but received no recommendations."

"Is that unusual?" Zimmerman asked.

"Very. It means they wanted him out." Caldwell sighed. "There's nothing illegal, per se, but Bishop is trouble and maybe you ought to find a way to get rid of him."

"I can't just fire him for no reason."

"Then I suggest you find one. Keep an eye on your email. Ray, watch yourself."

"Thanks, Doc. I'll take a look at what you got and figure it out. I'm glad you could help."

"You and me, both, my friend. Keep in contact with me, you got that?"

"I will. Talk to you later, Doc." Zimmerman ended the call and stared at his computer, waiting for the critical information to arrive. When it did, he opened the file and his eyes raked over the details. "Oh my God." His sights were lasered in on the screen and he hadn't noticed Pete enter.

"Chief?"

Zimmerman pulled his eyes away from the screen. "Pete. You're early."

"I know. I needed to get down here." He closed the door and continued inside. "You know something, don't you? What did you find out?"

"I don't want to jump to conclusions, Pete. There's a lot to take in here."

"I'm going out with Theo in the next 30 minutes. You owe me this. Am I in any kind of danger?"

"No. No, of course not. If I thought that was the case, I wouldn't hesitate to get the cops involved. Theo's had a troubled past. Just how troubled, I'm trying to ascertain now. I think it's best you go out there with him tonight and just keep it professional. You get a call, document everything. Even if you don't think it's worth noting, note it. Call me if you think anything smells funny." Zimmerman leaned over his desk and dropped his tone. "Don't let him think you know anything."

"I don't know anything because you won't tell me."

The chief raised his hands. "Don't act any differently around him. I mean it. I have a feeling if he thinks for one second we know what's what, he'll jump ship. And until I know more, I want to keep Theo as close as I can."

"Okay. I won't change anything. I'll do what I always do." Pete pulled open his jacket to reveal a gun tucked in his waist. "But until we know more about what the hell is going on here, I'm not taking any chances."

Zimmerman looked at the gun. "No. Absolutely not. You can't take that, Pete."

"I don't think you'd be saying that if you were me. I'll be all right so long as I stay alert and have some sort of defense."

"For Christ's sake, don't let anyone see it."

KATE INSERTED the key into the lock and opened the door of the condo she shared with Nick. It was 1am and all she wanted was to sleep. As she walked in, she spotted Nick on the couch with the television on. "You're still up?"

He spun back and stood. "I'm just going over some files we got today. I'm glad you're home."

"There was no point in me staying any longer because I have enough to create the profile. I started it on the plane, and I'll work on it tomorrow." She set down her purse and overnight bag. "Honestly, I don't think I've ever been so happy to leave a field office. You should've seen the agent I was assigned to. Man, that guy could talk. His boss, Surrey, he was all right. But wow."

Nick smiled and approached her for an embrace. "Sounds like you had fun, then."

"Sure. Fun." She held his gaze and his smile warmed her. It would have been the perfect moment for a passionate kiss. And she wanted to kiss him, but there was just too much space between them. His eyes expressed the same longing and the same hesitation. "You look like you could use some sleep. What's say we call it a night?"

"You're right. I've been at it for hours. I'll be able to look at this with fresh eyes tomorrow." He started into the kitchen and opened the fridge. "You want some water?"

"Please. I'll take it with me to bed." She met him half-way to the hall that led to their bedroom. "So, what are you working on?"

"Something a little unusual. I gave Fisher the download and he said to dig into it to see if it was something the team should offer assistance with."

"Who's the requesting office?" She asked before taking a large gulp of water.

"Houston."

6

Ray Zimmerman, the man in charge of the second shift EMTs, had learned enough about Theodore Bishop to know that the man needed to be terminated and the sooner the better. According to the records from Dr. Caldwell, Bishop's medical school marks were subpar at best, yet he was allowed to graduate. Never mind the complaints from his fellow students who suspected he cheated on the exams.

In 2015, Bishop began his residency at Our Lady of Mercy Hospital in Providence. During his first year, he had been disciplined three times by the attending physician for improperly documenting patient records. Examinations appeared to have been faked on some occasions, though that could never be proved.

It wasn't until his third year of residency that complaints from fellow residents were filed against him. Most stated that Bishop had erred in treatment protocols resulting in two patients coding, though they were saved.

The hospital did as the medical school had done—looked the

other way. Eventually, Bishop passed his licensing exams and his board certification after his third attempt.

As Zimmerman read on, it appeared more and more likely that Bishop had been underhanded throughout his entire medical career. One thing had been true, Bishop did not renew his license due to the cost of his malpractice insurance. However, the reason it had been high wasn't in this file. Pete was right to have been concerned. Now that Zimmerman had Bishop's details, it was enough to let the man go.

The second shift was returning as dawn emerged. Pete walked into the changing room at the station and pulled off his coat to hang in his locker.

Bishop approached his own locker. "It was a quiet night tonight. After watching the chaos of the wildfire, I thought I would welcome the mundane, but I guess I sort of missed being needed."

Pete tossed him a sideways glance. "You know how it goes around here. One quiet night means a busy week. I'm sure you won't be disappointed again."

"Oh, now, don't get me wrong," Bishop said. "It's not that I want anyone to need us."

"No. No, I get it." Pete closed his locker door. "I'll see you tomorrow night, man. Have a good one."

"You too, Pete." Bishop watched him leave and turned back to his locker. He kept a black bag inside with a change of clothes in case things got messy, which they sometimes did. He unzipped it and with a glance around to be sure no one watched, Bishop retrieved two syringes from his pants pocket and slipped them inside the bag.

Zimmerman entered the locker room. "Hey, Theo, you have a minute?"

Bishop quickly closed his locker door. "Yeah, sure, Chief." He followed Zimmerman to his office. "Is everything okay?"

"Take a seat." Zimmerman closed the door and returned to his desk. "Listen, Theo, I just got word from upstairs that we're cutting back on staff. Some bullshit about city budget cuts. You know how it goes."

Bishop nodded with a stone face.

"Anyway, man, since you're our most recent hire, I have no choice but to let you go. I'm really sorry. You're a good technician."

Bishop kept his eyes on the floor. "Is it because I went and volunteered at those two disaster sites?"

"No. Not at all. In fact, I used that as an argument to keep you on, but it has nothing to do with your work. It's the money. It always comes down to money, you know."

"So, that's it? No severance or anything?" Bishop asked, finally turning his sights to Zimmerman.

"You don't have enough seniority for that benefit. Like I said, I'm really sorry, man. This is the part of the job that I hate." He felt his pulse rise as he wondered if Bishop would escalate the matter.

"Well, I guess there's nothing more for me to say, except that it's been a real pleasure working for you, Chief." Bishop started toward the door. "And hey, if you know of anyone hiring..."

"You know I'll put in a good word for you."

"Thanks, Chief." Bishop walked through the station as if he hadn't just been fired. A quick stop to clear his locker and he continued on, saying nothing to his colleagues, and arrived at his car in the parking lot. As he keyed the lock, he spotted Pete sitting in his car.

Pete looked away in an instant and turned the engine. Little puffs of smoke drifted from his exhaust in the cool morning air and he pulled away.

Bishop kept his sights firmly on Pete's car as it disappeared in the distance. He huffed and shook his head. "Guess you knew it was coming and didn't bother saying anything." He slipped behind the wheel and started the car before peering at his belongings on the passenger seat, including the entire contents of his locker. The black bag sat atop all of it. With a wry smile, Bishop drove away.

❧

Detective Muncie with the Riverside police department rubbed the back of his neck while he listened to the M.E. on the phone. "How soon can you get me the lab results?"

"I'll send them over to you now. Let me know if there's anything else you need from me. I'll do everything in my power to assist you in this investigation."

"I appreciate that, Doctor. Thank you." It was in the hands of Detective Muncie who had already entered the first two cases into ViCAP. It was time to enter the third and make the call to the Houston FBI agent who had matched a similar investigation to his. "Good morning, can I speak with Agent Mitch Palmero, please?" He waited on the line for only a moment when the agent picked up the call.

"Palmero here."

"This is Detective Muncie in Riverside, Agent Palmero. How are you?"

"Doing all right, Detective, and yourself?"

"I'll be honest with you, I'd be feeling a lot better if I hadn't just gotten off the phone with the M.E.'s office up here. Looks like we got ourselves a bonafide serial killer, Agent Palmero. The toxicology came back on the third suspected victim and it matched the same poisoning that was in the other two."

"Along with what we have going on over here in Oakview, I'd say you're right about your assessment. Can you send me what you have? I've already put in a call to our experts in this situation, the

BAU in Quantico. I think we might have ourselves a real situation here, Detective."

"I'll send over what I have now."

"Good. And as soon as I know if our experts will be putting their hands on this, I'll get in touch with you and we'll probably have to have a sit-down."

"Whatever you need, Agent Palmero, you just let me know."

"Sounds good. I'll speak to you soon." Palmero ended the call. "Five dead. All poisoned. All from a possible volunteer. Shit. Scarborough's going to love this."

FISHER STOOD at the head of the table and tossed a file folder to each team member. "Okay. Here's what we know so far. We have two different disaster sites. A wildfire in Riverside, California and Hurricane Edward that hit Oakview, Texas. Both happened within weeks of each other. Both had hundreds of volunteers from all over the country. And now we know that during both events, a volunteer, or volunteers, are suspected of murdering at least five during the course of their supposed rescue efforts. There could be more, and likely are more, however, it remains to be seen if other connections in other locations have been made."

Kate flipped through the file. "The tox screen shows three victims were injected with poison. All differing poisons at that. A fourth victim died from lack of oxygen, and the fifth in Oakview, Texas, appeared to die from some sort of drug interaction. What makes this fourth victim different?"

"That drug interaction happened when the victim was given a high dose of potassium and with the existing kidney disease, led to a fatal outcome. Victim number four appeared to die from asphyxiation, though they're still awaiting what caused it and suspect it could even have been a possible allergic reaction to a medication."

"Our guy has medical knowledge," Walsh added.

"He does," Nick interjected but shot a look to Fisher before continuing. "Sorry, I don't mean to interrupt."

"Not at all, Scarborough. Go on. The agent in Houston reached out to you and brought this to us," Fisher replied.

"From what Mitch Palmero in Houston mentioned to me, the unsub, he believes, is either a paramedic or a doctor. Given the level of medical knowledge, it probably is someone with more in-depth knowledge than your average EMT."

"But they have no idea who this person, this volunteer is?" Duncan asked.

"That's where we have ourselves a real problem," Fisher replied. "The local investigators are already working on obtaining the names of the volunteers who registered. Of course, that doesn't mean all were registered."

"And if this guy went there with the sole intention of murdering people, what are the odds he stopped to fill out some paperwork?" Kate asked.

Walsh pressed his index finger on his nose. "Bingo. Where does that leave us, Fisher? Talk about a needle in a haystack."

"You got that right. But here's where I'd like to start. Now, we'll have help from the Houston Field Office as Agent Palmero is the lead investigator, but he has asked for our expertise. I think once we're all up to speed, we may want to head over there and get our hands on any DNA evidence those guys get off the bodies. Palmero has a team gathering statements from other volunteers to see if anyone got a weird vibe off the medical volunteers. We don't have a lot to go on right now."

"He's an opportunist," Kate said. "He wants the easy kill."

"I agree," Fisher said with an eagle eye trained on Kate. "What else?"

"Obvious medical training. He pretends to be the hero. I think he wants his victims to look on him as their savior. Not that all doctors are this way, but I think some of them like to play God. They like the power. This guy likes the power and he uses it against his victims."

"You believe he's a licensed physician?" Nick asked.

"That would be my initial guess." She turned back to Fisher. "If we get any DNA off the bodies, it won't be hard to track down the unsub. If he's a doctor, he'll be in the system."

"I wouldn't hold my breath," Walsh added. "I can almost guarantee this isn't the first time it's happened. He's careful. Pulling DNA is a pipe dream. There's a history here and I'll bet if we look deeper, we'll find a connection to other similar sites. I think that's where I'd like to start." He looked to Fisher. "Before we spend our resources heading to Houston on what little we know right now, I say let's gather everything we can from here first. It'll give Agent Palmero an opportunity to sift through his team's reports on the volunteers and it'll give Reid a chance to draft a profile."

Fisher folded his arms and nodded before turning to Scarborough. "What about you? Any other thoughts? He's your guy in Houston."

"Walsh is right. It's too early to bombard their office just yet. Palmero is coordinating with Riverside County too. I might make the suggestion they get the field office there involved in this too. This could span miles and years and is a lot to take on. We'll need those teams to do some of the legwork. In the meantime, I like where Walsh is going with this. But I'll defer to you."

Kate noticed and understood how difficult it must have been for Nick to concede. He was always in charge, since the day they met.

"I agree," Fisher replied. "Why don't you and I make a call after this to Palmero and let him know the plan and get his take. Thank you all for the valuable input. Let's get to work."

THEO BISHOP WAITED at the counter of the National Registry Office for EMTs in Charlotte, North Carolina.

"Here you are, sir. You are now officially registered in the state of North Carolina."

Bishop took the documents from the young woman behind the counter. "Thank you so much. I look forward to serving the people of Charlotte. Have a nice day." He walked to his car and stepped inside, peering at the certification before setting it on the passenger seat.

The chance that he would sail into another EMT position in Baltimore was a long shot. Word got around quickly inside the community and he was certain Pete Fryer had something to do with his being fired. His best option was to pick up and move. He'd done it before, just like Philly. No big deal. It wasn't like he had any ties in Baltimore. What ties he did have were far away and he wasn't the type to stay in touch. No family visits at Christmas. No birthdays to celebrate. Now he would be starting fresh in a new city. This time, he would be more careful.

The job interview had already been lined up and Bishop was on his way. Now that he had the paperwork, this should be a no-brainer. Most of these guys were impressed with Bishop because he was a doctor, even if he wasn't practicing. And it seemed no one questioned his reasoning for not currently practicing. Either that, or they just didn't care. It was probably the latter, but Bishop felt he was better than any of them. He could identify just about any medical situation they would come across.

Where he messed up with Pete, though, was his vagueness as to what transpired when the old woman croaked. Bishop saw it in Pete's eyes then. He knew the time was coming that he would have to pick up and leave again. Still, they could prove nothing. Bishop had gone to great lengths to ensure he left nothing behind and no witnesses.

The look in her eyes when she figured out his intentions. The thought of it now excited him. Her frail fingers clasping his wrist. She saw her imminent demise in his face, and it was the shot of adrenaline he needed. The power of taking a life. It was exhilarating.

Bishop arrived at the Charlotte Fire and EMS station where he was to interview with the paramedic and if he passed that test, he would interview with the fire chief himself. "Hello, I'm here to meet with Mr. Davenport with EMS. I'm Dr. Theodore Bishop here for an interview."

One of the firefighters wiped down the engine and gazed at Bishop. "You're a doctor?"

"I am."

The firefighter eyed him, then tossed his head toward the back of the station. "Head that way. Down the hall, third door on the right. Good luck, Doctor."

Bishop smiled and headed toward the door marked EMS and knocked.

"Come in."

He opened the door. "Hello, Mr. Davenport? I'm Dr. Theodore Bishop here for the EMT position."

"Yes, hi there. Why don't you close the door and come on in?"

Bishop offered a nod and a smile before closing the door. He sat down in a chair across from Davenport's desk.

"I understand you have the new certification from the state?" Davenport asked.

"Yes, sir. It's right here." Bishop handed him the document. "I'm also registered with the National Registry. They'll have my employment history as well."

Davenport perused the details. "I had a chance to reach out to your previous employer in Baltimore. A Ray Zimmerman."

Bishop's mouth dried and his eyes flickered for a moment. "Oh, good. He was an excellent supervisor and a good man."

"Unfortunately, he has yet to return my call, so I'll have to take your word for it. Tell me, Dr. Bishop, why are you an EMT when you're clearly a medical doctor?"

"It's a bit of a long story, but I'll just say that the cost of being a doctor acts as a hindrance. And frankly, I prefer to get out there and help where I'm needed most. Working in a family practice and writing prescriptions for antibiotics isn't the most exciting thing I've ever done." Bishop watched Davenport's reaction. Was he going to buy it, or keep pushing this line of questioning? Not that Bishop couldn't handle it. He'd been here plenty of times before. But the question remained, would Davenport give two shits about Bishop's past or did he just need a warm body in a truck?

"I'm sure your talents would be put to better use in an emergency situation. The kind we face every day. So, are you opposed to the night shift?"

Davenport cleared the way. Bishop relaxed his shoulders and wore a friendly smile. "Don't mind the night shift at all, sir."

7

Kate positioned herself in front of the whiteboard in her office. Photographs of the five victims were attached with magnets. Under each photo was a brief description and cause of death. There was no regional connection to the victims. The killer had used the cover of a natural disaster to hide his intentions.

"He would need the means, the money and time."

"Talking to yourself again, hey Reid?"

Kate spun around. "Eva. I guess I am." She turned back to the board. "What do you think?"

"I think that the Houston Field Office found no DNA left behind on any of the victims and they're still sifting through the list of volunteers; the ones who signed-in, anyway." Duncan gazed at the board. "I hope you can pull a rabbit from a hat. We need a profile. We need a place to look."

"There has to be someone who remembers him." Kate turned to her. "Has anyone talked to the triage doctors? Maybe one of them remembers who brought in these people for treatment. If we can't find a volunteer, maybe we find the doctors."

"Palmero might already be on it, but I can follow up on that." Duncan placed her hand on Kate's shoulder. "How are you holding up in here on your own?"

"I'm adjusting. I miss the back and forth I had with Quinn. He was brilliant."

"A brilliant, manipulative, asshole," Duncan replied. "You're pretty bright yourself. I'll leave you to your work and check up on those doctors. If I hear anything, I'll get back with you."

"Thanks." Kate returned to her board. "What am I not seeing here? Who the hell are you?" An idea took shape and she returned to her desk and pressed the intercom. "Levi, do you have a minute to come to my office?"

"On my way," he replied.

Kate waited for his arrival, which only took a moment.

Walsh entered. "At your service, Agent Reid. What can I do you for?"

She placed her fingers on her chin. "I think I've overlooked the obvious with our unsub."

"How do you mean?"

"I've been thinking this guy only uses the opportunity to kill during times of chaos. These natural disasters."

"Which we're looking into the past five across the country to see if any of those locations had similar deaths," he said.

"Right. And that's what we need to do, but what if the killer manages to pull off similar stunts with his own patients? We know he has medical experience, likely a first-responder, right?"

"I follow you," Walsh added.

"Emergency calls must be very chaotic, right? Lots of opportunities to overlook things, make so-called mistakes."

He nodded. "You know what you're saying, here, right?"

"That this unsub has killed a lot more people than we could possibly imagine. He would have had the means, the opportunity and a job that put him in a position of power over people when they need him the most."

"You think the unsub currently works in the medical field? Either a doctor or a paramedic. Something like that," Walsh continued.

Kate nodded. "I realize this gets us no closer to knowing who this is, but this case could be a hell of a lot bigger than any of us know. Duncan is asking around about the doctors who worked at the triage clinics in Oakview and in Riverside. I think one of them must have recalled who brought in the victims."

"You're assuming it was the unsub who brought them in."

"It would have to be," Kate said. "This person wouldn't risk someone else trying to revive his victims. He would wait until there was no possible chance these people could be saved. He kept them nearby, not allowing anyone else to intervene. Then, when all was said and done, he made up his story as to what happened, and handed off his victim to the appropriate people."

"Say you're right," Walsh began. "That would mean a lot of alone time with the victims to take his shot. A doctor might have that opportunity, but someone like a first-responder, an EMT, they're partnered up, from what I understand."

"Who's to say the partner wasn't needed elsewhere? Maybe the partner turned his or her back for just long enough. The possibility also exists a partner could be in on it," she replied.

"It's a possibility. I'll grant you. But like you said, it doesn't get us any closer to finding the unsub."

"Maybe we'll know more once Duncan has a chance to speak to some of these doctors. And, we're still waiting on Palmero and his team to finish going through their lists. I know we have a long way to go, but what I know of this unsub right now tells me he won't pass up on any opportunity to kill."

Hours had passed when Fisher walked into Kate's office to see her still peering at her board. "How's it going in here?"

Kate turned around. "Hey. It's going. I'm making progress." She pointed to the board. "You should've seen this a couple of hours ago. I was beginning to wonder if I was on the right track."

Fisher gazed at the board that now had question marks, scribbles and more photos plastered around it. "Looks like you've been busy."

"What's going on?" she asked. "Do you have anything new?"

"Actually, no. I wanted to stop by to see you on a different matter." Fisher pulled the toothpick from his mouth. "I just got off the phone with Agent Jonathan Surrey from the Denver Field Office."

She peered at him with raised brows. "Oh yeah?"

"Yep. He said they just captured the man who killed those three women and didn't hesitate to give you credit for the work you did on the profile."

"That's great news. I was beginning to wonder because I hadn't heard from my contact in a few days. I'm glad I could help. Surrey is an excellent profiler in his own right. I only built on the information he had."

"Somehow, I figured you'd shift the praise onto someone else," Fisher said. "It's what I've come to expect from you, Reid."

"I don't understand." She squared up with him. "Surrey had a lot of information already."

"I know that. I'm just saying that's what you do. You defer." He folded his arms. "Don't. You don't need to."

"Okay, I just wanted to give credit…"

"Reid, Surrey wanted you to know how much he appreciated your help. Take the compliment."

"Sorry." Her cheeks flushed as she turned away from him and back to her whiteboard.

Fisher pressed on. "I've looked at Surrey's file. He has a lot of experience and is very well respected."

"I have no doubt."

He placed the toothpick between his lips again and pushed it around before continuing. "I think he'd be interested in making a move to Quantico. What would you say to that?"

Her shoulders shrugged. "I'd say 'great.'"

"Well, he'd be a candidate worth considering is what I'm getting at. Assuming he'd be interested."

At this, Kate captured his gaze. "Who wouldn't be interested in making a move like that? This is where the best of the best come."

He cracked a crooked smile. "I'll remind you that you said that."

NICK PULLED out of the Quantico parking garage at 9:30 in the evening. Kate sat in the passenger seat and scrolled through her cell phone.

"Fisher mentioned you were forging ahead with your profile on the Houston case," Nick said.

Kate pulled her attention from the phone. "There are still a lot of variables, but I'm doing my best to narrow down the details."

"Good. He also mentioned the Denver Field Office captured their suspect, thanks in large part, to the work you did." Nick glanced at her. "Fisher was impressed."

"I've worked with him for almost a year and a half already. Why do I feel like I'm starting over? Like he didn't already know that I was good at my job."

"He's looking at it from a different perspective now. Before, you were an apprentice, learning the craft. Now you're on your own, taking charge and running things the way you want to run them."

She eyed him. "That's not entirely the case, though, is it? I think he just wants to see me either sink or swim and so far, I'm keeping my head above water. But Fisher wants to bring someone in over me. Not that I have a problem with that. I don't deserve to be the lead profiler. Not yet." Kate revealed a hint of a smile.

It was enough to loosen tensions between them as Nick continued the drive home. "I have a meeting later tonight."

"Tonight? It's already after 9," she said. "Have you eaten dinner yet?"

"No." He laughed. "Have you?"

"Well, no."

"I have to get in the meetings when I can. You know what our schedules are like. It's part of the agreement with the Bureau—and you."

"Right." Kate gazed through the passenger window at the night sky. "Maybe we should pick up some food on the way home then." She kept her sights on the stars above while her head spun with ideas about the killer. "Angel of Mercy."

"What's that?" Nick asked.

"This killer." She peered back at him. "He's an angel of mercy. Angel of death, however you want to look at it. This isn't new. There are many documented cases of serial killers who were nurses or doctors. Killing their victims because they could, or to look like a hero. First inducing a life-threatening situation, then attempting to save the victim."

"This unsub isn't trying to save any of them, though. He's doing this simply because he can," Nick added.

"Someone has to remember seeing him," Kate replied. "Otherwise, we'll be waiting for the next batch of murders. Who knows if they'll even be discovered? It can take years to find a trail and it's usually after several victims have already died."

"I know. You mentioned before that Duncan was working with Palmero to find the doctors who worked at those locations. You have to give her time to do her job. We have no other choice right now."

They arrived home and Kate held two bags of fast food while Nick opened the door. She set down the bags and pulled out two burgers and two fries. "You want a soda or something?"

"I'll take some water, thanks." Nick grabbed his food and sat down at the breakfast bar.

"Here." Kate handed over a bottle of water and sat down next to him.

He started into his food before noticing she wasn't eating. "I thought you were hungry."

"Yeah, me too." She dropped the burger onto its paper wrapper.

"We're not okay, are we, Kate?" He wiped his mouth and turned to her. "Do you think we'll ever be okay?"

"I don't think I can answer that right now. I know I put you on a pedestal. I always have and that's not fair to you. I get that. But to me, you're the best agent I've ever known. You've been my biggest advocate since the beginning, pushing me to be better. Insisting there's some greater purpose for me."

"Because there is," he replied.

"Stop. Please. Whether there is or not isn't the real issue. You know, there was a time, not so long ago, when you said to me you were afraid to work beside me because it might compromise your actions in the field. That you might hesitate out of fear I could be hurt."

"I remember," Nick said. "But I think I've done a pretty good job of overcoming that fear, that hesitation."

"I'm not so sure. I think the reason you did what you did in Rio was a direct result of the dangerous situation I faced. And not only me, but our entire team. That, combined with what Quinn was trying to do. It all boiled down to the fact that I was right there with you and you felt impotent about both situations. So you walked inside that bar."

"Kate, I'd been forced to drink with a drug runner. The desire came flooding back and I found it too great a pull on me."

"I'm sure that was part of it too. But if you had been in control of the situation both regarding the case and Quinn, I don't think you would've come close to opening that door and walking inside the bar. I was your downfall. And I don't know if I can live with that."

"I see." Nick closed his eyes and appeared to consider his next words. "I don't view it that way, but since you do, I guess it's starting to make more sense the way we've been around each other lately. I don't blame you for my selfish actions. I don't blame you for my being demoted. I'm at your mercy and you'll have to decide if you want to see this through." Nick stood up and snatched his keys. "I have to go to my meeting." He kissed her cheek. "I hope you're still here when I get home."

Bishop walked up the first flight of stairs to his studio apartment in the area known as Lakewood inside Charlotte. The rent was cheap and so was the apartment. He closed the door and secured the deadbolt and chain above. The sofa converted to a bed and as he sat down, the springs pushed against his backside. With the remote in his hands, he clicked on the old television. A 27-inch Panasonic that must've weighed 30 pounds. It sat atop a rickety credenza that looked to be on the verge of collapse.

The 10 o'clock news had just started. He'd spent the day preparing for his new job that started tomorrow night. Food was in his fridge, two towels hung over the rod in his bathroom and a pillow and blanket rested next to him on the sofa bed. More importantly, he had unpacked his boxes, what few he brought with him, and placed his scrapbook on the oak-laminated coffee table.

Next to his feet lay a black medical bag. The one he'd bought during his residency in Providence. He unzipped it and took stock of the contents. Syringes, gauze, chloroform to be used only in cases of emergency, and bottles of pills used to treat a variety of ailments from diabetes to liver disease. The collection had been amassed over several months, since his time working in Baltimore. It was difficult to steal from the trucks as everything had to be accounted for at the end of each shift. The chief had been meticulous about record-keeping. But Bishop had found a way to slip one or two things every other week or so, writing it off as being used on patients or sometimes, being stolen by patients. They handled their fair share of drug addicts who sometimes got aggressive, or so Bishop told Pete when Pete wasn't looking. He'd been far too trusting of Bishop to the point that Bishop felt bad for the guy. Turned out, though, Pete wasn't as dumb as Bishop thought. It was his fault he had to pull up roots once again. Maybe it was for the best. Can't stay in one place for too long without risking exposure.

Bishop picked up the large soda and sipped it through the straw before retrieving the scrapbook. He opened it and then the file next to it which contained news clippings. Mostly from the internet that he printed himself. Who bought newspapers anymore?

With a glue stick in hand, Bishop pasted the clippings under the heading he'd created that read, "Hurricane Edward." He'd also printed images from his phone and plastered them inside the scrapbook too.

Upon admiring his handiwork, Bishop turned the page and began a new section. "Wildfires – California/Riverside."

8

———————

Waiting around for answers from other people left Kate feeling helpless. As a new day arrived, word still hadn't come from Agent Mitch Palmero in Houston about any leads on identifying the angel of mercy or death, as the case seemed to be. Inside the breakroom, Kate poured coffee into her mug and added cream and sugar.

"There you are." Walsh entered wearing a grin. "I've been looking for you."

"You found me." She sipped on the steaming hot beverage.

Walsh gave her a sideways glance. "Is everything okay?"

"Everything's fine. I'm sorry. I didn't sleep well last night. Couldn't shut off my brain." Kate set down her mug. "What's up?"

"I thought you might like to know that Palmero is heading our way this morning. Apparently, he gathered a few leads and wants us to take a look. He also wanted to start putting names to faces and with this new information, get the ball rolling on an actual investigation."

"I thought Duncan was working with him?"

"She was—is. But Palmero made the call to Fisher and he authorized the flight. I just happened to be in the room when he took the call. I was on my way to see Duncan and give her the news," Walsh replied.

"That is good news. Probably the best I've heard in days."

"I'm glad I could bring a ray of sunshine to you, Kate." Walsh glanced at his phone. "Listen, I have a few things to take care of this morning before he gets here, so I'm going to run out." He started toward the doorway.

"When's he due to arrive?" Kate asked.

"Midday. You have time to polish up your profile." He nodded before disappearing.

Kate walked into the hall and started toward her office. "Hi." She spotted Nick approach. "I'm sorry I left without you this morning. I wanted to jump on a couple of theories that kept me up most of the night."

"It's fine."

She noticed the look on his face was anything but fine.

"I was actually coming to tell you that my buddy in Houston, Palmero, is heading our way as we speak," he added.

"I just heard the news from Levi. His visit is overdue. I was heading back to my office to finalize my draft."

"Then I guess I'll see you in the conference room at 1 o'clock." Nick started ahead.

Kate didn't know there was a scheduled meeting but didn't bother pursuing the conversation. He was clearly pissed that she took off without him this morning. It was no lie that she hadn't slept a wink and it had been a good call for her to steer clear of any human contact in that state.

When she returned to her office, a sticky note was placed on her computer. She pulled it off and read the message before leaving her office once again in search of the writer of said message. Duncan was on the lookout for her and asked her to come to her office when available. No better time than the present.

"Morning. You were looking for me?" Kate walked inside to see Duncan at her desk.

"Hey. Come on in. I popped in at your office but couldn't find you. Take a seat."

"Thanks. I needed a coffee and was in the breakroom." Kate sat down. "You heard about Palmero?"

"I did, which was why I wanted to talk. I've been going back and forth with Palmero on his team's progress and I know for a fact he's been keeping them focused. But he mentioned something to me just yesterday."

"What was that?"

"He's been coordinating with the FBI office in Riverside, California as well."

"Of course," Kate replied.

"Apparently, there was some concern on the part of the local authorities in Riverside that there might be someone who knows more than he or she is letting on," Duncan said.

"I'm not sure I get where this is going. About what, exactly?"

"His contact there says the local detective thinks one of the witnesses is reluctant. He thinks this witness might have a description for us."

"Then why isn't he volunteering to see a sketch artist?" Kate asked.

"I believe it's because he's illegal. At least, that's what the detective seems to believe."

"We're not looking to have anyone deported. Haven't the locals there made that clear? We have a possible serial killer on our hands. This information could prove critical." Kate shifted in her seat with growing irritation.

"Hey, you're preaching to the choir, Reid," Duncan added.

"What I'm getting at here, is Palmero wants us to pull some strings to help out this witness. He says his hands are tied and so are the Riverside agent's."

"What makes him think we can do anything about it?"

"I don't know. Maybe because we're here in Washington," Duncan replied.

"It's not like we personally know the higher-ups in ICE or DHS. I have no idea who those guys are," Kate added.

"All I'm saying is that we need to look into this. See if we can help out this guy so he'll cooperate. I realize it's a situation where we have a lot of moving parts, but I don't know what else to do. I don't want to risk the man fleeing and we get nothing from him."

"So he's using what he knows as leverage." Kate nodded. "Smart. Then I suggest we get on it and see what we can do. Let's try to have an answer for Palmero by the time he gets here."

Duncan smiled. "I know just where to start."

Nick had offered to pick up his former associate from Ronald Reagan airport, at which he now waited. It had been years since he'd seen Palmero, recalling the last time was at a continuing education seminar. This was back during his early days at the Washington Field Office, before Kate and before Dwight Jameson.

The moment he spotted a man approach, there no mistaking that it was Agent Mitch Palmero. He might have been a little older, they all were, but he had changed very little. The black hair was a little thinner, but still worn short on the sides and longer on the top. A bit gangly but he appeared to have more confidence in his step than in his younger years. And how could Nick forget about the bolo ties? The man loved his bolo ties.

With an outstretched hand, Nick stepped forward to greet him. "Mitch Palmero. How are you, man? You're looking good."

Palmero took his hand with enthusiasm and shook it firmly. "Doing all right, my man. You look soft. Like you been spending too much time rubbing elbows with the upper echelons of the Bureau. The Scarborough I remember didn't care about fancy suits and polished shoes."

Nick smiled. "Yeah well, I might dress better now but I'll take you on in a push-up contest any day. Soft, my ass." He chuckled and patted the man on his back. "Let's head out. You brought us one hell of a mess with this one. Better get down to business."

They caught up on old times on the drive back to Quantico. Nick appreciated seeing someone from his past. It was like he was a young and hungry agent again. It had been a long time since he felt that way. The fire in his gut pushing him through a case. He missed those days and hadn't realized it until now.

"Here we are." Nick drove onto the grounds and headed toward the Division's headquarters.

"Man, it's still hard to believe you're with BAU. That's the dream." Palmero gazed at the building. "I haven't been here in a while either. I think the last time was a few years ago to catch up on some training."

"That must've been before I was transferred. It's a good place to be, don't get me wrong, but there's a lot of politics here. It takes some getting used to."

"And are you used to it now?" Palmero asked.

"Nope." Nick pulled into the parking garage and cut the engine.

"Kate Reid, she was that agent who was abducted as a kid, right?"

"That's her. She and I live together."

"No shit? Oh, sorry man. I didn't realize. No disrespect."

"How could you know? Besides, none taken. Let's go inside and I'll make the introductions. I hear the boss wants to get started on a meeting right away." Nick stepped out of the car and Palmero caught up.

"What's the deal with all that because you were the Senior Unit Agent, right?" Palmero held up his hands. "If I'm overstepping, just punch me in the gut. That usually shuts me up."

"You're not overstepping. Yeah, it was my gig for a while, and I screwed it up. Cost me the job and might've cost me the girl too. That remains to be seen." Nick stepped onto the elevator and held the doors for Palmero.

The doors opened and Nick stepped off the elevator. "This is it. This is where it all happens." He smiled at Palmero. "You ready to get started?"

"Better believe it."

Nick led the way to his office. "You can keep your things in here until we can get you set up someplace else. How long are you planning on sticking around, anyway?"

"Just a day or two, tops. I'd like to hash out this list and see if we can get moving on a ground team."

"You got it." Nick glanced through the door of his office. "Right through here. I think they'll all be in the conference room waiting for us."

"Then let's not keep them in suspense. I'll follow your lead." Palmero grabbed the files he needed and waited for Nick to head out.

The team had convened in the conference room and awaited their arrival. Kate spotted their approach and the smile on Nick's face that she hadn't seen in a while. She didn't know this Agent Palmero but liked the effect he had on Nick already.

"Afternoon," Nick walked inside and gestured to Palmero. "I know most of you are already familiar with or have spoken to SSA

Palmero, but here he is in the flesh. Mitch Palmero, over there is Eva Duncan."

"Duncan, nice to meet you in person," Palmero replied.

"Back at you."

"That's Levi Walsh, our chief coordinator with the local authorities," Nick continued.

"Agent Walsh," Palmero nodded.

"Pleasure."

"This is Kate Reid, our resident profiler."

Kate nodded and smiled in response.

"And of course, you've spoken to Senior Unit Agent Cameron Fisher."

"It's a real pleasure finally getting the chance to meet you all. I'm looking forward to learning from each and every one of you and hope to hell we find whoever's out there taking the lives of the innocent," Palmero replied.

"Scarborough says you've stumbled across a few leads." Fisher gestured for the agent to sit at the head of the table. "And that you and Duncan have been coordinating on the list of volunteers."

Palmero opened his files and laid them out on the table before taking a seat. "That's right. Duncan and I have been working on identifying some of the doctors and volunteers from Oakview where Hurricane Edward hit the hardest. She has been at a distinct disadvantage with only the database at her disposal, while I've been able to get in facetime with the local authorities on scene during the evacuations and rescue missions. That said, she phoned me late yesterday to ask that I follow up on a doctor whose initial statement had been overlooked." He eyed her. "Agent Duncan."

"A Dr. Andrew Valente. I questioned Agent Palmero if the man had been interviewed again given his initial statement that he recalled an EMT bringing in one of the victims."

"And I indicated that it looked as though Oakview might

have let that one slip, so I took the lead and ran with it." He pulled out a picture of the doctor. "This is Valente. A respected surgeon in Galveston who volunteered his time to aid in the rescue and recovery missions. The good news is, he recalls the EMT."

"By name?" Walsh asked.

"If only we could be so lucky," Palmero replied. "No. Not by name, however, we know he was an EMT and one crucial element the doctor recalled was the man's uniform indicated it was a facility in Baltimore."

"Now we're talking," Nick said.

"Exactly," Palmero replied.

"On that note, something hit yesterday, and it looks like now is the opportune time to discuss it," Duncan added. "Riverside."

"Ah yes, the Riverside Field Office," Palmero interrupted.

"You got it." Duncan pulled up in her chair. "Reid and I had a brief discussion on this as well, so I reached out to your contact in Riverside and spoke to him about his probable witness."

"Wait, we have a witness?" Walsh asked.

"A reluctant witness," she added. "The man who came forward is here illegally. He's essentially asked that in exchange for his cooperation, he'll be guaranteed a green card."

"He won't help us find a killer until he gets a green card?" Nick asked.

"That does seem to be what he's asking for and the agent in Riverside asked if we could make that happen," Duncan added.

"Here's the thing," Kate began. "We need this Riverside witness. If we can get Dr. Valente in Oakview to meet with a sketch artist, we can find out quickly if we're dealing with the same person. It would, without a doubt, connect the two cases and we'd have a face." She looked to Fisher. "The question is, can we make that happen?"

"Getting a guy a green card?" Fisher shook his head. "I have no idea. As you all know, that is absolutely not our department."

"I might know someone who can help if that's how you want to proceed," Nick said. "It won't be a quick process, though. If the man won't cooperate until he gets a card, we're screwed."

"If you think we can do this," Duncan began. "Then I'll inform the Riverside agent, or Palmero can, if he prefers, and we can see if he can convince the witness to move forward pending the immigration details. I think that's all we can do."

Fisher cast his sights around the room. "Since we have Palmero here, I think the thing to do is have him work with Scarborough and Duncan to get something in writing on the green card. Whoever you know, Scarborough, it might be best to put a local face on the situation. We don't have the Riverside agent here, but Palmero is working the same case. It might help. I think Duncan will need something to take back to the agent to offer assurances to his reluctant witness. In addition to that, Dr. Valente in Oakview will need to be put in front of a composite artist and come up with something we can use." He looked to Palmero. "Is there anything else you need to do from here with our help?"

"I would like to sit down with Reid to review her profile." He looked to her. "Unless you have something we could go over right now?"

"I have preliminary information I've compiled for everyone's review. We can start there."

"Sounds good," Palmero said. "Let's hear what you've come up with."

Kate had been prepared for this. While it was still early in the investigation, she had shared her initial thoughts with Nick and as she peered at him, he nodded for her to continue.

"Okay then." Kate opened her files and placed photos of the victims on the table. "We're dealing with an angel of mercy, or angel of death, it depends on your school of thought, but both are essentially the same thing. A person in a position of power over another, specifically in a medical setting. That person then exerts his or her power to bring harm to the victim. Now, there are different types of these particular murderers. Some truly believe they are showing mercy by putting someone who is terminal or otherwise in a great deal of pain to death. Then you have the ones who create a health crisis in a victim only to save that victim to look like the hero."

"Which one do you think we're dealing with here, Agent Reid?" Palmero asked.

"The third type, which is the one who exerts power over a victim just to watch that victim die. This person seeks out the most vulnerable. The ones experiencing a crisis that will result in death without medical intervention. Or even precipitate that crisis to expedite the victim's demise. This person is completely without mercy. He or she has the means, the skillset and the desire to be a god. And, if you'll note, the victims have been killed through various means. Poison, asphyxiation, medicine interactions. He'll use whatever he has at his disposal. We will find no consistent pattern among his victims. No commonality."

"That won't make it easy for us to find this killer," Walsh said.

Kate nodded. "So, what else is new?"

9

As the new guy, Theo Bishop wanted to impress his colleagues and the firefighters at the Charlotte firehouse, so he volunteered to cook the night's meal. Everyone took their turn cooking for the ten or so men and women but the next in line willingly gave up his turn for Bishop.

"I hope you guys like chili. I don't cook for myself much, but I used to make this for the study group back in med school." He ladled out hefty portions for everyone. "There's some cornbread on the counter too."

"Thanks, Bishop. This looks great," one of the EMTs replied. "Glad to have you on the team." The man reached for the TV remote and turned it on. "News okay with everyone?"

"Sure. Maybe there's a fire we don't know about yet," another added with a chuckle.

When all the bowls were served, Bishop sat down in the back of the room.

"Hey, aren't you eating?" A firefighter asked.

"Chili gives me a bad case of heartburn. I'll just eat the cornbread."

"Suit yourself. It is damn delicious, though." The fireman set his sights on the television mounted on the wall and shoved a spoonful of chili into his mouth. The evening news began to broadcast. "Oh, good. Janine's on tonight. I like her."

"You like her ass," a woman replied.

He creased his brow. "I can't even see her ass. She's sitting down!"

"A wrongful death suit has been filed in Baltimore this week by a family who claims an employee of an ambulance service failed to resuscitate their elderly mother. The victim had a history of heart problems and the Emergency Medical Service in Baltimore says it will fight this suit."

"That figures," one of the EMTs began. "You do the best you can and you get sued. I mean, can you believe this shit?"

Bishop remained in the back of the room with his eyes glued to the TV. The reporter had already moved onto another story, but her words replayed in his head. *"Wrongful death. Lawsuit. Baltimore."* While he couldn't be certain it was the same woman who ended up as a DOA, it sure sounded like it had been. This was bad. How long would it take for his old boss to find him here? He would be dragged into court. He was sure of it. Then they'd look into his history.

Bishop shot out of his chair and headed into the bathroom.

A co-worker noticed him leave. "What crawled up his ass?"

"Who knows? Maybe he just has to take a dump," another said.

At the end of the day, Fisher had decided to treat the team to dinner, including their guest, Agent Mitch Palmero. They arrived at a bar and grill in Quantico that was frequented by agents and trainers at the Academy.

"Man, it's kind of weird all these Feds hanging around," Palmero said. "I leave my office in Houston and go out and... hell if I see anyone. But here, it's like you're surrounded by them."

Scarborough laughed. "It takes some getting used to." He pulled out a chair at the table set up for the group.

Kate sat next to him and Palmero took his place across from her.

When everyone managed to find their seats, Palmero began. "I'm impressed by what you've come up with so far, Reid. You're very talented. I can see why Scarborough dragged your ass to Quantico."

She glanced at Nick. "I wouldn't say he dragged me here. I wanted to be here and learn from the best."

The waiter placed glasses of water in front of everyone. Palmero took a sip before adding, "Well, I can only imagine your past experiences must play a role in your current insights. You see these people for who they really are. These killers."

"It's what I was trained to do." She took a drink. "But I can't deny that what I've been through has given me a unique perspective."

"Kate's come a hell of a long way," Nick added. "I don't think we'd be as good a team if she wasn't here."

"I second that." Walsh raised a hand.

Kate's eyes were drawn to the television when the closed caption displayed words and a banner scrolled across the screen at the bottom. "Baltimore."

"What's that?" Nick asked her.

"The news. Something about a wrongful death suit filed

against a Baltimore EMS firm." She turned to him. "Dr. Valente said the EMT who brought in a victim wore a Baltimore EMS uniform. Don't tell me that's a coincidence."

Palmero noticed the others watching the TV. "What's going on?" His back was to the wall, but he turned around. "What is it? You see something?"

Kate peered at him. "Some family in Baltimore is suing an ambulance service for wrongful death. That was all it said, but an EMT and wrongful death?"

"Really? Did we just get a break in this case?" Palmero asked.

Kate nodded. "I think we did."

ON RETURN from his first shift with the Charlotte EMS, Bishop sat in the locker room and slipped on his coat. His partner, Desmond Brown, opened the door to his locker and placed his shoes inside.

"You did good, tonight, Theo." He pulled out his Nikes and slipped them on. "You handled yourself well. Glad to have you in my truck."

"Thanks, Desmond. It was a quiet night, but it gave me a chance to get to know the city. It's best to know a place at nighttime."

"Cause that's when all the freaks come out, yeah?" Desmond added.

"You got that right." Bishop furrowed his brow. "I didn't see Lucinda tonight. I could've sworn she was at dinner."

"Oh, she was. Got sick or some shit and went home." Desmond closed his locker. "It's not like her to bail on a shift. She must've been suffering pretty bad. I'm sure she'll be all right though. Hey, man, I gotta jet. Catch up with you on the next shift."

"Sure thing, get some sleep." Bishop noted the sun rising on a new day. He closed his locker and started toward the door.

"Night, or Good morning, Theo," another of his colleagues said. "Hope you don't get whatever took down Lucinda. That's all we need is a virus to take us out, huh?" The man laughed.

"No doubt. I'm pretty sure I don't have any sick time either." Bishop waved and walked out into the parking lot. The sun hurt his eyes and he placed sunglasses on his face. His car was easy to spot because it had Maryland plates. As he approached it, the story from the news last night reminded him to get those plates changed. So far, he'd heard nothing from anyone about this so-called wrongful death suit, but an internal investigation would most certainly take place. Chances were good that the chief would tell the authorities it was he who treated the woman.

He slipped onto the driver's seat and peered through the wind-shield. "Shit. The registry." Bishop was on the National Registry and that would be the first place they'd look to pin down his current location. "Damn it!" He slammed the wheel. He'd screwed up and now he needed a way out. It would be days, a week if he was lucky, before EMS Baltimore would track him down. His only saving grace was that the suit was a civil one. Although, that could change on a dime if presented with certain evidence.

Bishop arrived at his apartment building and inserted the key in the main door. The lobby inside was only accessed by the residents through the use of a key. Any visitors had to be buzzed in. His shoes squeaked across the checkered lobby floor until he reached the stairs. One thing he'd already learned was that it was quicker to take the stairs. The elevator was unreliable.

He jogged up the staircase to the second floor and quick-stepped down the corridor. The narrow hall was lined with faded green doors on either side. The numbers on the doors were either hanging crooked or had fallen off altogether. His studio unit was at the end.

Bishop cast a nervous glance, but no one was around. It was 8am and most people were probably already at work. Those around here who had jobs, anyway. The rest were probably still asleep.

With the key in the lock, he used his shoulder to push open the door as it stuck to the frame and needed a lot of force. Inside, he secured the deadbolt and the chain. No one was after him that he knew about, but it felt as though they were.

The remote to his television rested on the old oak coffee table. He picked it up and tuned in the news. "Come on. Give me something." With his cell phone in hand, he scrolled through his news feed in search of his next location. Getting burned while he was still here wasn't going to happen. Bishop had been careful for this long and this little hiccup wasn't going to finish him off.

"That's what I'm talking about." He nodded as he peered at his phone. "The Bahamas. Of course. They always get hit." He read the story and hadn't heard much about it on the news, then again, it hadn't been that bad.

Nassau took a hit, albeit, not a direct one from Hurricane Florence. Only a Cat 3, but enough to do some damage. Help had already begun to pour into the island to sift through their already derelict neighborhoods. The resorts, it seemed, sustained only minor damage. The people who lived there were the ones who appeared to suffer the worst of it.

"This looks like the place." Bishop needed to lay low for a while. It was unlikely he'd be given the time off of a job he'd started only the previous day. However, his time was up already. They'd find him soon enough. But if he left before anyone knew what he'd done, he might stand a chance.

W<small>ALSH WAS</small> the one who coordinated with the local authorities. His responsibilities included opening lines of communication, ensuring jurisdictional concerns were addressed and all the political maneuvering that no one else really enjoyed doing. But Walsh thrived on it. He had a great appreciation for the state and local cops, and they picked up on it, showing their own gratitude in return. When Fisher asked him to head over to Baltimore, he opted to leave first thing this morning. Best case, he could get there inside of 90 minutes, unless there was an accident.

As luck would have it, the roads had been clear, and he arrived at the law offices of Hickman, Brown, and Meyers at 9am sharp.

"Good morning." Walsh retrieved his credentials. "I'm here to see Mr. Hickman regarding the wrongful death suit against EMS Baltimore. FBI Agent Levi Walsh."

"Of course, one moment, Agent Walsh." The young woman picked up the phone and pressed a button on the console. "Mr. Hickman? I have FBI Agent Walsh here to see you." She waited. "It's about EMS Baltimore. Okay, thank you." She returned the phone to its cradle. "He's on his way. Feel free to take a seat."

"I've been on my backside for the last hour and a half. I wouldn't mind stretching my legs for a minute," he replied.

"Be my guest."

Mr. Hickman, the senior partner in the law firm, approached with an outstretched hand. "Agent Walsh. I'm afraid I wasn't made aware of your impending visit."

Walsh shook his hand. "That's on me, sir. I left the office first thing this morning before you opened your doors."

"Okay, then. So, what can I do for you?" Hickman wore a navy blue 3-piece suit with a patterned red tie and looked every part the lawyer.

"Do you mind if we have a sit-down in your office? I won't take up but a few minutes of your time," Walsh added.

"Of course. Right this way." Hickman looked at his receptionist. "Be sure to hold my calls, would you, Jennifer?"

"Yes, sir." She smiled at Walsh as he walked by.

He smiled in return and felt a mild heat rise in his cheeks. He was much too old for that young woman who couldn't have been over 25. But for a man in his early forties, it was flattering when a pretty woman smiled, even if it was her job. "I should apologize for the intrusion, Mr. Hickman."

Hickman walked into his office. "That's entirely unnecessary, Agent Walsh. Anything I can do to help out you folks, I'm more than happy to do." He motioned to a guest chair. "Please, have a seat and tell me what it is I can do for you today."

Walsh sat down. "I work in the FBI's Behavioral Analysis Unit in Quantico. Essentially, that means we offer assistance to other FBI offices who need help in areas where we specialize such as serial killings, among other violent-type crimes."

"Oh my. I see," Hickman added.

"We've been working on a situation with the Houston office and while working on that case, my colleague happened to notice a news story regarding a case your law firm is heading up."

"We have several cases going at any given time, Agent Walsh. Don't suppose you can be a little more specific?"

"We're particularly interested in the civil suit against Baltimore EMS."

"The wrongful death claim," Hickman added.

"The very one. See, there's a suspect out there who, well, I don't want to get into too fine a detail, but suffice it to say, we'd like to know more about your case and your client."

"I'll tell you everything I legally can, Agent Walsh."

KATE WRAPPED her knuckles on Duncan's open office door. "Good morning."

Duncan peered up. "Hey. I haven't seen you all morning. Did you just get in?"

"No. I've been keeping my nose to the grindstone on this mercy killer."

"Is that what we're calling it now?" Duncan asked.

"That's what I'm calling it." Kate walked in and sat down. "I wanted to run something past you."

"Shoot."

"I know you've had to make this whole Riverside immigration deal a priority, but I was hoping you might be able to jump in and help me out with something if you have the time," Kate said.

"I made my calls to the Riverside people and handed everything to Scarborough. It'll be up to him to pull the right strings. So, I guess what I'm getting at is, yeah, I have some time. What are you thinking about?"

"Levi will probably end up getting what we need, but in the event the case in Baltimore doesn't jibe with ours, I think we should still move forward with other leads."

"I couldn't agree more. Never put all your eggs in one basket, right?" Duncan added.

"Something like that." Kate chuckled. "This will be time consuming, but what do you think about looking into previous disaster sites to determine if similar situations exist?"

"You mean, check for other suspicious deaths?" Duncan clarified. "I thought Walsh had considered that angle already?"

"With him getting pulled away, I don't want it to slip through the cracks. I mean, look, there's no way this guy is a beginner. I think he could have been at this game for a long time. And if that's the case, there are bound to be similar deaths over the past few years and if there is, someone might remember the who, where and when."

"I agree. If it so happens that we find examples of such cases, and Walsh comes back with a name, we might be able to build one hell of a solid case against whoever this mercy killer is."

Fisher appeared in the doorway. "Good. You're both here. I'm not interrupting anything, am I?" He walked inside.

"Not at all. Just spit-balling," Duncan replied.

"Then I'd like to run a name past you both. As discussed, I'm working on filling Quinn's position and someone just handed me a pretty strong candidate to consider."

"Anyone we know?" Kate asked.

"Agent Mitch Palmero." He sat down next to Kate.

Duncan looked at him with a furrowed brow. "He wants to make a move?"

"He was so impressed with Reid's profile and picking up on that news story last night, he thought it would be an honor to work with her. And the rest of us, of course."

"That's very flattering, but does he have the right kind of experience?" Kate asked. "Look, I'm not one to talk, I get that, but I don't think he's particularly known in the field of profiling. Is he?"

"There's a whole world outside of D.C., Reid. A lot of extremely talented agents who do exactly what you do in their field offices. They don't get the opportunity to coordinate with other offices as we do, but from what I know about Palmero, he's worked in Violent Crimes for more than six years. Before that, Kidnapping. He has a lot of wins under his belt."

"I wasn't aware," Kate said. "I guess it's your call. You're the boss. I'll work with whoever you think is best for the position."

Duncan eyed her before returning her sights to Fisher. "I get that Reid came here under the assumption she would be an apprentice for Quinn. That's been blown out of the water, but why do we need to fill the spot right now anyway?"

Kate smiled and lowered her head as if embarrassed Duncan was singing her praises.

"We're a team here," Fisher said. "And that team needs a strong profiler in the position. Don't get me wrong, Reid, you are strong, there's no doubt about that. But I'm not an expert and you need someone who is. Look, I'm just building a candidate list right now. Nothing is final, nothing's been decided. I'm kicking ideas around and I wanted to get your thoughts."

"I like him," Kate said. "I think he would fit in well and I certainly would have no problems working for him. But like I said, it's your call, Boss."

Fisher pushed off the chair. "Well, I'll let you two get back to the business of finding killers. Thanks for the input."

Duncan waited for him to be out of earshot when she turned back to Kate. "You're okay with him finding a replacement for Quinn?"

"How can I not be? One thing I'll never say about Quinn was that he was bad at his job. Look, I am not qualified to do this on my own. Not yet anyway. Fisher has to do what he has to do."

10

In the backroom of a laundromat, Theo Bishop sat on a stool with a white sheet hanging behind him and a camera on a tripod in front of him. His hair had been dyed to a light brown and was cut shorter. Stubble scattered across his face, though it had come in his natural shade of black. He needed a new look for his new passport.

"Don't smile." The man behind the camera wore a dingy grey t-shirt beneath a black plaid button-down. He was a scrawny man whose apparent side-hustle was creating fake travel documents. "You're done. I'll be right back."

Bishop got to his feet and walked to the nearby desk where he waited for the man's return. With an envelope stuffed with cash, he counted the amount due. His cash reserves were dwindling thanks, in part, to the move to Charlotte. It hadn't seemed a great concern because he'd gotten a job quickly. However, the lawsuit changed his circumstances. Getting out of town had become his top priority.

The man returned and tossed the newly minted fake US passport onto the desk. "Your name is Eli Parnell. You live in Lexington, Kentucky."

Bishop studied the document. "Looks good."

The man scoffed. "Yeah, I know. Five grand, like we talked about."

Bishop handed over the cash. "How do I know this will pass muster?"

"Because I say so. Look, man, you came to me. I gotta assume you did your research. You're not happy with the results, feel free to find someone who will do it for less. I guarantee you, you won't."

"Fine." Bishop tucked the passport into his coat pocket and headed to the door.

"Have a safe trip," the man said.

Bishop pushed through the door of the laundromat and returned to his car. On the passenger seat was a large black duffle bag. He sat down on the driver's seat and placed the passport in the side pocket of the bag. As he checked the time, his flight to Nassau was due to leave in less than five hours.

Leaving town wasn't in his initial plans, but he'd screwed up in Baltimore. Actually, he was pretty sure Pete must've alluded to a mishap with the old lady to her son. The reports had been meticulously written. Everything documented. T's crossed and i's dotted. There should have been no reason to consider the incident had been some sort of wrongdoing on Bishop's part, but there it was. He knew it had to have been Pete. He saw the look when he told his partner the woman was dead. It was a look he'd seen before.

He arrived at the Charlotte airport and left his car parked in the long-term lot. It would be weeks before anyone would realize it was his. What to do when that time came, however, was something Bishop hadn't worked out just yet. Although, he needed to remember that his name was Eli Parnell. That was kind of a big one.

The security line was longer than he had expected. Charlotte's airport wasn't a particularly large one but maybe it could be a good sign for him. TSA workers would want to keep the lines moving and might just be a little less careful in their screening. Bishop hoped that would be the case. If not, he might find himself spending the night in jail and who knew what after that. "This better be good," he whispered to himself.

The man who crafted the false passport had come highly recommended by a local immigrant Bishop had come across in his apartment building. The man wouldn't dare say a word if the cops came knocking because his own documents had been faked.

"Next." The TSA agent at the podium motioned for Bishop to approach. "Where are you headed to, sir?"

"Nassau. I'm a volunteer...."

"Business or pleasure," the agent continued while he placed the passport face down on the scanner.

"I'm a medical volunteer for the hurricane clean-up efforts," he replied.

The agent glanced at the photo and then at Bishop.

Bishop swallowed down the lump in his throat when the comparison took too long.

"Have a safe trip, Mr. Parnell." The agent handed back the passport.

"Thank you." Bishop walked past the podium with notable relief. The worst was over. Still, the conveyor belt awaited. He had been smart enough to check his duffle bag, knowing his supplies inside could have given cause for a search. That search could have led to something more.

"Come on through." Another agent signaled for Bishop to walk through the x-ray machine. "Stand with your arms up and feet placed on the marks below."

Bishop waited inside the machine while it took photos of his body.

"Thank you. Step through, sir. You're good to go."

And that was it. Bishop was clear. He gathered his belongings and headed toward the gate.

WALSH WALKED into the Baltimore EMS station and approached one of the staff. "Excuse me, is Ray Zimmerman in this afternoon?"

"He's the supervisor for the second-shift," the man replied as he scarfed down a ham sandwich. "He usually gets in around 6 but his shift doesn't start until 8 tonight. The first-shift supervisor is here."

"You know what, I'll try to catch Mr. Zimmerman later this evening. Thank you for your help." He left the building and held his phone to make a call. "Hey, it's Walsh. I left the law office where the suit was filed and thought I'd head over to the EMS office. Unfortunately, the man named in the suit doesn't work here anymore, according to the attorney, but that the supervisor would know where he went. But I struck out. The supervisor's not here either. I'm thinking I'll head back and make the call to him later."

"Sounds good. We'll see you back at the office in a couple of hours." Fisher ended the call.

Walsh wasn't ready to call it quits just yet. The attorney had no reason to believe what had happened to the woman had been intentional, in fact, his suit suggested it was simply negligence and human error. But it was just too damn coincidental. Kate was right to think this was connected. Her hunches were usually spot on. Not everyone on the team had felt that way, but then Quinn was no longer part of the team.

He returned to the station and spotted the same man sitting at the same table. "Excuse me again, sir. I'm sorry to keep interrupting. I think I would like to see the supervisor on shift now if that's okay."

"Sure." The man pointed to the door ahead. "That's his office right there."

"Appreciate the help." Walsh headed toward the closed door and knocked.

"Come in."

He opened the door. "Afternoon. I'm Agent Levi Walsh." He displayed his credentials before continuing. "Do you mind if I ask you a quick question?" The supervisor wore a concerned expression and Walsh added, "it's about an EMT who I don't believe works here any longer.

The man's face returned to that of someone with only mild concern. "Okay. Who are you talking about?"

"Theodore Bishop. Dr. Theodore Bishop. Are you familiar with him?"

"Yeah, of course. He worked second shift, but I guess he was let go oh, about a week ago, maybe, two. You'd have to check with Zimmerman. He was Bishop's supervisor but works the night shift."

"I need to head back to my office, but I was wondering if there might be a way to find out where Dr. Bishop is currently employed."

The man cast his gaze toward the ceiling. "Well, he'll be registered." He turned back to Walsh. "You could check with the National Registry. If he's working as an EMT now, they'll know where."

Walsh smiled. "That's good news. Thank you so much for your help." He started to leave.

"Is this about that wrongful death suit?" the man asked.

"Yes, it is. Thanks again." Walsh returned to his car.

NICK WAS on his phone while Palmero sat in the office and waited for him to finish the call. "And you can issue a visa for now, is that correct?" Nick nodded. "And when it runs out, what will happen? Uh-huh. Okay, so interviews and statements. Got it. What are the chances it'll be turned down?" Nick waited again while the person spoke. "I see. So long as he can prove self-sufficiency. Okay. Well, I can't thank you enough. This is going to bring us that much closer to solving this case." He laughed. "Oh, I know how much I owe you. Believe me, it won't be forgotten. Thanks again. Bye." He set down his phone.

"Well? It sounded positive," Palmero said.

"They agreed to issue a temporary visa. It's all we can do for him for the time being. The rest will be up to him."

"I hope that will be enough," Palmero replied.

"There's always a way we can turn the tables, but I don't think either of us wants to do that."

"Threaten him with deportation if he doesn't talk," Palmero added.

"That's right. I'd rather catch flies with honey but if this won't do it for him, it could get ugly."

"I don't know how you did it, but I think this will do the trick. I should let the agent in Riverside know where the FBI stands." Palmero pushed off the chair. "I'll bring Duncan in on the conversation since she's been working with him too."

"Okay. Good luck. We need it." Nick watched as Palmero walked into the corridor. But before he could turn away, Walsh appeared.

"Palmero, you need to hear this too," Walsh said as he stood outside Nick's office. "We all need to hear this. Is everyone here?" he asked Nick.

"I believe so. When did you get back?"

"Just now. We should gather in the conference room for five minutes. I'll round up everyone."

"Okay." Nick stood and met Walsh in the corridor. "Just an FYI, we got a solution to our immigrant blackmailer."

"Blackmailer. That's a strong word," Walsh replied.

"Withholding information to get what you want. What else would you call it?"

"Politics? I don't know." Walsh patted Nick on the back. "Good work, Boss."

"I'm not the boss anymore." Nick followed.

Walsh didn't respond and continued to round up the rest of the team. "I'll meet you in the conference room in five." He headed toward Duncan's office. "Hey, can you spare a minute for a quick rundown in the conference room?"

"Sure."

"I'm gathering everyone now. Meet you in there." Walsh disappeared.

Within minutes, the team waited in the conference room for Walsh to return. Kate was the last to enter and Walsh trailed her.

"Thanks for dropping everything," Walsh began. "Dr. Theodore Bishop." He held up a photo of Bishop that appeared to come from an ID badge from his previous employer. "According to the attorney representing the family in the wrongful death suit against Baltimore EMS, this is the man who they allege was neglectful in his treatment of the elderly woman, and mother to the man who filed the case."

"They must not have anything to point to criminality," Kate said.

"They do not," Walsh added. "Which makes this more difficult for us because we are going to have to run on the assumption this man here is the same man who killed five others at two different humanitarian efforts."

"How can we prove this man also aided in those disaster zones?" Duncan asked. "We still need our witnesses to sit with a composite artist to get us a rendering."

"You're right about that. However, I have a call into Bishop's previous supervisor who I will ask to confirm whether Bishop was given leave to offer assistance."

"He doesn't know?" Nick asked.

"I didn't get to speak to him. He wasn't there. However, some folks were very helpful and suggested I visit the office of the EMT National Registry. As luck would have it, Bishop is a registered member."

"Are you saying we know where he's at?" Kate added.

"That's what brings me to call on all of you now. We have a name. We have a reason to suspect this individual is our unsub, but what we don't have is proof. Not yet and not until we, at the very least, get our hands on a sketch. What I need to know is how confident everyone is that we should approach this man who now happens to work for the Charlotte fire department as an EMT." Walsh looked around the room. "Fisher, this will ultimately be your call, but I thought a general consensus would be helpful."

Fisher nodded. "If we drag this guy through the mud and it turns out not to be him, we'll have likely damaged his reputation and career and will face a substantial lawsuit."

"You're saying we have to wait until we get corroborating testimony from our two witnesses before we approach him?" Kate asked.

"In this situation, Reid, I'm not sure we can run on circumstantial. I'm not saying your theory is wrong. I know you and I know how reliable your insight is. But we might have to sit on this until we know more." Fisher glanced at the other team members. "Unless anyone has a better idea? I'm open to all options."

Nick set his sights on Palmero. "We have two potential witnesses. It might be best if you head back to Houston and get with the Oakview detective to help him run down Dr. Valente." He turned to Duncan. "You've been in contact with the Riverside field agent. If Fisher's good with it, you and I can meet up with him to get his witness to come forward. Since it's my State Department contact who pulled the strings, it would be a good idea for me to go with you to offer assurances to his man." Finally, Nick looked to Fisher. "Walsh and Reid can keep track of Bishop in Charlotte while continuing to gather evidence to support Reid's theory. What do you think? It's your call."

Nick had just taken charge again and Kate wondered if Fisher noticed. Hell, they all must've noticed. She believed in Nick's plan. It was the right course of action, but it wasn't Fisher's idea. And by the look on Fisher's face, he knew it. The team waited for his response and Kate was sure the temperature in the room dropped 20 degrees in that moment.

"I agree with Scarborough. It's a good plan. Let's do it." Fisher left the room before anyone else.

Palmero got to his feet and looked at Nick. "What was that all about?"

"It's a long story, my friend."

Kate approached Walsh. "Hey, so I guess it's you and me, huh?"

"Always." He leaned in and lowered his tone. "That was awkward as hell."

"Tell me about it. Fisher made the right call, though. He's a good man and I don't envy him his position."

"I think your boyfriend might have a different take on that."

Walsh put his arm around her. "Let's find out more about the good Dr. Bishop, shall we?"

Nassau's airport had opened for humanitarian and rescue missions the day following Hurricane Florence. The majority of the island was without power. Tourists flocked to the airport in droves in search of ways to leave the island. Some were allowed to board the cruise ships that arrived at the port to offer assistance. Others tried to arrange charter flights to Miami.

When Theo Bishop, whose name was now Eli Parnell, arrived, he slipped through with ease thanks to the bedlam. The last thing he needed was local police asking questions as to his purpose on the island. He'd yet to secure any identification that would associate him with one of the humanitarian convoys that had already arrived. That was first on his list of things to do.

At the baggage claim area, several people waited, huddled around the conveyors in a swarm. Bishop kept his eyes out for anyone with a Red Cross emblem, Doctors without Borders, anyone who looked like they were part of the rescue efforts. When his eyes landed on a young woman, a nun, who appeared to be on her own, he waited for her to move toward the conveyor and when she did, he approached.

"Excuse me, Sister, can I help you with your luggage?" He pointed to a bag that was coming near. "Is that one there yours?"

"No, it's that one, just there. Blue."

Bishop smiled and stepped toward the conveyor. He pulled off the blue bag and set it next to him.

"That one there as well, if you'd be so kind," she said.

"You got it." Bishop reached for the second bag and once he had both, he rolled them toward her. "Here you go, Sister." He spotted the name of a church on her luggage tag. "Are you here to offer aid to the hurricane victims?"

"As a matter of fact, yes. I am traveling with others; however, I was the only one with checked bags. Supplies for the victims, of course."

"Of course."

"Thank you for your kindness, sir. Might I ask your name?" She pulled her bags closer.

He paused a moment and quickly recalled his new name. "Eli Parnell. It's nice to meet you, Sister."

"It's Anne. Just Anne." She retrieved a card from her carry-on bag. "If you need anything or wish to join us in our efforts, feel free to reach out to me. This is my number."

Bishop peered at the card. "Our Lady of Mercy." He smiled.

"That's right. We're based in Miami, but of course, we go where God needs us most. Good day, Mr. Parnell."

"Good day, Anne." Bishop held the card between his fingers and twirled it. Was it a coincidence he used to work at a hospital with that very name? He turned his gaze to the ceiling. "Maybe you just know where I am at all times."

11

The resorts offered rooms to anyone associated with the humanitarian efforts. Bishop arrived at the Blue Vista Hotel.

An islander in a uniform top that had a striking resemblance to a bowling shirt smiled at him. "Good evening, sir. How may I help you?"

"Good evening. My name is Eli Parnell. I'm here with the Our Lady of Mercy mission to aid in the hurricane recovery efforts." He set down the card the nun had given him. "That's my supervisor who can vouch for me if required."

The man examined the card. "That won't be necessary, Mr. Parnell. I'll get you checked in. We welcome all who come here to help our Bahamian brothers and sisters. We are grateful to have you." He turned to his computer.

Bishop scanned the lobby. Only a few people were there, and all looked as though they were there to help. He couldn't spot a single tourist. "You must be pretty empty right now."

"Oh, we are, sir. Everyone evacuated when the first warnings came. The rest of us call this place home. There was nowhere else for us to go."

"I'm very sorry to hear that. I hope your home remained intact."

The man smiled again, only this time it was a closed lip grin that revealed the answer to Bishop's question. "I'm afraid not, sir." He reached for a keycard and wrote down the room number. "You'll be in room 3729. As you can see, we are extremely under-staffed, so all we ask is that you are patient with us and understand we may not have the ability to change linens or clean your room on a daily basis. We will do our best, however."

"Please. It's totally unnecessary. I can take out my own trash. I'm here to help, not to be a burden. Thank you." Bishop took the key and rode the elevator to the third floor. While the hotel was a three-star at best, it beat the hell out of his studio apartment in Charlotte's questionable urban area. Bishop walked inside and set down his bags. It was already late and there would be nothing for him to do tonight. First thing in the morning, he would find the ones who needed him the most.

WALSH WALKED into Kate's office with his hands tucked into his pockets. "Hey, it's getting late. What's say we call it a night and grab some food?"

Kate pulled her attention from her computer and checked the time. "Oh, wow. It's almost ten." She sat back and raised her arms in a long stretch. "I could use some food." She closed the lid of her laptop and grabbed her coat and purse. "I just want to stop in and see Fisher on the way out. Is that okay with you?"

"Be my guest. After you." He stepped aside and waited for her to leave the office before following.

"What about that supervisor?" Kate looked over her shoulder. "Did you talk to him yet?"

"He hasn't called back. But I called right after he supposedly got on shift and he didn't answer."

"That's odd. You'd think when a badge wants to talk to you, it might be a good idea to return the call."

"It's right up there with the rest of the dumb shit people do," Walsh added.

They arrived at Fisher's office and Kate walked in. "Hey. I see you're still here too."

"Still here." He gazed at them. "Looks like you two are heading out."

"We're going to grab a bite to eat," Walsh began. "Care to join us?"

"You know what, I think I will. Thanks for the invite." Fisher shut down his computer and stood. "Oh, by the way, I just got a call from Duncan. She and Scarborough arrived in Riverside and are going to get checked into a hotel then meet up with the agent first thing in the morning."

Kate nodded. "Oh. Good. I was wondering if they'd arrived yet." Nick hadn't called her and in any other circumstance, he would've texted his arrival at the very least, followed by a call before he went to bed. She wondered now if even that would happen.

"You ready, Reid?" Walsh asked.

"You bet. I'm starved. Mind if I hitch a ride with one of you? I drove in with Nick this morning."

"I'll take you. I can drop you at home too. I'm closer to you than Walsh," Fisher replied.

"Thanks. I appreciate it."

Kate stepped into the passenger seat of Fisher's Infinity Q80. It was a far cry from her Ford Explorer, which she'd splurged on after her transfer to Quantico. "Thanks for letting me hitch a ride. If we'd known Nick was going to fly to California, we would've taken separate cars."

Fisher pressed the ignition button. "Hey, no worries. These things come up in our line of work. Walsh said we were going to go back to the Bar and Grill?"

"Yeah. I guess he likes it there. And it's close." Kate hadn't been chummy with Fisher and certainly not in the way she was close to Walsh. Of course, she and Walsh tended to be teamed up more frequently, but maybe it was long overdue for her to forge a bond with Fisher. "You know, about finding a lead profiler, I want you to know that I'm on board with whoever you choose."

"I appreciate that, Reid. And just so you know, I wouldn't want to bring on anyone you weren't comfortable with."

"Hey, I get along with virtually everyone." She turned to him. "Well, except Quinn. That whole thing started off on the wrong foot and had nothing to do with you or the others on the team."

"I don't pretend to know all that went on between you two, but I knew Quinn pretty well and I was aware of his tactics. I'm sorry you were subjected to them."

"Don't be. I let him get too close and I paid the price. So did Nick. But that doesn't mean what I did in response was acceptable. I get that it wasn't, and I know I face a censure hearing."

"Cole has his way of doing things that I don't always agree with, but I'll be there in your defense if you need me to be. I guarantee you that."

"Thanks. That's nice to hear. I know we don't say much to each other, but I want you to know that I have no animosity about you taking on the Senior Unit Agent spot. None. You were here long before Nick and maybe it wasn't fair for him to swoop in and take over."

"Cole had his reasons. Take earlier today for example. Right off the bat, Scarborough pulled together a comprehensive plan to approach this case. The guy's smart. He knows what he's doing. He's been in a leadership position. I haven't until now. But I hope I can live up to Scarborough's reputation at the Bureau. Minus this most recent situation. I don't want to let any of you down."

It was the first time she saw Fisher. Saw who he really was. He was a good guy. He had his flaws, but they all did. Nick among them. Maybe it was time Kate remembered that he had been a good guy too. Nick was smart and knew how to handle a case. In all of this, she'd forgotten that about him. He screwed up. But who among them hadn't?

To LOOK at the clear blue skies now, it had been difficult for Bishop to believe Mother Nature had unleashed a devastating hurricane on the people of this island. He stood outside a market-place with downed awnings and splintered wooden carts scattered about the sidewalks and streets. Debris littered an area the size of a football field.

His reason for being here now was a far cry from the others who had gathered, traversing the area with saddened faces and dried tears on their cheeks. Bishop didn't care about any of that and he wondered if this had been the right call. Where were the first responders? Where were the people being carted in with life-threatening injuries?

"Excuse me," Bishop approached a Red Cross volunteer. "I'm with Our Lady of Mercy church and have medical training. Might I be of use somewhere else?"

"Please, come with me." The volunteer started toward a nearby station that had been set up. The tent displayed the Red

Cross insignia. "Good morning. This gentleman has a medical background. Is there a need for him at another location?"

The woman smiled, pushed her glasses up on her face, and studied Bishop. "Absolutely. There is another area much harder hit where medical aid is currently being rendered. I can take you there. It is not far."

"Thank you. Anything I can do to help." Bishop followed the older woman to a Jeep and stepped up onto the passenger seat.

"You are a doctor?" The woman turned the engine and pulled ahead.

"I am, yes," Bishop replied. "Dr. Eli Parnell."

"Well, Dr. Parnell, they will be most grateful to have your assistance."

Bishop held onto the handle above the door of the Jeep. The roads undulated through the city. The woman swerved to avoid large rocks that tumbled from the hills and landed in the middle of the lanes, which were scarcely wide enough to handle two cars passing at once. "How much farther?"

"Another mile. You won't find any luxury resorts where we're going. The hardest hit areas were the neighborhoods that already struggle to find fresh water from the community wells. Most of the homes had already suffered damage from previous storms and had yet to be repaired. Those were the ones who failed to withstand Florence's wrath."

Bishop had grown tired of listening to this woman speak of the plight of the locals and bided his time until they finally arrived.

She pulled the Jeep to a stop as close to the command station as possible. "We are here, Dr. Parnell. I will show you inside and leave you to do your best to help."

He followed her to the tent. This was what he had been waiting for. When she approached one of the doctors, he interrupted and made the introduction for himself. "Dr. Parnell. I'm here to help in whatever way I can."

"Perfect." The doctor looked to the Red Cross volunteer. "You have no idea how grateful I am that you brought him here."

"My pleasure, but I must get back." She turned to Bishop. "Dr. Parnell, these fine men will see to it your skills are put to use. Good luck."

Bishop nodded and when she disappeared, he began. "Where do you need me?"

"Have you worked in an ER, Dr. Parnell?" The man asked.

"I have."

"Good. Then I'll take you to the triage tent where they are bringing in victims of the building collapse that occurred late last night. Many were trapped."

"The storm ended two days ago," Bishop said.

"Yes, but the building was in desperate need of repairs as it was, and the people stayed when they were asked to leave. When you have no place else to go, what choice is there, really? Around 2am, the stress had become too great and the dwelling fell. Many are still missing." He walked inside. "Here we are. Dr. Rami, this is Dr. Parnell. He is at your disposal."

"Dr. Parnell. Good. We're shorthanded."

"I'll leave you to it." The doctor left.

The tent teemed with injured people and as Bishop gazed around, he spotted only three doctors. It was exactly as he needed it to be. "Where should I start?"

The door of the tent flew open with two men carrying a middle-aged woman on a stretcher. "We need help!" one of the men shouted.

Dr. Rami pointed to them. "Dr. Parnell, you should start there."

Bishop hustled toward the men. "Let's bring her over here."

He led the way to an empty gurney and examined her. "Lacerations to the extremities, facial contusions." He used scissors to cut open her right pant leg. "Crushed femur." He looked at the men. "I got it from here. Thank you."

When they left, Bishop watched the other doctors tend to several other patients in the tent. He was free to do as he wished and cast his sights to the injured woman.

Her eyes captured his. They welled with tears that fell and stained her grimy cheeks. "Please help me."

Bishop smiled warmly and placed his hand on her head, smoothing down her hair. "Of course, I will. What's your name?"

"Jacinda Wells."

"Jacinda, I'm going to have to run some tests first. Okay? How about I start you on some pain medicine to ease your suffering?"

She smiled and nodded. "Thank you. Thank you, Doctor."

"That's why I'm here, Jacinda. I'm always here to help." Bishop placed latex gloves on his hands and prepared her for an IV mainline. A small metal table lay next to the gurney and contained the necessary equipment to start the fluids. "You're going to feel a pinch." He slid the needle into the back of her hand and watched her wince in pain. A tingle shot up his spine as he peered at her. "There you go. All set."

Bishop kept an eye on the doctors around him before he looked at Jacinda again. "I'm going to give you something for the pain now."

"Yes, please. I need something now," she replied.

He leaned in to within inches of her face. "I'm sorry. What was that you said?"

"Medicine for the pain. Please, Doctor." Tears shed down her face as she winced once again.

"Of course. I'm here to help you. I can see how much you're suffering, and I want to end that suffering for you." He wiped away the tears from her cheeks. "Do you want me to help you, Jacinda?"

She creased her brow in confusion. "Yes, doctor. Please." She moaned. "Please give me the medicine. I beg you. I am in such pain."

Bishop studied her. "I know. I know it hurts. I can make it stop."

Dr. Rami approached from behind. "What is the status of your patient, Dr. Parnell?"

Bishop spun around. "I was just about to administer pain medication, then draw blood for testing before I dress the superficial wounds."

"Good. I want you to get her on a truck to transport to the nearest hospital. I can see she will need x-rays at the very least." Dr. Rami continued making the rounds to the other doctors.

Bishop had gotten lucky and couldn't afford to waste any more time. "Well, that was close, wasn't it, Jacinda?"

Her eyes widened with fear. "Wait. Wait. Please..." She turned her head in search of the other doctor and as she was about to speak, she shot back at Bishop as he squeezed her hand.

"Shhh... They're all very busy. It's best not to disturb them while they're helping other patients. You're my patient, Jacinda and I'm here to help." Bishop inserted a needle into the mainline IV drip. "There you go. You'll be all better in just a minute. I promise."

The woman began to convulse, and Bishop held her down. It wouldn't last long but he scanned the area for anyone who might take notice. No one had. "Relax, Jacinda. I know what's best for you. I'm your doctor." He placed his fingers on her carotid artery to check her pulse. He knew that if he pressed hard enough, he could induce a blackout, which would silence her more quickly, yet look as though he had done nothing wrong.

He kept his fingers in her neck, pressing hard, and watched her eyes widen with the knowledge that she knew he was about to kill her. She continued to twitch. He smiled and waited. The only part that mattered was when they understood what was happening. That he had complete control of their lives and he could extinguish them in a heartbeat.

Jacinda stopped twitching. Her pulse slowed, her eyes fluttered closed and she lost consciousness.

Bishop waited until the last beat. Ten seconds passed, twenty. One minute. Nothing. He turned back and wore fear on his face. "No pulse! I'm losing her! Dr. Rami, please help!"

The doctor rushed to his side. "What happened?" He grabbed Jacinda's wrist to check for a pulse.

"She must've had internal bleeding. I don't know. I did everything by the book."

"Damn it." Rami looked back. "I need a crash cart over here!"

Bishop knew it was too late. The poison had done its job and no resuscitation efforts would work. He would stand back and allow Rami to take the appropriate measures. But his job was done.

12

Noah Quinn's office had remained exactly as it was the day he left. There were no family pictures on his desk. Quinn wasn't married and didn't have any children. Kate never even knew if he had brothers or sisters. Maybe he had been an uncle. She would never know because she would do everything in her power to stay as far away from him as possible, unless of course, duty called, and she was forced to partner with him. Although that scenario seemed improbable.

She stood in his office and looked at his desk with only the Bureau-issued laptop resting on it. A small meeting table in the center of the room. A dry-erase board on an easel at the back. And lastly, file cabinets that held case files. Recent ones only. Cases older than two years were sent into archive.

Everything was in position for the next Noah Quinn, whoever that might be. For now, though, Kate went inside this office for one reason; to remind herself that someday it would be hers. No matter what had happened and how Quinn had forced her to question herself, she knew she was better. Fisher had made it clear last night as they drove to the restaurant that it was protocol to fill the position. She understood that and wondered who it might be sitting in that chair. Would that person be able to look beyond her storied past and look only at her record? More importantly, would she be able to learn something from this unknown person?

To think of Fisher's current prospects, it was too difficult to answer that question. Mitch Palmero seemed like a decent guy. Jonathan Surrey was a little more of an enigma. She hadn't spent much time with him at the Denver office, but he was apparently impressed with her work.

Kate could ponder the question all day, but there were leads to run on to find her Mercy Killer. She turned to leave and noticed Walsh approach. "Hey, Levi."

"Morning. Were you just in Quinn's office?" he asked.

"I was. Just taking stock. Listen, I wanted to get into this National Registry system with you if you have a minute. I'd like to trace Theodore Bishop back to medical school and start pulling some records. I have a feeling, if this is our guy, he'll have a few stains on his history to answer for."

"Agreed. I finally got a call back from the Baltimore EMS supervisor, Ray Zimmerman."

"Oh yeah? What did he have to say?" Kate asked.

"Not enough. Walk with me." Walsh continued into the hall and toward his office. "He said Bishop was let go because of budget cuts."

"Budget cuts?" Kate followed him inside.

"Yes, ma'am." Walsh sat down and gestured for Kate to do the same. "I asked him if he had any concerns about Bishop, considering he was named in the wrongful death suit."

"And what did he have to say about that?" she pressed on.

"Get this. He said he hadn't read the entire suit and hadn't realized Bishop had been named in it."

"If that doesn't sound suspicious..." Kate added.

"Tell me about it. I think the guy's trying to cover his ass. He must suspect Bishop had a hand in the wrongful death and didn't want to look like he was admitting to anything. He said if I needed any more information on Bishop that it was best to contact the city's lawyer about the case."

"So we aren't getting any cooperation from him?" Kate asked.

"Not an ounce." Walsh pulled up to the edge of the desk. "But we have the National Registry, and your idea of getting in there and finding some history on Bishop—that's what we need to be doing. Not only will the registry tell us where he's working now, assuming he is, but we'll be able to access previous employment records."

"I'd like to pull med school records too," Kate said.

"Good. Then it looks like we'll have our hands full today. I'll look at employment, you can find his medical school files."

"You got it." Kate began to leave.

"Oh, hey, have you heard from Scarborough?" Walsh asked.

"We talked briefly last night. It was late and he was pretty tired. He said he'd contact me after getting with the Riverside field agent and their prospective witness."

"Good. Maybe I'll touch base with Palmero and see how he's coming along on his end."

"What do you think about him, by the way?" Kate asked.

Walsh shrugged. "I don't know him that well. Why?"

"Fisher mentioned he'd like to include him as a prospective candidate for Quinn's post," she replied.

"Really? I didn't know he had the appropriate background."

"Neither did I." She started ahead. "I'll catch up with you later."

∽

FROM THE CONFINES of her office, Kate pressed on in the search for anything related to Theodore Bishop. Her biggest fear in doing this was that he wasn't the guy. She'd weaved the thinnest of threads between the Baltimore EMS wrongful death suit to the Oakview murders and the Riverside murders. All of which had nothing more in common than occurring around the same time frame. Until they got their witnesses in front of sketch artists, there was zero connection of Theodore Bishop to either of those events outside of the lawsuit. Now Kate was trying to pin multiple deaths by poisoning and various other methods to a guy who might've just been piss poor at his job and someone died as a result.

Nick and Eva had flown over a thousand miles away to run down a lead. Agent Palmero returned to Houston to talk to a doctor who thought he remembered a guy with the victim.

It was all circumstantial and it had all been Kate's idea. The worst part was that Nick had backed her up. When he did that, Fisher agreed because he didn't want to appear biased against the former boss.

It was up to Kate now to find something against Theodore Bishop that would make the connection tangible. With help from the medical licensing department, she'd discovered Bishop was first licensed in Providence.

"Hello, yes, I'm FBI Special Agent Kate Reid. I'm conducting a background check on a Dr. Theodore Bishop."

"How can I help with that, Agent Reid?" The man on the line asked.

"I understand he attended medical school there in Providence. It would be very helpful if I could speak to the school directly as it relates to Dr. Bishop."

"Let me see here." Typing could be heard through the phone. "Yes, he did attend Fieldbrook Medical School and I can give you the number to the Dean of Admissions."

"That would be great, thank you." Kate grabbed a pen and paper. "Whenever you're ready." She listened as he relayed the number and jotted it down. "I appreciate your cooperation." Kate ended the call and headed toward Fisher's office. She spotted him at his desk and began, "I don't suppose you can pull some strings for me?"

Fisher looked up from his computer. "That depends. What do you need?"

"A warrant." Kate walked in. "I need the med school records on Theodore Bishop and I can't get them without one."

"That is a fact." Fisher shook free a toothpick from the box on his desk and placed it between his lips. "You sure you don't want to wait to see what Scarborough and Duncan come up with on a composite drawing? Palmero's expecting one too. You'll know if we're dealing with the same unsub."

She dropped into the chair across for him. "I did think about that."

"I appreciate you wanting to nail down this unsub, but if you jump through hoops now and it turns out to have been for nothing, we'll have burned favors. We always need favors, Reid," Fisher replied.

"Then what do you suggest? I hate waiting. You've probably figured that out about me already."

"I have. But look, our team is working on this. You have to let them do their thing."

"It's just if Walsh is able to discover where Bishop's working, I want to get to him before he knows we're looking," she added.

Fisher studied her. "If I was sitting here talking to Quinn, he'd have already gotten the warrant. He wouldn't have asked Scarborough."

"He wasn't the type to ask for permission. I'm not him. I trust in the process. Don't get me wrong, I've been known to sidestep a time or two, but I want to be better. I know I can't behave like I'm running a one-woman show. I've done that and have learned my lesson. What I'm asking is, do you trust me enough to believe that I'm right about Bishop?"

"Trust has nothing to do with it. I trust you with my life. I also know that Scarborough gave you a long leash. No offense."

"None taken. In all fairness, he did that because I am usually right."

Fisher smiled. "Now you're starting to sound like Quinn."

"I'm sorry. I don't..."

"Don't be sorry. When you ask for something, you need to be all-in. Don't waver. If you do, I'll see that you doubt yourself. I need you to be the type of agent who doesn't doubt herself. Ever. That doesn't mean you won't be wrong sometimes. That happens to the best of us." He sat up and pulled out the toothpick, aiming it at her. "I want you to come in here, tell me what you want to do and why. Stick to your guns, Reid. Don't let anyone tell you any differently." He sighed. "I'll make the call and get the warrant. But you better be right about this man. It'll cost you if you're not."

Kate stood. "I'm right. I might not have been sure when I walked in here, but I am now. Thank you." She turned to leave.

"Do me a favor?" He asked and waited for her to turn back. "Remember who you are and don't second guess yourself."

"I won't." Kate left his office, confident in the direction she wanted to take. Running things by Nick for his approval was now a thing of the past. She'd always depended on him to restrain her actions or dissuade her, or just simply to get his endorsement. She had needed Nick's approval and it was the very thing Nick, himself, had warned her about years ago with Marshall. The conversation they'd had was so clear to her again.

"I saw how you looked at Avery back there. Seeking his approval; wondering if he thought it was a good idea for you to come

along with me this morning. Now I'm not saying that's what he expects. My guess is, he doesn't. But that's how you are when you're around him."

Fisher was telling her that same thing. Why hadn't she seen it before now, or more importantly, why hadn't Nick seen it? Kate knew the answer to that. When she'd fallen in love with Nick, she fell into the same pattern as she had with Marshall. He let her because he thought it meant keeping her safe. Safe from her own decisions, apparently.

Kate walked back to her office understanding that if she ever wanted to occupy Quinn's old office, that pattern had to be broken. It wasn't Nick's fault any more than it had been Marshall's fault. They did what men do, which was great unless you also happen to work for those men. It was up to her to decide what she wanted more. The job or Nick Scarborough.

THE RIVERSIDE FIELD AGENT, Miles Denton, ended his call and looked across his desk at the two BAU agents who had recently arrived. "He's here."

Eva Duncan and Nick Scarborough traded glances before he spoke up. "If he doesn't agree to this…"

"He already said he would," Denton replied. "All we can do now is hope his memory is intact. Let's go set him up with the sketch artist."

They made their way to the first-floor forensics unit where the composite artist sat at his computer.

"He's in the lobby. I'll bring him in." Denton left the room.

"You two are with BAU Quantico?" The artist asked.

"Yep," Duncan replied. "We flew in last night with the hopes

Denton's witness would cooperate. Agent Scarborough pulled a lot of strings to get him what he wanted."

"I hope it's worth it for you folks." The man turned back to his computer. "I'll get this ready to go and see what I can pull from him. Why don't you two take a seat over there? This will take a while."

"We have all day," Nick replied.

Agent Denton, a young hotshot looking to make a name for himself, returned with the man who'd basically blackmailed Nick into promising a green card in exchange for his testimony. "Have a seat right here, Mr. Ramirez."

Denton got him settled in and returned to Nick and Duncan. "You two want to stay down here and wait or you want to head back up? This will take at least an hour. We can grab lunch if you're hungry."

"I can wait," Nick began. "I want to make sure he doesn't renege on the deal."

"Suit yourself." Denton sat down at another desk and waited.

Ramirez took a seat while eyeing the BAU agents. He'd leveraged himself and appeared to understand that if he didn't come up with something good, the deal would be taken off the table.

"Okay, Mr. Ramirez, I'd like for you to tell me about the man you witnessed," the artist began. "We'll start off with the shape of his face. Was it round?"

"No, it was more pointy. He had small, squinty-eyes, too." Ramirez gestured using his face as an example. "Black hair."

"Okay. Good." The artist began to draft the sketch.

Nick leaned closer to Duncan. "Do we know where Ramirez was when he spotted who we think was Bishop?"

"According to Denton, he said Ramirez was serving food to the rescue workers when he noticed several people being brought to a nearby triage tent for burns and smoke inhalation. He swears he remembers the victim and the man who brought him in."

Nick grunted. "I guess we'll see soon enough."

Agent Denton walked toward Ramirez and the sketch artist and peered at the computer before looking at Nick. "Where's your photo of the man in question? The guy you think is the same one who volunteered?"

"I emailed it to you before we flew out," Duncan replied.

"That's right." Denton pulled out his phone and scrolled through his emails. "Here it is." He opened the image and held it next to the monitor. "It's a little too early to tell, but I am seeing some similarities."

"We're a long way from finalizing this," the artist began. "I'm going to need you to step back a minute and let me do my job."

Denton raised his hands. "Sorry, man. Do your thing."

Agent Mitch Palmero walked into the lobby to meet his witness. "Dr. Valente, thanks for coming down. Please, follow me." He started back to his office. "I can't tell you how much I appreciate your cooperation on this."

"You believe someone was impersonating a doctor during the hurricane rescue efforts?" Valente asked.

"Something along those lines, which is why we need your help." He held open his office door. "Right through here. Please take a seat." Palmero followed him inside and sat at his desk. He straightened his bolo tie and smoothed back his short dark hair. "What can you tell me about the man you spotted wheeling in the elderly gentleman who had passed?"

Valente crossed his stumpy legs and folded his arms in his lap.

"Well, I can tell you that he seemed perfectly normal. Legitimate. Not like he was there for any other purpose than to help."

"What made you believe otherwise?" Palmero asked.

"It wasn't until I received a call from the Oakview Police Detective. He asked if I recalled seeing this man and I said I had. The wife had been rescued, as had her granddaughter. But what struck me was the look on his face. I can't put words to it exactly." Valente turned away to gather his thoughts. "We were all very solemn. Many people had died, and our hopes had dwindled that we would find anyone else alive. When the woman was brought in, the rest of us, myself included, were filled with hope. But what I saw on that man's face was, well, sinister."

"Sinister?" Palmero asked. "In what way?"

"Like he was happy the man was dead. Triumphant, I would dare to say."

The agent nodded. "And you recall his face?"

"Oh yes. I do indeed."

It was easy to lead a witness one way or another and Palmero had to be very careful he didn't mention Bishop by name or show him the picture Walsh had gotten from Bishop's former employer. He needed Valente to recall his version of this man all on his own. It was the only way to be sure. "Then we should get started," Palmero replied.

13

The reluctance of some of Bishop's previous employers to disclose his history was a red flag for Agent Levi Walsh. While this task was outside his wheelhouse, as he generally coordinated with local authorities on crisis protocols, the team was stretched thin and his experience prior to joining the BAU lent to his credibility.

Walsh served as an Army Intelligence Officer in the mid-1990s before joining the Bureau in 2003. After 9/11, everything in the intelligence arena had changed and Walsh's tradecraft had been honed to the point that he had been courted by the CIA. But protecting his homeland was critical to Walsh, so he opted to pursue a career at the Bureau.

Knowing when someone was evading and deflecting came with his background. That was exactly what at least two of Bishop's previous employers had done. The Baltimore EMS station and the EMT contracting service Bishop had signed onto about a year prior. Before that, he'd been a medical resident at Our Lady of Mercy Hospital in Providence. Walsh got nowhere with them due to privacy laws. This was where he hoped Kate had made progress.

He stood outside her office and looked in on her. Kate hadn't noticed him as her eyes appeared glued to her computer screen. "Hey."

She glanced at him. "Levi, you startled me. Come in."

He walked inside. "You looked pretty intense. I obviously interrupted something."

"I was just reading an email." Kate waited until he sat down. "How's it going? Are you making progress?"

"As a matter of fact, things are moving along at a decent clip. I thought we should compare notes and see what we need to do to keep our momentum." He set down a file on her desk. "This is what I have so far on Bishop's employment history. A lot of foot-dragging and vague responses."

"Interesting. Sounds like his employers might be a little worried about what they did or didn't do," Kate added.

"You could be onto something. What about you?"

"Fisher got a judge to grant us a warrant for Bishop's medical school records," she replied.

"Well, hell, it's about time." Walsh adjusted his suit coat. "When's our flight?"

She laughed. "I'm not sure Fisher will let us go until we get those sketches from the two witnesses."

"Any word on when that might happen?" he asked.

"Let's find out." Kate picked up her phone. "Hey, it's me. I'm sitting here with Levi. Did you two get it?"

"It's hot off the presses. I'll send it to you now," Nick replied. "Stay on the line and take a look."

"I'm going to put you on speaker." Kate set down her phone and pressed the speaker button.

"Okay, it's been sent," Nick replied. "Hey, Walsh. How's it

going?"

"Doing all right over here. You and Duncan?"

"I think after you two see the composite sketch, we'll be on the next flight home."

"I got it." Kate opened the email. "Levi, come take a look."

Walsh walked behind her desk and waited for the file to load. "Well, I'll be damned."

Kate left open the photo of Bishop she received from the National Registry and next to it, opened the sketch. "I'm not saying it's a perfect match, but it looks like Dr. Theodore Bishop to me. Levi?"

"That would be a great big affirmative from me. Hey, Scarborough, you and Duncan should head on back. We got ourselves a match."

Fisher sat at his desk and examined the photo alongside the sketch. "And what have you heard from Palmero in Houston?"

Kate sat in the chair across from Fisher while Walsh leaned against the credenza on the back wall. She'd been in this very spot many times with Nick. Presenting her argument, asking if it was enough to move on a lead. Here she was again doing the same thing with Fisher. "He indicated that Dr. Valente was finished with his description and that his composite artist was cleaning up the image. We should have it any minute now."

"Is it a match, too?" Fisher asked.

"According to Palmero," Walsh began. "Yes."

"Then I don't see much point in waiting on confirmation. Go. Both of you take the plane to Providence and get those medical school records."

Kate stood up to leave. "Thank you."

"Don't thank me. Just get some proof we can use to bring this guy in."

Walsh followed Kate and placed a hand on her shoulder. "Great job, Reid."

As they stepped into the hall, she turned back to him. "Now all we have to do is piece together Bishop's life and find out where the hell he is right now."

It had been almost a week since Theodore Bishop, now known as Dr. Eli Parnell, arrived in Nassau. His time was running out thanks to an administrator from the volunteer group he had latched onto who had figured out he wasn't, in fact, with the group at all. A bill for the hotel arrived under his door this morning. It was time to go.

Bishop threw his belongings into his duffle bag. His supplies had run low in any case and perhaps it was best to call it off. The idea of going back to Charlotte, though, seemed risky. The law firm that filed the wrongful death suit would've tracked him down at his new place of employment. He would certainly be fired. The one thing he needed to remind himself of was that this had been a civil suit. He had been charged with nothing illegal. However, as the case progressed, it would become clear Bishop was guilty of a crime, several, in fact.

He slung his duffle bag over his shoulder and walked into the corridor. Many of the volunteers were already onsite continuing with their work cleaning up and helping the injured. Most of the victims who had been missing had already been recovered, the dead and the living.

Upon stepping off the elevator and into the lobby, Bishop eyed the front desk. He needed to slip out unseen. Since it was still early in the morning, he stood a reasonable chance as there were several volunteers still in the process of heading out for the day or heading home. As people milled about, he weaved through the crowd and made it to the doors where he slipped away. That might have been the easy part. Bishop needed to get on a plane, but would he return to Charlotte?

He started on foot toward the city center which had remained virtually intact after the hurricane. There were few, if any, volunteers there and he could catch a ride to the airport in a cab with just a few dollars. On consideration, maybe the best option was to return to Charlotte. Maybe he'd overreacted and could explain away the lawsuit. After all, could he really be fired for just being named in the suit? If he was going to be fired, it would be for the fact that he took off without asking for leave. He might not have a job to go back to, but he still had his belongings at the apartment. Rent had been paid until the end of the month. He could lay low and figure out a plan.

WALSH PULLED to a stop outside the building in downtown Providence. "This is the place. Let's go talk to these guys." He opened the driver's side door and stepped onto the sidewalk that fronted the building.

Kate stepped out to join him, securing her overcoat and tucking the files beneath her arm. "Ready when you are."

Walsh approached the door and pulled it open. "After you."

Kate approached the man behind the desk. "Hi. I'm Special Agent Kate Reid." She held out her credentials. "This is Special Agent Levi Walsh. We'd like to take a look at the records of one of your former students. A Dr. Theodore Bishop."

The man eyed them. "I'm afraid I can't give you that information without some sort of a warrant."

"It just so happens that I have one." She placed it on the counter.

"I see." He looked over the document. "Let me get my supervisor for you."

"Sure thing." Kate watched as the man walked into the back and turned to Walsh. "Should we mention the pending litigation?"

"Let's just wait and see what they'll offer up. We have a warrant that has nothing to do with the Baltimore case. We'll have to play this by ear."

The man returned with his supervisor. "This is the Dean of Admissions, Dr. Reese. Dr. Reese, this is FBI Agent Reid and Agent Walsh. They have a warrant to pull the records of Theodore Bishop."

The woman examined the warrant and looked at Kate. "Can I ask why the FBI needs Dr. Bishop's records?"

"We're conducting an investigation." Kate was purposely vague in her response understanding that she didn't want rumors to spread and end up reaching Bishop. If that happened, they'd squander all tactical advantage.

"Oh, I see. Please follow me back and I'll get them for you."

"Much appreciated," Walsh added.

"This seems quite serious," Reese began. "Dr. Bishop graduated only a few years ago. I'm sure there must be some sort of misunderstanding." She keyed a locked door and pulled it open. "We keep the student records in here." She continued inside to a room lined with file cabinets and two workstations. "I'll just need to locate the files. It'll take me a moment on the computer."

"We're in no rush, Dr. Reese." Kate stood beside Walsh and waited for the woman to find the files. "From what I understand, this is one of the best medical schools in the country."

"Yes, it is. We're very proud of our success rate." Reese jotted down something on a sticky note. "Here we are."

Kate approached her. "Are the files in this room?"

"Oh yes. Only files older than ten years are sent to storage." Reese stood. "Come. Right this way." She walked along the south wall near the back and pulled open a cabinet. "His records are in here, according to the database."

Kate watched as the doctor thumbed through the files until it appeared that she finally landed on the correct one.

"I believe this is what you're looking for, Agent Reid." Reese turned to her and handed over the files. "This is everything we have on Dr. Theodore Bishop."

"This is great. Thank you. Do you mind if my colleague and I take a look in here?"

"I'm afraid I'll have to ask that you go into one of our conference rooms. These files are all confidential."

"That won't be a problem, Dr. Reese," Walsh began. "Thank you."

She led them to a small conference room. "If there's anything else you need, please don't hesitate to ask the front desk. They'll be more than happy to track me down."

"We'll need copies of these as well," Kate added.

"When you're ready, I'll have them copied for you." She closed the door.

"If your hunch is right, we'll be in Providence for a while." Walsh sat down.

"What makes you say that?" Kate took a seat next to him.

"Because if we find negligence in these files, then I'll have no doubt we'll find them throughout Bishop's career. Including his time at the hospital here in the city. So let's get started."

They split up the duties, each reviewing the files in chronological order from the time Bishop finished his bachelor's degree and headed into medical school to his graduation.

Walsh shook his head. "You know what I'm seeing here? Our guy is smart. His grades are impeccable. He graduated in the top 1% of his class. How do you do that and then throw it all down the drain?"

"I don't know. With what I'm looking at, he was a problem at least to some of his professors." She pulled out the papers. "These are disciplinary actions written up on multiple occasions. Three are from the same instructor; a Dr. Simmons." She peered at him. "I bet he still works here. Should we talk to him?"

"Why not?" Walsh stood up.

Kate followed him to the front reception area again.

"Excuse me," Walsh began. "We'd like to speak to one of your professors. Dr. Simmons. Is he available?"

The man appeared anxious but picked up the phone anyway. "Sorry for the interruption, Dr. Simmons. Two FBI agents would like to speak with you. Do you have a moment?" He listened and nodded. "Great. I'll send them your way. Thank you." He ended the call. "Dr. Simmons is in his office." He pulled out a map of the grounds. "You're here. Dr. Simmons is right over here within walking distance."

"Thank you." Walsh grabbed the map and walked through the door. He turned up the collar on his coat and buttoned it. "Bishop graduates with exceptional grades, gets accepted into a residency program at one of the top hospitals in the state, but somehow for some reason, got under the skin of at least two of his instructors. So much so that they wrote several disciplinary reports."

"Which didn't count against him," Kate said. "What top-notch hospital would accept a resident with that kind of history?"

"Maybe the kind that didn't know about the disciplinary

actions," Walsh added. "This is the place." He opened the door for Kate as she walked inside.

"Dr. Simmons, I'm Agent Reid, this is my partner, Agent Walsh with the FBI."

The man stood and appeared nervous. "Yes, hello." He offered his hand. "I understand you're here about Dr. Theo Bishop."

"That's right. Do you have a moment to answer a few questions about him?" Walsh asked.

"Of course. Anything I can do. Please, sit down." Simmons returned to his chair. "Dr. Bishop was an excellent student."

"That's what we understand." Kate removed her coat and placed it in her lap as she took a seat. "However, we noticed in his records that you filed disciplinary actions several times. Can I ask why that was?"

Dr. Simmons appeared reluctant. "Agent Reid, I have many students and while I do recall Dr. Bishop as being one of my brightest students, I'm afraid whatever I wrote in his file, I can't seem to recall exactly."

"Let me refresh your memory, Doctor." Walsh retrieved the files. "On the third of October 2012, you wrote that Theodore Bishop had been thought to have played a very serious prank on another student. One that states here you couldn't prove."

"Oh, yes. I recall now." The doctor pushed up the glasses on his nose. "It was some time ago, but I recall a student coming to me insisting the reason he missed his exam was due to an illness. That illness, he indicated, was a direct result of Theodore Bishop placing some sort of laxative in his food. Of course, it's a harmless college prank until it results in someone's grades suffering."

"Sure." Kate nodded. "And then less than six months later, near the end of the first year, Bishop was written up for suspected cheating on an exam." She peered at him. "Given Bishop's grades, why would he have needed to cheat on a test?"

"I don't suppose I'm the person who could answer that, frankly. But the test results were considerably better than all of the other students. And it appeared, while there was no concrete proof, that Bishop, in fact, obtained the answers in some form or another."

"And nothing was done in either of these incidents?" Walsh asked.

"These were unproven infractions. Notating them in the file was the only course of action," Simmons replied.

"And then this last one was written near the end of his medical school training and involved a cadaver," Kate added.

Dr. Simmons cast down his gaze and fidgeted with his fingers. "Yes, well, that was an unfortunate situation wherein Theo took it upon himself to use the cadaver in a fashion deemed unacceptable by the school."

"Unacceptable? Can you elaborate on that?" Walsh asked. "The report doesn't go into much detail."

"I'm not sure I can recall the precise situation, other than the fact that he conducted unauthorized tests on the subject. It rendered the cadaver useless. Cadavers are quite expensive for medical schools."

"I can accept your responses, however, that doesn't explain how Bishop still managed to graduate near the top of his class and then get accepted into a residency program at Our Lady of Mercy, which I understand is a top teaching hospital," Kate said.

"Again, I don't think I'm the person to answer that question. Perhaps that should be directed at the administration."

Kate glanced at Walsh. "The administration?"

"Well, yes. They're the ones who transmit the student's records and transcripts. Every hospital he would've applied to would have received Theo's transcripts." Dr. Simmons peered at them. "Is there anything else I can help you with? I'm afraid I have a class starting soon, if not."

They stood from their chairs before Walsh added, "I think we'll stop back in at the front office. Thank you, Dr. Simmons. This has been very enlightening." He offered his hand.

"Yes, it has." Kate also shook the doctor's hand before following Walsh to the door.

"Can I ask you something, Agent Reid?" Simmons said.

Kate turned back. "Yes?"

"The obvious question would be for me to ask if Theo Bishop was in trouble with the law. After all, the FBI doesn't request private records for nothing. Has he done something wrong?"

"That's what we're trying to find out." Kate nodded. "Thank you for your time, Dr. Simmons."

As they walked along the grounds back to the administration office, Kate began, "I wonder if the hospital was given the reports on Bishop?"

"You think the school withheld them so he could get into a good residency program? What would be the point in that?"

"I don't know." She peered at him. "Maybe they were covering their asses."

"Covering for what?" Walsh added.

"I say we talk to Dr. Reese again and find out."

"Then maybe head over to the hospital and see if we get any similar stories about Bishop," Walsh said. "If we get the goods on Bishop, combined with what the witnesses have said? I think that'll be enough cause for us to bring him in for questioning."

14

Senior Unit Agent Cameron Fisher made the trek to Unit Chief Cole's office. Cole had been at BAU Quantico almost since its inception. He'd helped spearhead the department structure that ultimately became the three units inside of the Behavioral Analysis Unit. Cole had seen it all and seemed to know exactly how to move forward when others didn't. When he brought in Nick Scarborough, a Washington Field Office transplant, Fisher didn't question him. That wasn't entirely true, but he didn't overstep the bounds of authority. That wasn't who Cameron Fisher was. Not when he was a first-rate detective back in New York and not now.

"You wanted to see me, Chief?" Fisher stood in the open doorway.

"I did. Come on in. Take a load off," Cole replied.

"What can I do for you, sir?" Fisher asked.

"I wanted to check in and see how things were progressing on the case out of Houston." Cole leaned back in his chair and rested his hands over his slightly oversized paunch. He was pushing 60 and seemed to have put on a fair amount of weight over the past couple of years. Still, Cole was a distinguished man with nearly white hair and deep "eleven" lines between his eyes.

"The team is spread out right now. Scarborough and Duncan are on their way back from Los Angeles. Walsh and Reid are in Providence filling out the suspect's history."

"You've settled on a prime suspect?" Cole asked.

"Yes. We have enough corroborating evidence to suggest the man we're interested in is a Dr. Theodore Bishop. At the very least, we want to track him down and ask questions."

"That's good to hear."

Fisher studied him. "I've worked for you for a long time, sir. This case wasn't the only reason you wanted to see me, was it?"

"Not entirely," Cole began. "I wanted to know how the team was—getting along—with you at the helm."

"So far so good from my perspective. Scarborough's been nothing but professional. I didn't expect and haven't seen anything to the contrary. We have a good team in place."

"What about Quinn's replacement? Have you put together your wish list?"

"I have a couple of names in mind, although I haven't spoken to the entire team about them, mostly just Reid. Not even the prospective candidates themselves."

"And she's handling the transition well?" Cole added. "She's been under Scarborough's wing for some time. I'm not sure how she'll do now that she's out of his shadow."

Fisher smiled. "I'm not sure she's out, not completely, anyway. But I have no doubt Reid will pick up the ball and run with it. I think this is the opportunity she needed, frankly. Quinn wasn't the right mentor for her and the relationship with Scarborough only complicated matters. No. Reid will be just fine and she's open to whoever the candidate is."

Cole sat up in his chair. "Keep me informed on the progress of your investigation."

"I will." Fisher stood and headed toward the door but stopped. "There is one other thing." He turned back. "What I just said about Scarborough and Reid. About it having complicated matters."

"Yes?" Cole pressed on.

"I think that could happen between Duncan and me. I don't want it to."

Cole nodded. "I am aware of your relationship and you might be right, Cam. Look, I understand the demands of this job better than you might know. The toll it takes on any relationship is great. Let alone on a relationship with a member of the team." He sighed. "The closeness that can grow out of this way of life is almost inevitable. But if there was to be another situation like the one between Scarborough and Reid, I'm not sure the team could repair itself. Do you understand?"

"You aren't sure I can be an effective leader as a result of my relationship with Duncan."

"After the hoops I just had to jump through to keep Scarborough here and Reid off the chopping block? I don't want to go through that again. I won't sit back and watch my agents implode. What I'm saying is, this is all still fresh, and you'll forgive me if I'm gun-shy on the matter. All I ask is that you take my words under advisement."

Fisher nodded. "I will. Thanks, Chief."

Our Lady of Mercy Hospital was just ahead. Walsh pulled into the visitor parking lot and cut the engine. "The school insists all records were transmitted here. All we can do now is talk to these guys and get their take on Bishop."

"We don't have a warrant to request Bishop's records here," Kate added. "I wasn't sure we'd get this far. But now that we have, how do we go about this?"

"We can ask questions about Bishop. They can choose to answer them or not. But yeah, we won't get his personnel records." Walsh unlatched his seatbelt. "Then again, we may not need them."

Kate opened the door and they walked to the hospital entrance. She was ready to haul in Theodore Bishop for the murder of at least five people. The profile on this guy was almost textbook. Angel of Death. God complex. Whatever anyone wanted to call it. Theodore Bishop killed those people because he wielded the power. Kate didn't like to come to such a certain conclusion without so much as having spoken to the suspect. In this instance, she was positive about who Bishop was. She just needed the proof to back it up.

Almost from the moment Walsh said the name, Theodore Bishop, the nurses and doctors who worked with him wore fear on their faces. But fear of what? Bishop himself or had they feared they were complicit in his actions similar to what Kate believed had happened at the medical school?

"And you were partners with Bishop during your second year of residency?" Walsh asked the man.

"I was. We weren't friends, not by a long shot. Bishop tried to undermine me every chance he got. He wanted the fellowship, which wasn't even an option until third year. I don't know. He had a hero complex or something. Like he had to be the guy who got it right every time. That's not the way this works, you know?" The doctor dropped his cigarette into the ashtray around the back of the hospital.

"He was ultra-competitive. Is that what you're saying?" Kate pressed on.

"Oh, it was more than that. Look, I heard some shit about him. Didn't pay much attention until this one time when we were working on a case together. Easy. Some college kid came in with appendicitis. Simple stuff, right? Well, I'll tell you, the kid ended up with almost complete organ failure within two days of his surgery. Bishop insisted it was an infection from the op." He swatted away the notion. "That was bullshit right there. No, man. It wasn't an infection. It was Bishop."

"Are you saying you believed Dr. Bishop did something to the patient?" Kate asked.

"Hell, yeah. Not that anyone believed me. Oh, I took it to the top. They were all like, 'we'll look into it.' And 'that's a serious allegation.' Well, no shit it's serious. I mean, really?"

"No one did anything with it?" Walsh added.

"Nope. Not a damn thing."

"Why do you think that was?" Walsh continued.

"Lawsuits. Plain and simple. The hospital pays a shit ton of money for medical malpractice. No one wanted to face that."

"So what did the patient do?" Kate asked. "Did he sue the hospital?"

"I have no idea. I was told it wasn't mine to deal with and I should keep my nose out of it, so I did."

"Interesting." Kate looked to Walsh and back to the doctor. "Thank you for your time." She handed him a card. "If you think of anything else, or maybe if you'd be good enough to make a statement when the time comes…"

"Look, Agent Reid, I'm an attending now. I, uh, I'm not sure…"

"Don't worry about it." Walsh placed his hand on Kate's shoulder. "We got it from here. Thank you again for your help." He nodded for Kate to move on.

She was reluctant but played along until they were out of earshot of the doctor. "What was that about?"

"We don't need him right now. The patient he was talking about obviously survived the incident. But what this does is establish that pattern we were talking about. I think we have enough, don't you?"

"I suppose so. Are we going back then?"

"Unless I'm missing something. We need to get moving on tracking down Bishop and having a chat with him."

THE WRONGFUL DEATH lawsuit was a problem; however, Bishop would need to see how it would play out. He'd covered his tracks just as he had with his previous victims but there was a chance that he missed something. Something stupid.

Becoming Eli Parnell had been useful in order to leave the country. No one could possibly find out his real identity there which would give him the cover he needed. Now that he was back, it became clear there was no scenario in which he could continue his way of life without being Dr. Theodore Bishop. The National Registry for EMTs was a nationwide database that required fingerprints. Those prints were kept in the FBI's database. Eli Parnell would be his go-to in the event he was forced to leave the country again.

For now, he would return to Charlotte and ask for forgiveness in missing the five days from work. It had been for a good cause, he would insist. And the suit? Well, that was all just a misunderstanding.

The sun fell below the horizon meaning Bishop's shift was due to start. He walked into the station and straight to his supervisor.

"Well, you're back," the man said. "I wasn't sure if we would see you again. Did you even look at your phone for my messages?"

"I am so sorry for the trouble. I was called away on a family emergency, but I've taken care of everything now and would like to ask for a second chance."

"You worked here for what, a day? And you want a second chance?" He eyed Bishop. "Your hair is different. Did you dye it or something?" He brushed off the remark. "Never mind. You really put me in a bind, Bishop. You get that, right?"

"I do, sir. I'll take on any extra shifts you need me to. I'll cover for whoever needs it. Please. I can't afford to lose this job. It was truly a family emergency. I swear it."

"Fine." He sat up. "But this will be the only time this will happen. Look, Bishop, I know about the wrongful death suit. I'm sure you're on edge about that, but it happens, okay? I don't know the whole story and I haven't been contacted by anyone, but sometimes the things we do out there go south. It can't be helped. You just need to push through it and do your damn job."

"I understand." Bishop started to leave. "Thank you, sir, for giving me a second chance."

"You won't get a third, Bishop. Don't screw this up."

He nodded and made his way to the locker room and dropped his bag onto the bench. A few of the other EMTs prepared for their shifts. It became clear he'd been singled out and those around him maintained silence. That was, until Bishop opened his locker door. A hand-drawn image depicting a stick-figure leaning over another stick-figure on a gurney. It was supposed to be him, and he held what looked like a defibrillator in his hands. A bubble caption read, "This won't hurt at all, but it will kill you."

Bishop slammed the metal door and shot a look around. The other techs chuckled under their breaths and looked away. They'd found out about the lawsuit.

"Bishop, glad to see you're back. They all thought you took off because of the lawsuit. Ran scared." Desmond Brown glared at the others. "If it was them, they would've done the same thing. They're just screwing around with you, man. Don't take it personally. Come on, you ready to roll out of here, or what?"

"Yeah. I wouldn't mind getting the hell out of here." Bishop followed him as they headed to the truck.

As KATE and Walsh returned to the office, the elevator doors opened and inside was almost deserted. It was 9pm and the place had cleared out.

"You want to meet with Fisher before heading home?" Walsh asked.

"Let me make a pit stop at my office and then I'll meet you at his in ten minutes?"

"Sure thing." Walsh headed to his office.

Kate started into the corridor when she spotted Nick emerge from the kitchen. "You're back, too?"

"Just got in about 30 minutes ago, actually. Fisher said you and Walsh were on the plane, so I didn't bother making a call to you. How'd it go?" Nick asked.

"Better than I expected. You?" Kate asked.

"We got what we needed. You were right about this guy, Kate. He's the one," Nick replied.

"I hope so. Listen, Levi and I are going to brief Fisher. Have you and Eva sat down with him yet?"

"No, not yet. We figured we would wait for all of us to get here. So, now that we have, we should meet up. I'll let Fisher know we're all here." Nick smiled and ran his hand down her arm. "I'm glad you're back."

"Same here." Kate continued on.

Nick had always been a sounding board for her and offered his take on things. It was one thing she loved about their relationship, the back and forth. Bouncing ideas off one another. They thrived on it and it often brought great results. It couldn't be dismissed. Nick had been a reliable resource, a confidant, and a lover. But Fisher's words resonated. Could she separate the two and find that resource from another?

"Hey," Duncan leaned into Kate's doorway. "Welcome back."

"Same to you," Kate replied.

"Fisher's ready. We're meeting in the conference room."

"Right behind you." Kate gathered her files and followed Duncan.

"Okay, folks. It's late. We're all tired and want to go home," Fisher began. "Let's get up to speed on the day's events so we can start fresh in the morning. Scarborough, why don't you get us off the ground."

"Duncan and I flew out to L.A. and met with the Riverside field agent. An agreement was reached to allow his witness to obtain a temporary visa in exchange for his statement." Nick reached into his files. "This was the sketch they came up with."

"I immediately got on the phone with Agent Palmero in Houston where he transmitted the sketch that he received from Dr. Valente. I have that right here." Duncan slid it toward the middle of the table.

"And this is what our primary suspect looks like." Walsh tossed a picture onto the table. "It looks to me like we have ourselves a match to one Dr. Theodore Bishop."

"But it doesn't stop there," Kate began. "Levi and I were in Providence and tracked down the medical school records of Bishop after Fisher was kind enough to call in a few favors to get us a speedy warrant. We also talked to a few people at the hospital where Bishop served his residency."

"It turned out that most everyone who either worked with him or went to school with him knew there was something off," Walsh added. "But no one did anything about it. Bishop skated through his medical training. None of the higher-ups bothered to call him out when something smelled funny."

"Are we all in agreement then?" Fisher scanned the room. "We hunt down Bishop and bring him in as a suspect?"

"We need Palmero's help," Nick said. "This was his initial investigation and while it appears to span across California as well, I think it has to go to Palmero to bring him in."

Fisher nodded. "Agreed. Does anyone happen to know where we can find Bishop?"

"According to the National Registry, Bishop works for a station in Charlotte," Kate said. "We should gather the team and head to Charlotte." She peered back at Nick. "Palmero can take the lead."

"Just bear in mind that we're still a long way from proving anything right now," Fisher added. "We have no conclusive evidence that it was Bishop who intentionally caused the deaths of these rescue victims. Only that he was spotted with them. And the validity of at least one of the witnesses could be in question."

"Riverside's witness," Nick said.

"Yep."

"What about the wrongful death suit?" Kate asked.

"Wrongful death implies negligence, not intentional homicide," Fisher replied. "What we need is hard evidence. Without a doubt, there's enough here to bring him in for questioning, which is what I suggest we get lined up now. Scarborough, let's huddle up in my office and we'll call your buddy, Palmero. We need him to head to Charlotte where the rest of us will meet up with him."

Fisher looked around. "Let's all go home and get some sleep. I have a feeling tomorrow will be a wild day."

15

When Nick and Kate were at home together, they relished in each other's company. The moments were rare, and they took full advantage of them whenever possible. Tonight was different. They returned home separately, and Nick was already inside when Kate opened the door.

"You beat me." She secured the door behind her.

Nick was in the kitchen with his head in the refrigerator. He pulled up. "Hey. I noticed you and Walsh talking and didn't want to interrupt so I just took off. You hungry? I can whip up something for us."

"No, thanks. I'm fine." She placed her coat on the hook near the door and set down her carrier bag. "Wouldn't mind a big glass of water, though." She walked into the kitchen.

Nick filled up a glass from the fridge. "Here you go."

"Thank you."

"Well, I'm starving. You don't mind if I make something, do you?" He pulled out a package of hotdogs and buns.

"Not at all." Kate returned to the living room and kicked off her shoes before dropping to the sofa sectional. "Fisher seems to have a handle on the investigation, don't you think?"

"Absolutely. I appreciate how he's handled all of this. Considering this was a buddy of mine who asked for help." Nick pulled the dogs from the microwave and lined them with ketchup inside the bun.

"I don't know if I'm supposed to say anything, but Fisher asked me what I thought of Palmero."

"Why would he ask you that?" Nick shoveled half the dog into his mouth while standing at the breakfast bar.

"He thinks Palmero might be a suitable candidate for Quinn's job," Kate replied.

Nick choked down the food. "What? I had no idea Palmero was interested in a move to Quantico, let alone in that position."

"I'm not sure he is. Fisher made it seem like he might consider it though, were they to discuss it."

"It would be a promotion for him." Nick wiped away a spot of ketchup from his lip. "Palmero's a hell of an agent but this would be a new challenge. I'm surprised Fisher would take him into consideration."

"Well, it could be a case of just trying to fill a list." Kate sat up when Nick returned to the sofa. "I like the guy. I just don't know him well enough to make an assessment. I might get that chance, though, since he's meeting us in Charlotte tomorrow." She studied his face and with her thumb, gently rubbed at the corner of his mouth. "You missed a spot." She held his gaze and smiled. "So much has happened. So much has changed."

"Change isn't always a bad thing," Nick replied. "We can get better. We can be better."

"Nick, I know this demotion has affected you. How could it not? But you don't talk about it. You haven't gotten mad or yelled or screamed about it. I have no idea how you feel because you won't tell me."

"How can I get mad at something I brought on myself? It's not fair to Cam. It's not fair to the team, or you. I made my bed, Kate. What can I do but accept it and move on?"

"Maybe I want you to be mad." She turned away. "Maybe I want you to feel something about what happened in Rio. About how angry I was with you when you sided with Quinn."

"I didn't side with him…"

"You did. You said I shouldn't have asked Dwight to follow him and that he had the right to be concerned by that. I mean, the guy was blackmailing us. What was I supposed to do?"

"I don't want to go through this again," Nick sighed. "We've been having this argument for months now and nothing changes. You get pissed, I feel like shit and we go to bed and start all over the next day as if none of it happened. You're facing censure, Kate. You should be preparing for the hearing. The outcome could change the trajectory of the rest of your career."

"I know that. Quinn gets a nice cushy transfer. I get censured."

"Not yet you haven't. It hasn't been decided yet," Nick added. "But that doesn't change the fact that you haven't forgiven me for what I did in Rio. I haven't forgiven myself either. But the idea you haven't; that's what I can't take."

He was right. They'd circled around this same argument for months and it was usually Kate who brought it up. It had just become so infuriating that Nick refused to get angry about Cole's decision to demote him. But maybe what it was really about was that he refused to get angry at her. He wouldn't engage her, and she felt she had beaten him down as a result. It was as if he'd become a man with no fight left in him. A man who had given up on his dream; given up on her.

Kate turned back to him and placed her hands on his cheeks.

"You were a man to be reckoned with. A man who stood down for no one if he thought he was in the right. When we first met, and you barged into my hotel room and Marshall was with me. The look on your face. I'll never forget it. You looked at him as if he should have been ashamed of himself."

"I was a different man then. Yeah, I knew he shouldn't have slept with you. He was a cop and you were the victim. But on looking back, how am I any different now?"

She pulled away her hands. "I'm no longer a victim, for one thing. But I need to know you still have that fire inside you. That fight to stand up for what you believe. You pulled me out of a hole I'd fallen in after Marshall died. You convinced me I was on this earth for a purpose and you showed me that purpose. I'll never be able to repay that. But something changed somewhere along the line."

"I fell in love with you. I did everything in my power to protect you from the Bureau and from yourself."

"But I didn't need to be protected," Kate said. "That's where all this went wrong. It isn't just about the drinking. It isn't just about Rio. It's about who I am supposed to be and maybe I've been diverting my attention from the heart of the matter. Blaming you for putting the team in danger in Rio."

"I did."

"You didn't. We were all quite capable of handling ourselves, but I put it on you. That wasn't fair."

"Kate, what do you want me to do? Scream at you? Will that make you feel better? Do you want me to fight for my old job back because I'm sorry to say, that ship has sailed." He paused for a moment and studied her. "Do you want me to quit?"

"No. No, of course not." Kate stood from the sofa.

Nick rose and faced her. "You want me to be who I was when we met. Hungry, wanting to catch every bad guy out there. You want to see the fire in me again." He moved closer to her and wrapped his arms around her, pulling her tight against his chest.

Kate was surprised by the move and hesitated to give in. Desire quickly overcame her need to pursue the pointless argument. Nick had that effect on her even still. This wasn't the way to provoke change; they both knew that. But it seemed that once again, the root of the problem would be pushed aside for another day.

BISHOP'S SHIFT ended as his partner pulled into the station. He jumped out of the truck and grabbed his reports and medical bag. The sun peaked over the horizon amid the partly cloudy skies and brisk air. Most of the city still slept, but for the few who witnessed the orange and yellow-streaked sky, it made working nights just a little more tolerable.

"Hey man, I'll see you tonight, right?" Desmond asked. "You aren't going to bail on me again?"

"I won't. I'll see you tonight. Get some sleep." Bishop watched as his partner left the building. He had other plans and walked into the locker room. "Morning." He said to another tech.

"Did you just get back?" the man asked.

"Sure did. It was a pretty quiet night though," Bishop replied.

"Good. Maybe today will be quiet too." He slung a bag over his shoulder. "I gotta roll out. Catch you later, Bishop."

"Catch you later." Bishop had suspected who it was who left the troubling image in his locker. And he waited for that person to come on shift.

Bishop walked into the breakroom and poured a cup of coffee, keeping a close eye on the back door where the employees entered. It seemed as though his wait was growing too long. His coffee was finished. But then, the man in question arrived.

"Bishop? I'm surprised to see you still here. Shouldn't you be heading home?" The man asked.

"Yeah. I was just finishing some reports to hand in to the boss. Hey, is that your Mustang out there?"

"It is. She's a beaut, right?"

"Sure is. I wouldn't mind checking it out if you have a minute," Bishop said.

"Sure, why not? Come on. I'll show you what she's got." He grabbed his keys and walked into the parking lot. "It's cold as shit out here this morning."

"Yes, sir." Bishop walked behind him a step or two until they approached the black newer-model Mustang. "Now that right there is a work of art." He looked to the man. "How the hell did you afford something like this on our salary?"

"The wife and I live with my parents."

Bishop eyed him, figuring he must've been in his mid to late 20s. "Oh, cool. You're married, huh?"

"Two years. No kids though. Wifey wants to move out of the folks' house before we start having kids." He unlocked the driver's side door. "Get behind the wheel, if you want."

Bishop smiled and slipped onto the black leather seat. "Nice. Leather seats, too. Very nice." He caressed the leather-wrapped steering wheel and ran his fingers across the buttons on the center console. "Man, I sure could use some wheels like this." He stepped out again and pointed to his car. "That's my piece of shit over there." While the man gazed over at the car, Bishop grabbed the needle and plunged it into his neck.

He cried out as he grabbed his neck. "What the fuck, man? What did you just do? You crazy son of a bitch!"

"You think I don't know it was you who drew that picture? You have no idea what I'm capable of." He held the man's gaze. "Well, I guess you do now."

As the man's legs wobbled, Bishop lowered him onto the driver's seat. He checked for onlookers, but no one was around. Upon turning back to the man, he shook his head. "I'll bet your parents will be glad you won't be taking up space in their house anymore. Maybe your wife can find a real man." Bishop closed the car door and headed to his own car, pulling away before anyone noticed what had happened.

It had been an impulse move. An idea he couldn't shake during his shift last night. There was nothing he despised more than being mocked. These pissants who thought they were smarter than he was. If he'd planned it right, thought it through, he could've covered his ass, but the guy pissed him off. Just like his co-worker Lucinda had before he left for Nassau. She'd laughed at something he'd said at dinner. The first dinner he made for the department, and so he put eye drops in her chili. She missed two days of work and thought she had the flu. No one suspected a damn thing. This time wouldn't be so easy to cover up.

THE TEAM WAS on the first flight to Charlotte. Agent Palmero was en route and scheduled to arrive an hour after their flight. A briefing had been arranged with the Charlotte FBI Field Office in order to bring up to speed the local office and the Charlotte Police.

On arrival, the operation would split into two. One team to go to Bishop's apartment building and one team to go to his place of employment. In the early hours of the morning, Walsh had been on the phone with the Charlotte Police who said they would assist in Bishop's arrest when he returned from his shift. No one wanted to spook him, and the operation had to be covert.

The landing gear dropped, and Kate flinched. She'd gotten better at controlling her nerves while flying and only occasionally reacted.

Nick squeezed her hand. "Almost there."

She smiled in return. Last night had brought back the man Kate wanted, if only in the personal sense. He'd summoned a passion she hadn't felt from him in too long. Maybe they were breaking through the wall between them. Maybe this was the first step, reestablishing the love they had for each other. It seemed as though that was never really in question. They could love. It was the rest of it that had begun to crumble around them.

The door opened and the team deplaned from the private jet operated by the BAU.

"The Charlotte Field Office sent a car for us," Walsh said as he started into the aisle. "We'll wait for Palmero there."

"Good. Thanks." Nick followed behind while Kate waited for Duncan.

"I expected to see Fisher with you," Kate said as Duncan walked along the aisle.

"He decided to hang back and didn't think we needed him to come along for this," she replied.

"Oh." Kate started ahead. "Guess I should get used to Fisher's management style."

"He might be wanting to play it safe for right now. Hands off and all that," Duncan added. "But I wouldn't count on it staying that way."

They made their way down the staircase and onto the tarmac where a woman stood in front of an SUV.

"Morning. I think you're our ride." Nick offered his hand. "I'm SSA Scarborough. This is the team. Agents Walsh, Reid and Duncan."

"Good morning. I'm Agent Bingham, Sarah Bingham. Hop in. I'll take you to our office."

Kate hadn't worked with a lot of women at the Bureau, with the exception of a handful. Vasquez, for one and now Duncan. There was Georgia Myers, but Kate preferred not to think about her if she could help it. So she was always pleased to meet another female agent. She'd come to learn that it was sometimes easier to get certain things accomplished with a female counterpart than a male one. All stereotypes aside, it was no lie that male agents tended to assert themselves more. As if they felt less secure in who they were. Women didn't do that so much, not from what Kate had seen so far.

"What area do you work in, Agent Bingham?" Kate asked as they stepped inside.

"CID. Narcotics trafficking."

Kate nodded. "Nice."

The FBI's Criminal Investigative Division, or CID, was part of a larger department inside the Bureau and handled a wide range of investigations. Drug trafficking was just one.

Bingham started the engine. "The office isn't far. Should take about half an hour to get there."

Nick was in the passenger seat. "Another agent is flying in from Houston and should be here in about an hour."

"I'm aware. They're sending another car for Agent Palmero." Bingham pulled away from the curb. She looked to be in her early thirties and wore her blonde hair in a pixie cut; very short, but neatly styled. Her skin was fair and dotted with light freckles at her nose. The conservative cut of her pants suit complimented her boyish figure.

"There's a lot of buzz at the office right now," Bingham said. "Lots of people are excited to meet the experts from Quantico."

"We're only here to assist Palmero. This is his investigation," Walsh said from the backseat.

"Well, I have a feeling you're all about to get the star treatment. Just be forewarned." She smiled.

They arrived at the Charlotte office where Bingham led them inside. Several agents stood in the lobby as though waiting for royalty.

"See? I told you." She continued inside. "There's nothing to see here, guys. Get back to work. Our friends from Quantico have to get set up."

"I like her," Duncan whispered to Kate. "She should be on the list too."

"What list?" Kate asked.

"You know, to replace Quinn."

"Maybe so." Kate smiled.

"Right through here, everyone." Bingham headed into the main open space of the first floor. "I'll show you to the conference room and grab ASAC Jones for you. Does anyone want a coffee or anything?"

"I'd love one," Walsh said. "But I can grab it. Just point me in the right direction."

"Straight down that hall. It's the second door on the left. Plenty of coffee and I'm sure you'll find donuts in there too."

"Count me in." Kate followed him.

When they walked into the breakroom, Kate grabbed two mugs from a cabinet. "So, Bingham's interesting."

"She is." Walsh took the mugs from her and poured the coffee.

"Not bad looking either," Kate added.

"What?" He furrowed his brow.

Kate held up her hands. "I'm just saying. She's cool. Cute, obviously smart."

"Uh-huh. And lives how many miles away?" He took a sip. "Where are those donuts?"

"Seriously, though. We have to pull this off fast before Bishop catches wind of what's going on." Kate's phone buzzed and she grabbed it. "What the hell?"

Walsh checked his phone too. "Oh shit." He set down the coffee, nearly spilling it, and hustled out.

Kate was right next to him when they returned to the conference room.

Nick stood inside next to Bingham. "One of the local detectives called. He knew his captain was coming here for this meeting this morning. Apparently, they got a call about a body inside a car."

"Okay." Kate waited for him to elaborate.

"It was located at the EMS station where Bishop worked."

"Have they talked to him?" Walsh asked.

Nick shook his head. "He's gone. Cleared out. We just lost our window."

16

In the parking lot of the EMS station, local police cordoned off the area. Agent Palmero stood in front of the black Mustang with his hands on his hips and his bolo tie flapping in the wind. "Damn it. He was right here, and we missed him."

Nick stood near. "We were getting our ducks in a row, building a case so we could bring in Bishop for questioning. Something like this wasn't even in our purview. If we weren't sure of his guilt before, we sure as shit are now."

Agent Bingham approached them. "Charlotte Police is getting a statement from the supervisor. He said someone played a joke on Bishop and put this up in his locker." She held up her phone with a picture of the hand-drawn image.

"Nice. I'm sure that was what set him off," Nick replied.

"You don't think it had anything to do with the work we've been doing to track him down?" Palmero asked.

"No one knew about it. There's a chance someone from the hospital where he worked might've reached out to him after my team made contact, but from what Walsh said, no one liked the guy. They all suspected something was wrong with him. And, nothing's been leaked to the media." Nick sighed. "I think this was a situation where Bishop lost control. It was bound to happen sooner or later. The lawsuit, being taunted by your co-workers. We're not talking about a rational man here. Now one of his coworkers is dead."

Kate walked around the car and returned to Nick's side. "Scarborough's right. The lawsuit must've been weighing on him. Then this guy makes a joke." She turned back for a moment before continuing. "I heard the supervisor had mentioned something about Bishop just taking off for a few days. Then he comes back and does this."

"Did he know what Bishop did during that time?" Palmero asked.

"He claimed it was a family emergency," Kate replied.

"That's something we should delve into," Nick added. "For now, the priority is to find Bishop. He has to be stopped."

Walsh examined the body while the Charlotte Medical Examiner prepared to load it onto the truck. "How long before you get back DNA results?"

"I understand the urgency, Agent Walsh, and my people will do their best to expedite the testing. However, it all depends on the lab. I'll keep on top of them," the doctor replied.

"Thank you." Walsh retrieved a business card. "Call me as soon as you have something. Please."

"Of course." He looked to his assistant. "Let's get him loaded up."

The team gathered near the entrance of the EMS station and waited for the Charlotte detective to finish his interviews. It was time to make a call on the next move.

"You two know the most about him. What do you think his next move is going to be?" Nick asked.

"Levi, what do you think?" Kate respected the chain of command and Walsh was her senior.

"It has to be all-hands-on-deck. The Charlotte police, Bingham, you and your team and us. There's no telling how long or if he'll stay here. My guess is, once he sees this on the news, and he will," Walsh pointed to the news truck pulling away, "I don't think he'll be stupid enough to stick around."

"I think you all should set up shop in our field office," Bingham began. "We let the local police be the boots on the ground and we work to find surveillance footage, banking transactions, anything we can to pinpoint a location." She looked to Walsh. "Time is running out and from what you all have said, he won't stick around."

BISHOP WAS WASTING DAYLIGHT. He needed a plan to get the hell out of Charlotte. Someone would've found his coworker's body by now and the story would probably be on the evening news in a matter of hours.

Dr. Theodore Bishop was still a highly educated man. He could find a solution. And as he peered at the passport used to get him in and out of the Bahamas, the answer stared back at him. "Well, Mr. Eli Parnell, we meet again."

He had the identity, some money stashed away, and now he needed a new ride. He was a doctor, not a car thief. The anatomy of the human body was ingrained in him, not the anatomy of a combustible engine or how to start one without a key.

This would present a challenge. He peered outside of his

second-story studio apartment, sure the police would surround it soon. A bus stop was just below. "Public transportation." Bishop zipped up his duffle bag that he'd only just unpacked a day earlier. Whatever medical supplies he had were tossed inside too. He'd used a lot of in Nassau and unexpectedly used some on his coworker. The plan had been to replenish his stores on shift tonight. That was out the door.

He walked downstairs and waited for the bus. It looked like the 210 would take him into downtown Charlotte. "Nope." He peered again at the routes posted inside the bus stop overhang. "Raleigh? Maybe." Eli Parnell could blend in there for a while. No one was looking for him. "Raleigh, it is."

The bus was due to arrive at any moment and he was alone at the stop. He would avoid the commuters if he played his cards right. The bus plodded along the roadway and slowed as it neared.

When the doors opened, Bishop smiled and dropped the money into the slot. He would have to take this to the depot where he could slip onto another bus that headed into Raleigh. The plan was to be there before nightfall. It would be close.

Duncan slipped into the hall outside the room that had been set up for the team. "Hey. Thanks for calling me back."

"What's the latest?" Fisher asked.

"Bingham is coordinating her people in the hunt for closed circuit video, credit card usage, anything like that that will give us a clue as to where Bishop's going."

"That must mean he fled his apartment already?"

"Yes. Charlotte police headed there as soon as the body was found, but he was gone."

"What about the media?" Fisher pressed on.

"The field office here has a media coordinator who has been working with the local news. So far, they've avoided giving them any idea that Bishop is tied to a wrongful death suit in Baltimore or is suspected of killing anyone else for that matter."

"I want to keep it that way," Fisher replied. "How's Scarborough doing?"

"Same as always. He's taken the lead, which is fine. He is the ranking agent. If you're asking me if he's got his head on straight, then yes, he appears to. Which leads me to my next question. We've got Palmero here from the Houston office, our team, and the Charlotte field office. That's a lot of agents who might not be certain whose case this is," Duncan replied.

"As far as we're concerned, this is still Palmero's investigation. He is who we will defer to. That said, it'll be up to him to determine what role Bingham's team will take. That's not our concern. Our concern is finding Bishop. Let them decide who's taking the credit, or the fall."

"No doubt. We may want to steer clear of that should Bishop slip through our fingers," she added. "I'd better get back inside. Will you be staying put?"

"For the time being but keep me up to speed. I don't want to be the micromanager. We already had one of those."

"Bye." She walked back into the room where Bingham stood next to one of her agents. "Any hits yet?"

"Not a one. He must've had some cash on hand because no one's found any transactions, bank or credit card. And he ditched his car. Charlotte police found it at his apartment."

"Shit. We might be too late." Duncan spotted Kate and the others huddled near the back of the room and made her way to join them. "Bingham says they don't have anything yet."

"We've been discussing our options," Nick began. "It's safe to assume since he's ditched his car that he'll be on public transport."

"You don't think he would've tried to get another car? Borrow one from a friend or something like that?" Kate asked.

"He's new here," Walsh added. "I'm not sure he had any friends. Not friends who would cover for him like that anyway. I think Scarborough's right. He's on the road. We should check the airport, and bus, and train stations."

"Where's Palmero?" Kate peered around the room. "This is his show. He needs to know what's going on."

"I'll track him down." Nick started out the door and into the halls of an office he wasn't familiar with. Palmero stood just inside the office of ASAC Jones and noticed him approach.

"Scarborough. What's up? Did something hit?"

"Not yet, but we have some ideas. You want to come join us?" Nick peered inside. "Sir."

"Agent Scarborough," ASAC Jones said. "Palmero was just filling me in on what's been happening, but by all means, you two do what you need to do. I'll be here if you need anything."

"Thank you." Palmero headed into the corridor again with Nick by his side. "That guy's a piece of work. He tracked me down and insisted on hashing out who was going to be paying for this operation. Seriously?"

"I'm not surprised," Nick added. "It's part of the job—justifying expenditures."

"Sounds like you speak from experience," Palmero added.

"Sadly, yes. But no longer. Come on. We need to lay this out," Nick opened the door and Palmero walked inside while he followed. "No one's found anything that will point us to a location, but my team and I were discussing hitting up public transportation."

"I like it." Palmero joined the others. "What's the plan, folks? I'm all ears."

BISHOP ARRIVED at the bus depot in Charlotte and headed into the restroom. Inside his bag, he retrieved a baseball hat and slipped it on. It would be enough to keep his face hidden from the CCTV cameras dotted around the area. He opened his wallet and pulled out a bank card, twirling it through his fingers. "I can't. They'll find me." He slipped the card back inside his wallet and pulled out some cash.

A final check in the mirror and Bishop walked out of the restroom and headed toward a kiosk. "One ticket to Raleigh, please. The next bus, if possible."

The man behind the counter typed on his computer. "Looks like we have one leaving in an hour." He peered at Bishop. "That'll be $113.67."

Bishop handed over the cash and when the man slid the ticket across the counter, he gave a final nod before leaving. Now he had to wait for an hour and the only way to ensure he wasn't spotted was to keep his head down. He had shaved off the stubble grown for Eli Parnell, but his hair was still light brown. That might be enough to keep him from being identified if the hat came off.

He peered at his ticket. It was issued to Eli Parnell, Bishop's new alias. This was who he had to be now if he wanted to break away clean. However, that meant no longer working as an EMT, or doctor or anything relating to the medical field at all.

As he waited for the bus, there was one person Bishop wanted to reach out to if for nothing else than to reassure her whatever she was about to hear on the news wasn't true. He wasn't who they would say he was. He had been engaged to her once a long time ago, before he started his residency at the hospital in Providence. Bishop held his phone and peered at the screen. She had loved him, though he had been incapable of reciprocating. He pressed the button and the line rang.

"Hello?" she answered.

"It's Theo. How are you, Holly?"

"Theo?" She paused for a minute. "Why are you calling me?"

"Is this a bad time? Are you at work?" he asked.

"No. My shift doesn't start for another two hours. Theo, I haven't heard from you in more than a year."

"I know. I just thought after everything..."

"You mean after I left you?"

"Despite what you think, we meant something to each other once, didn't we?"

"Money. Is that what you need? Are you in some kind of trouble, Theo? After what they all said about you at the hospital. They all knew what you did to those two patients."

"If I'd done anything wrong, I'd be in jail by now and I'm not. No one proved anything. I told you that long ago."

She laughed. "Yeah, well, I think we both know the reason why that was. Theo, I don't have any money to give you, okay?"

"I don't need your goddamn money, Holly." His voice was raised. "I thought... screw it..."

"Whatever feelings I had for you are long since over. I know who you really are, Theo."

He heard the line drop. "Holly? Holly?" Bishop pulled the phone from his ear. "Bitch!"

"*Bus 618, leaving at 3:42pm, headed for Raleigh is boarding now in Bay 15.*"

Bishop pushed off the bench and walked outside to Bay 15 where his uncertain future awaited. "Raleigh?" He asked the bus driver.

"That's right. Ticket?"

Bishop handed over the ticket.

"Thank you, Mr. Parnell. If you'll take a seat."

Bishop headed through the aisle and all the way to the back of the bus. He was going to make it out of Charlotte before the evening news aired when his face was sure to be plastered all over the city. Holly would know exactly who he was then.

Kate rubbed the back of her neck as she sat at the table alongside Walsh and Duncan. Nick had opted to go with Bingham and Palmero to check out the various locations where Bishop might attempt to flee.

"I haven't found anything," Kate began. "No airline ticket purchases, no train tickets..."

"No bus tickets," Walsh added. "Yeah, me either."

"It's like he vanished," Duncan said. "I wonder if Scarborough and those guys are having any better luck."

"If they had, I'm sure we would've been the first to know," Walsh replied. "Scarborough was right. Our window closed. Dr. Theodore Bishop is in the wind."

"No. There has to be a way to track him down. With the sheer volume of surveillance footage, he's bound to turn up somewhere."

"He's smart, Reid," Duncan replied. "You said so yourself. He's a doctor who managed to slip through various jobs and training doing exactly what he's accused of doing now, only he came out clean."

"Because no one wanted to admit they screwed up," Walsh said. "Everyone we talked to was so concerned about their own jobs, or lawsuits. Even the medical school allowed him to graduate with the allegations brought forward. They were afraid too. Everyone has turned a blind eye to what Theodore Bishop has done."

"That makes it all the more important that we don't do the same," Kate said. "He's been emboldened by inaction on the part of his superiors and the authorities. That's what allowed him to slip into the volunteer sites virtually unnoticed. No one questioned his credentials. They needed help and who would think a doctor would be there to kill people?"

17

Twilight settled over the city as Agent Bingham drove back to the Charlotte field office. Traffic was heavy going the opposite direction as commuters headed out of downtown. Agent Palmero sat in the passenger seat while Nick was in the back. No one spoke. The mission had been a bust.

"I hate going back empty handed," Bingham said. "I thought we'd pick him up on CCTV somewhere."

"Bishop's gotten used to being unseen," Palmero replied. "He knows how to play the game."

"He's gotten away with it for his entire career," Nick added. "We still stand a good chance of someone calling in a tip. That story is about to air on every local channel. We should be prepared for the incoming calls."

"I'll make sure any tips are funneled through to me," Bingham said. "What are you going to tell your people?"

Palmero looked back at Nick. "I assume they haven't found anything, otherwise, they would've made contact."

"I managed to put in a brief call to Reid about an hour ago.

They were still combing through surveillance footage. Nothing yet, though."

"State police can help us get out a BOLO," Bingham continued. "We need to think about casting a wider net. He's not in Charlotte anymore, I'd stake my career on it."

"I agree," Palmero said. "Chances are good, however, that he's still in the state. TSA has his details. They would've alerted us if his ID was checked."

"I wouldn't discount that he might be getting help," Nick said. "What do we know about his family?"

"That's a good question." Bingham pulled into the parking lot of the field office. "Let's discuss that with the others." She cut the engine and walked inside.

"Hey," Palmero reached for Nick's arm and pulled him aside. "We did everything we could out there today and so did your team."

"I know."

"It's just that you look, I don't know, pissed off or something," Palmero added.

"I'm not pleased he slipped through our fingers if that's what you're asking."

"Nah, man. It's more than that. Look, I know we haven't touched base in a long time, but I know who you are, and I know what kind of agent you are. What's really going on, Scarborough?"

"I'm just trying to figure out where I fit now."

"I'm sure it was a hell of a blow what happened with your team's shakeup. It would set anyone to question where they stood."

"That's all this is." Nick started toward the entrance as he noticed Bingham waiting for them. "I'll tell you though, it felt good being out there today. From the sense that I didn't feel like the world rested on my shoulders. That's one good thing about not being the boss. I can focus on solving cases."

"There you go." Palmero patted him on the back. "Gotta look at the silver lining, mi amigo."

"It's about time," Bingham said. "Thought you two just wanted some alone time for a minute." A smirk played on her lips.

Inside the operations room, the rest of the team continued to sort through the city's CCTV in hopes of picking up Bishop somewhere. When the door opened, Kate's attention was drawn away. "You're back."

"And by the look on your faces, you had just about as much luck as we did," Walsh added.

"No dice," Palmero said as he walked inside. "But Bingham thinks it would be a good idea to toss this to the State troopers and have a BOLO issued."

"I hate putting out something like that over the scanners," Kate said. "All ears will be listening, including civilian. This will blow up if we do that."

"I'm not sure we have a choice, Reid," Bingham replied. "If Bishop leaves the state, we're screwed. We have 24 hours, at best, if we hope to find him. After that, all bets are off. So, we can weather the storm of the media, or we can let Bishop sail on out of here and hope he'll pop up again when there's another disaster."

Kate furrowed her brow. "Now there's an idea."

Duncan nodded. "Wait for another disaster?"

"Any flight he tries to board will be flagged," Walsh said. "So, we stand a good chance of getting at him before he hops on a plane."

"We do. But what you just said about another disaster means we need to establish this as his pattern of behavior. He'll need money to travel as well. That's where we might yet find credit card usage and purchases," Kate replied.

"Okay, that's all well and good," Walsh said. "But we need to find him now. I have to agree with Bingham. The state cops need to issue a BOLO. It's our only shot at getting to him before he skips out."

The team turned their sights to Nick, who was the senior agent and since Fisher wasn't around, the only boss they had.

"Let's call Fisher and present our ideas. He's the boss and he'll need to make the call. Escalating this with the involvement of state police will bring significant changes in how we operate from here on out. And Bishop will know we're on the hunt for him without a doubt," Nick said.

"He must already know," Kate replied.

"The cops, sure. But the FBI? Probably not." Nick turned to Bingham. "You have a line we can jump on with everyone?"

"Sure do." She pulled the speakerphone from the rear credenza and placed it in the center of the table.

Nick made the call.

"Fisher here."

"Hey, it's Scarborough. I've got the team here and you're on speaker."

"Great. What's the word?"

"No luck on tracking down Bishop at any of the transportation areas. No airport either, which means it's likely he's still in the state. The idea was floated to let state police issue a BOLO."

"Okay. It doesn't sound to me like there's any other choice," Fisher replied. "Unless someone has another idea?"

"It's Reid here. My concern is, as always, the case blowing up on social media and news feeds. The story has already aired here on local news about the murder at the EMS station. We're fairly certain Bishop would've seen it somewhere."

"And by broadcasting over the scanners that there's a BOLO out, you think it'll only amplify the coverage?" Fisher asked.

"It'll become a national story and I believe he'll go into hiding," Kate added.

"That's where Reid and I differ in opinion," Bingham said. "This is Sarah Bingham."

"Well, Bingham, tell me what your thoughts are," Fisher replied.

"Reid is correct in that the enhanced coverage could force Bishop into hiding. I think by getting the story out there, people will know to be on the lookout for him. We need eyes, Agent Fisher. Everywhere."

"And what are your thoughts on this, Scarborough? You're the senior agent. I'd like to know what direction you want the team to take. Bearing in mind you have a lot of resources at your disposal currently."

"We do. Yes." Nick cast a glance to Kate. "There is another theory and that is Bishop would likely head to another disaster site."

"And what if one never develops?" Fisher asked. "He's already killed a coworker and I'll bet if we look hard enough, we'll find that the wrongful death suit will turn out to be a murder. We need to act now." He paused a moment. "Bingham's right. Take it to the state police. In the meantime, what do we know about any family he might have? Someone who might help him get from point A to point B?"

"That was our next objective," Nick added. "We're on that now."

"Good. Keep on it. We need all the help we can get to find Bishop."

"Got it," Nick said. "We'll keep in touch." He ended the call and peered at the others. "There you go."

"I'll work with Bingham and the state police," Palmero said. "We can still get out that BOLO tonight."

"That'll leave the rest of us to work on the family members Bishop might turn to." Nick checked the time. "Palmero, you and

Bingham can work with the police, but then I suggest we call it for tonight. It's late. Too late for us to keep calling around. We'll meet at 6am tomorrow."

"Copy that," Palmero said. "Looks like my field office is footing the bill for a hotel stay. I had my people arrange some rooms at the Doubletree."

KATE WALKED into the hotel room with Nick closing the door behind her. She removed her coat and set it on top of her bag. "Glad I brought the overnight bag."

"You never know where a case will lead." Nick pulled off his coat and tie and slid off his dress shoes. "You all did good work today."

"We didn't get our guy," Kate said.

"Since when does it ever happen that easily?" He reached inside the bar fridge and grabbed a bottled water. "Palmero will be happy I'm drinking an $8 bottle of water." He smiled and gulped down most of it.

"Are there any peanuts or candy bars in there?" Kate asked. "Let's give him a nice, fat bill at the end." She smiled.

"You haven't eaten," he said.

"Neither have you." She picked up the phone. "How about room service?" A knock sounded on the door. "That was fast. I haven't even placed the order."

Nick walked to the door and opened it. "Hey, man. Come in. Kate and I were just about to get room service. You want anything?"

Walsh walked inside. "Actually, I was thinking you two, myself and Duncan should huddle up downstairs at the bar for a few minutes."

"Sure. Is everything okay?" Nick asked.

"As far as I know. I just think it'd be a good idea to come to a consensus within our team." He looked at Kate. "You game?"

"Yeah. Of course." Kate stepped back into her ankle boots and waited for Nick to put on his shoes.

They followed Walsh to the elevator.

"Duncan's waiting for us already. I told her to get a drink while I fetched you two. She looked like she needed one."

"I think we could all use one," Nick said.

Kate shot him a look.

"It was just a joke, Kate," he replied.

Walsh noted the uncomfortable exchange. "Well, I'm dying for a beer. I see Duncan over there." He waved.

"I'm sorry—I didn't..." Kate began.

"Don't worry about it." Nick dismissed her and caught up to Duncan. "Hey. Good work today."

"Thanks." She sipped on her bottle of beer. "I'm exhausted as hell, Walsh, so I hope you have a good reason for calling this little pow-wow."

Walsh slipped into the booth while Kate sat next to Duncan.

"I think we need to present a united front," Walsh said.

Kate's brow creased. "Isn't that what we're doing?"

"Eva, what do you think about Bingham's suggestion?" Walsh began.

"About the BOLO?" She shrugged. "It's probably the right call. I mean, Cam agreed. It's too late to change it, Levi. Palmero and Bingham are already on it."

"I know," Walsh added.

"Then what are you getting at?" Nick asked.

"Look, I didn't want to upstage Palmero. This is still his investigation. And I didn't want to say anything in front of those guys and not even Fisher until I knew more. Which I do now."

"What is it?" Kate pressed on.

"I just got off the phone with a guy. I called in a favor and he just got back to me. He's NSA and I asked him to run facial recognition on passports for any flights departing from the east coast in the past week."

"That's a big job," Kate began. "You think Bishop took off somewhere during this supposed family emergency? The one he told his supervisor about? I thought TSA had been alerted."

"I think he went somewhere. I asked him to check Bishop's photo against passports that had been scanned."

"What did your contact say?" Duncan asked.

"He said Bishop's passport hadn't been used in years and nothing came up as far as a driver's license. So my friend ran the facial recognition software. He picked up a passport photo that was a 95% match to Bishop. There were a few others that weren't nearly as close, so I said, let's move on that one. The name on that passport was Eli Parnell."

"Son of a bitch," Nick said. "He got himself a fake passport probably after the lawsuit was filed because he feared other connections would be made." He turned to Kate. "That's why you guys haven't found banking transactions, or credit card charges. He's got himself a brand-new identity."

"If your NSA contact got a match, where did he go?" Kate pressed on.

"Well, you're never going to believe this." Walsh eyed them as if to build the tension. "There was a hurricane that hit the Bahamas a few weeks ago."

"Oh shit. I remember that," Duncan said.

"Yes, ma'am. Dr. Theodore Bishop, aka Eli Parnell, flew there. I can only guess as to why."

"Oh my God. He did the same thing there, didn't he?" Kate asked. "We have to get in contact with the authorities there and try to make the connection. I'll bet we'll find more unexplained deaths."

"This BOLO isn't going to do much for us now, is it?" Duncan asked. "It'll be issued for a guy who fell off the grid."

"We need to be looking for Eli Parnell," Kate said.

"We do, but here's my concern," Walsh continued. "I don't think we can let this be known. Not yet, anyway."

"Why?" Duncan asked. "We need everyone to keep their eyes open for him. This is Palmero's case too."

"Yeah, it is. Just hear me out." Walsh raised his hand. "The media already has this story out there. Bishop knows we're looking for a guy named Theodore Bishop. He's already taken care of that problem. But he doesn't know that we're now looking for Eli Parnell. It's our leg-up. And the only one we have at the moment. Any aliases that get out into the open will force him to either create another one, or just get the hell out of the country and hope we don't find him."

"I don't like either one of those options," Nick said.

"You and me, both, pal. We keep this inside our team, just until we can get a lead on where he might be. Look, I don't like keeping the lead investigator in the dark any more than you guys, but we've got way too many fingers in this pie already. The more people who know about this, the more likely we'll spring a leak." Walsh looked around. "Are we in agreement?"

"Mum's the word." Nick raised his water glass as if to toast.

"I'll back you, 100%, Levi," Kate added.

"Same here. Looks like we're all in," Duncan said. "What about Fisher? What are you going to tell him? I don't think it's right to keep this from him too."

"Give me till morning. That's all I ask," Walsh said.

"What's happening in the morning?" Duncan replied.

"I need to give my contact time to scour DOT surveillance

footage for Bishop. North Carolina's transportation department collects CCTV from public transportation terminals, red light cameras, interstate cameras, all of it. If Bishop has left the state, we'll know by morning. When I have that, I'll call Fisher myself and give him the good word. And, we'll let Palmero in on what we discovered. Can I count on you, Eva?"

"Always."

"Good." Walsh raised his hand to get the attention of the bartender. "Who's ready for a drink?"

It felt good to be united on the decision. While Fisher hadn't been there or known about it, Kate knew he would have agreed. Some things were best kept close to the chest. It was what made the BAU team so successful.

Drinks were ordered and a few appetizers arrived. It was a rare occasion they spent social time together and that felt good too. She'd screwed up with her response to Nick's supposed joke. He hadn't deserved her derisive gaze for saying something that to anyone else would have seemed completely innocent. And it lingered between them now.

But when the time had come to break up their party, Kate also knew the time had come to issue her apology. When they returned to their room, Nick hadn't said a word. He shed his clothes and stood in only boxer shorts and walked to the bed.

"It's late. We should get some sleep while we can," he said.

Kate unbuttoned her blouse and slid off her dress pants and shoes. She pulled on a t-shirt and stood over him as he crawled under the covers.

"What?" His tone was quiet, not harsh, but concerned.

"I'm sorry about earlier when Levi brought us downstairs." She held his gaze. "The look I gave. It was—unacceptable. I silently derided you right there in front of him and I should never have done that."

"He didn't notice."

"I'm not so sure." Kate sat down on the edge of the bed while Nick pulled up and leaned against the headboard.

"You liked being out there with Palmero today, didn't you? I could see it in your eyes when you returned. You looked—happy."

"Yeah, I guess it felt pretty good to be out there again. It's been months since we've been in the field."

"You used to say you were tired of the legwork, the fieldwork. That was why you wanted to be at Quantico—to lead the team, not lead field investigations."

"You're right. I did want that. Until all the bullshit got in the way. Politics, rules."

"There've always been rules, Nick. That hasn't changed." Kate smiled and placed her hand on his arm.

"That's true. Maybe they just have been feeling more restrictive than usual. It was nice to be away from it all for a while."

"Well, anyway, I guess we should call it a night." Kate stood up and Nick placed his hand on her hip.

"I'm so proud of what you've become, Kate. The agent you've grown into. I knew it was in you. I always knew."

Kate smiled and walked around to her side of the bed and crawled under the covers. He had known and he'd been right. She only wished she could see his path as clearly. All she could see now was Nick drifting farther and farther away.

18

The state police issued the "Be on the Lookout" warning for Dr. Theodore Bishop. Every cop in North Carolina was keeping their eyes peeled for "Dr. Death," as they'd come to call him. It was 6am and the BAU team arrived as scheduled back at the Charlotte field office.

According to Walsh's NSA contact, the scope of the search had taken longer than expected and had yet to yield results. Right now, they were no farther ahead on this investigation than they had been last night. The only upside was that they knew Eli Parnell was his alias.

"We have to find any family members." Kate sat at the conference table surrounded by all the agents. "We should consider that he hitched a ride with someone he's either related to or has close ties to. That's what I would do if I was him."

"I agree that has to be the next step," Nick added. "What about the Nassau ME? Have you received word back from him?"

"It's still early there. I've got a couple of hours before I would expect to hear from him," Kate replied.

"Okay. Then I suggest we all go about finding Bishop's family," Nick said.

Kate stood up and headed into the breakroom for a cup of coffee. Her phone buzzed in her pocket. "Reid here." She listened. "Yes, of course, Dr. Schroeder. What can I do for you?" She nodded while he spoke. "I see. Yes, of course. It's very helpful. Do you have an address?" She pulled up the notes on her phone and typed in what he'd relayed. "Thank you. If I have any other questions, can I count on your continued support?" Kate smiled. "Thank you, Dr. Schroeder. Thank you very much." She returned her phone to her pants pocket and started into the corridor before running into Bingham. "Have you seen Agent Scarborough?"

"He was in the operations room a minute ago," Bingham replied.

"Perfect. Thanks." Kate headed into the room and spotted him. "Hey, I need to go back to Providence."

Nick pulled her aside. "Why? What's happened?"

"I just got a call from the doctor Levi and I met with the other day. The one who had made the complaints against Bishop, but no one acted? He suddenly recalled something of value."

"Suddenly?" Nick looked at her with uncertainty.

"I'm sure the news story prompted his recollection," Kate said. "Looks like it hit the national news. He knows someone who was once close to Bishop."

"Who? Is it family?"

"No. A former girlfriend," Kate replied. "Now the current girl-friend of Dr. Schroeder, the one we met with."

"Well, that is interesting," Nick added. "Okay. Take Walsh with you..."

"Nick. No. I can handle this on my own. We don't need to pull resources away from the hunt. It's just a conversation but I want to be sure to keep anyone from finding out, mainly, the press. Until I know more, I can handle this on my own. Please."

"You're right. Get on the next flight and get it done. Keep me posted."

She nodded and turned away.

"Hey," Nick said. "Get in and get out."

"I will." Kate started into the hall once again, only this time she was leaving.

Walsh spotted her in the lobby. "Hey. Where are you off to?"

"You remember the doctor in Providence? Dr. Schroeder?" she began.

"Sure."

"He called. Apparently, he's involved with a woman who used to be with Bishop. The woman wants to talk."

"Great. When do we leave?"

"Levi, I'm going alone. I got approval from Nick. I can handle this, and I expect to be back before nightfall."

Walsh placed his hands on his square hips. "I don't think that's a good idea. You think Fisher would be okay with it?"

"I don't see why not. He told me he had faith in my intuition. Come on. You know I'm more than capable of talking to a person of interest on my own. There's enough here to keep everyone else busy. I can do this."

He nodded. "You're right. Of course you can. But if you need anything, you call me. Good luck and I'll see you back here tonight."

Kate smiled. "Thanks, Levi. I'll see you soon."

THE FLIGHT LANDED and Kate hurried off the small commuter plane as it arrived in Providence. What Kate had hoped to gain was to learn if Bishop had been in contact with either this girl-friend or someone she knew. It was the first time in a long time Kate had been given a chance to follow up on something alone. Not since Los Angeles, that she could recall, had she been given such an opportunity. It was time to show Fisher what she was capable of.

The witness, a woman named Holly, had agreed to meet alongside the doctor at the hospital. Kate made her way to the airport curb and hailed an Uber. "Our Lady of Mercy hospital, please." She stepped inside.

She scrolled through her phone for any messages from the team, or calls from the Nassau ME. Still nothing. It was nearly 10am and she should have heard from the medical examiner by now. With the phone to her ear, she made the call again. "Yes, hello, I'm Agent Reid. I need to speak with Dr. Knowles. I left an urgent message for him yesterday. Is he available?" She nodded. "Thank you."

The line was transferred, and a man picked up. "This is Dr. Knowles. Agent Reid, I'm so sorry I haven't returned your call."

"I understand how busy you must be, Doctor, but this is extremely urgent. Have you had a chance to review your cases to see if you have a match to several of ours here in the states?"

"I have, Agent Reid. There was one. However, I'm awaiting a final report, but the circumstances surrounding this particular victim raised many eyebrows."

"Can you send what you have to my email?" Kate asked.

"Of course. But you should also know something else, Agent Reid. The doctor in question did not go by the name of Theodore Bishop..."

"Did he happen to go by the name of Eli Parnell?"

"How did you know?" the doctor asked.

"A hunch. Thank you. Please send the details as soon as you

can. I'll keep an eye out." Kate ended the call and noticed the hospital in the distance.

The driver pulled to a stop at the main entrance. "Here you are, ma'am."

"Thanks so much." Kate opened the door. "I'll be sure to give you 5-stars." She closed the door behind her and headed into the building.

The man she'd been waiting for had also been waiting for her. Kate walked inside and spotted the doctor right away. "Dr. Schroeder."

"Agent Reid," He offered his hand. "Thank you for coming. Follow me. I'll take you to see Holly."

Kate followed him into his office. She noted the sign on the door. "Attending Physician."

Inside, a slight woman, possibly only 5 feet 4 inches, who couldn't have weighed more than 110 pounds, sat on a small sofa perpendicular to the doctor's desk. She stood.

"You must be Holly." Kate approached with her hand extended.

"Yes. I'm Holly Drier and you're Agent Kate Reid. I appreciate your willingness to come here and so quickly. This isn't something I would want to get out if you understand my meaning."

"Of course."

"Why don't we have a seat over here." The doctor pulled out two chairs at a small table near the center of his office. "Holly. Agent Reid." He motioned for them to sit before he finally took his own seat.

"So, what is it you wanted to say to me, Holly? As you know, many people are out looking for Theodore Bishop. Has he contacted you?"

"Yesterday." Holly looked away as if ashamed she'd waited to bring forward her information. "When I saw the news..."

"Did he say where he was?" Kate pressed on.

"No. I tried to, well I thought he was calling to ask for money or something. When I tried to get more details out of him, like where he was or what kind of help he needed, he refused to say."

"Why was that?" Kate asked.

"I imagine he thought I'd run to him." She pointed to Dr. Schroeder. "Which, of course, I did."

"When were you and Bishop dating?" Kate asked.

"About a year into his residency here at the hospital. I'm a nurse and well, that was how we met. But here's the thing, Agent Reid, I left Theo after all this stuff came up, you know? After what Dr. Schroeder said about the kid with the appendectomy, and what others had implied. It got to the point that I was afraid to even speak to Theo about it. Dr. Schroeder—David—told me you and another agent came here to talk to him and that was when I knew Theo must've really screwed up." She looked to the doctor, who nodded for her to continue. "There's something else too. I—um—I can't be sure, but I think Theo might've been trying to poison me while we were together."

"Did you go to the police?" Kate asked.

"No. I know that sounds crazy, but I couldn't prove it. We'd been dating for about 6 months or so. I had just moved in with him. I thought we were going to get married. But a month or so later, I started getting terrible headaches. Migraines."

"She thought it was just stress from the job," Schroeder added.

"And of course, Theo tried to convince me that was the case. But I'd never had migraines before and there was nothing that had changed in my job to make me think it was stress."

"So you thought it was Bishop? That he was, what, putting something in your food?" Kate asked.

"Something like that." She eyed Schroeder. "I had heard the stories about him. The cases that were just too coincidental. I knew it was him. I just knew it. But I had nothing to take to the cops."

"You left him after that?" Kate asked

"After a couple of more months. Yes, I left him. He then left the hospital, lost his license and that was when I started dating David." She reached for his hand.

Kate jotted down notes. "Your migraines...did they stop?"

"Yes. Within a week or two of Theo moving out. They were gone."

"I see. Does he know you and Dr. Schroeder are dating?"

"He does. I honestly don't know why he called on me. It was like he was searching for a part of himself that just wasn't there anymore."

Kate nodded. "Does he have any family?"

"His mom. No one else that he's ever mentioned to me. But I, apparently, didn't know him as well as I thought I did."

"Do you mind if I look at your phone?"

Holly retrieved it and opened it to the call. "That was him. I had long since deleted his contact from my phone, so when I answered, I had no idea it was his number."

Kate examined the call log. "Unknown number." She peered at them. "He was smart enough to block it."

"Agent Reid, Theo is a very smart man. He's gotten away with horrific things and I think if you suspect he's done something awful, and he knows you suspect it, I doubt very much that you'll find him," Holly said.

"With your permission, I'd like to contact your cell phone carrier and request the tower logs from that line."

"Of course. Anything I can do to help. I'm sorry I waited. It's just that, well, I was afraid," Holly replied.

"I don't blame you. If we can find out where this call came

from, it'll help us a lot in figuring out where he was, and where he might be going."

ON THE PLANE back to Charlotte, Kate viewed the email from the medical examiner in Nassau. A man who said he was a doctor, who went by the name Eli Parnell, injected a woman with what turned out to be a drug intended for heart patients. The resulting cause of death was heart failure. Kate had seen this before in another of Bishop's victims.

According to the medical examiner, when Bishop had been questioned about his credentials by the doctor in charge of the triage unit, he claimed they had been in his hotel and he left to retrieve them, against the doctor's wishes. Bishop, or rather, Parnell, never returned.

"Same guy. Same M.O.," Kate said.

The man in the airline seat next to her began, "Excuse me?"

"Oh sorry. I was just talking to myself. Hazards of the job," Kate replied.

"What do you do for a living?" the man asked.

"I'm a federal agent."

"Oh. Wow. That's interesting. Are you working on a case?" the man's eyes widened with interest.

"As a matter of fact, I am. But I'm afraid it's all confidential at the moment. QT. You understand."

"Sure. Sure. Yeah, hey, do what you gotta do. And—thanks for, you know, for your service, I guess. I mean, I know you're not like military..."

Kate smiled. "Thank you. I appreciate it." She felt the plane begin its descent into Charlotte and peered through the window at the setting sun. Her promise to return by day's end had been intact.

Nick was there to pick her up and pulled curbside when he spotted her. When she opened the door, he smiled. "Glad you're back."

Kate slipped inside and closed the passenger door. "Good to be back. It was worth the trip. Thank you."

Nick pulled away from the curb. "No need to thank me. Just tell me you got what you needed."

"I think so. What's been happening today?" she asked.

"More of the same. The captain with the state police came in and offered additional assistance. Fisher said he'd hold off for now. Said there were a lot of people already working on finding Bishop. Walsh is still keeping a lid on the Parnell alias for the time being, but I'm not sure how much longer we can hold onto that information. We tried to track down any family and got a hit on the mother. She hadn't seen or heard from Bishop in almost 5 years."

"Do you buy that?" Kate asked.

"I'm putting a pin in that for the moment," Nick replied. "We'll likely need to pull her phone records and look for a connection to Baltimore or Charlotte since we don't have a phone number for him."

"And the call to his ex-girlfriend, Holly? Do we know where the call originated from yet?"

"Based on the details you provided us, Walsh and Palmero have been coordinating with the cell phone provider. What I do know is that Walsh's NSA contact is currently running recognition on security video at the bus terminals. We should have an update on our return." Nick glanced at her. "You could make a strong case to not replace Quinn, you know."

Kate scoffed. "Not a chance. Fisher already said I didn't have the experience. I can't argue with that. Besides, I don't pretend to know everything."

"I know you don't. I'm just saying when I was made SSA for the Washington Field Office, I didn't know what the hell I was doing. I just did it. And it turned out okay."

"In all fairness, you had the years put in already. I don't. And especially not for BAU. It was practically a miracle I was offered a position in the first place."

"If you say so." Nick pulled into the parking lot and cut the engine. "Still, Fisher should know you can handle yourself."

"I hope everyone on the teams knows that." Kate stepped out of the car and waited for Nick to join her. "I'm sorry. I didn't mean that the way it sounded."

He grinned. "I know you didn't. But you're right. Everyone should already know what you can do. I certainly do." Nick started inside.

When they arrived back at the ops room, Walsh stood from his chair and wore a wide grin. "God bless you, Reid. I knew you could do it."

Kate was surprised by his praise. "What? Did you find where the call to the ex came from?" she asked.

He walked back. "You're damn right we did. He might've hidden his number, but you can't hide a call's location. According to the cell phone provider, the call Bishop made to his ex-girlfriend pinged back to a cell tower right here." Walsh pointed to the monitor.

"That's really close to that bus depot," Kate added.

"Yes, ma'am. So Palmero over here." Walsh gestured to him. "He decided to head over there for a visit and wouldn't you know..."

Palmero placed his hand on Walsh's shoulder. "The bus operators had their own security footage. Cameras behind the ticket counters. We got surveillance footage of a guy buying a ticket. Looked an awful lot like Theo Bishop. He purchased a bus ticket to Raleigh."

"He's still in North Carolina." Kate smiled.

"He's still in North Carolina," Walsh added. "So, we're packing up and heading to Raleigh."

"Great. When?" Kate asked.

Duncan walked toward them. "Right now. I just got us a car. We're leaving now."

19

Theo Bishop had started off with noble intentions, wanting to leave a mark as his father had. A well-respected doctor, his father had saved lives during the Gulf War before returning to the U.S. and eventually becoming the Chief of Surgery at Our Lady of Mercy Hospital. That was the only reason the younger Bishop had been granted residency.

Bishop had envied the way his father's patients admired him. They looked at him as though he was their savior. That was how it started.

Holly had been merely an experiment. How far could he go without ending a life? She had been the guinea pig. It turned out that Bishop had no capacity for love in that manner. Only a need to be loved and idolized.

Now, as he sat on the edge of his bed inside the Super 8 in Raleigh, Bishop needed a way out. He had his new identity, Eli Parnell, but Parnell had no medical degree. He wasn't certified as an EMT. This left him with no way to slip into a role that would grant him access to the people who needed him, or rather, the people he needed. Not to mention that he'd murdered a colleague, and the cops were after him. No medical degree or certification in the world was going to help him escape that. The longer he remained in North Carolina, the greater the odds were of him being captured. He'd seen the news reports. He knew they were after him, although they had been looking for Dr. Theodore Bishop.

He tossed his bag onto the bed and reached inside, pulling out his EMT certificate. It would take time and meticulous care, but it was possible to alter the name on the certificate. While that alone wouldn't be enough because it would only take a quick search on the database to see it had been falsified, it could be enough to get him in the door outside the country.

He could use his alias passport to purchase a bus ticket to Mexico where the forged EMT certificate wouldn't be questioned. It was extreme, but the time for extreme measures had arrived.

Bishop pulled back the heavy curtain and gazed out into the parking lot. Streetlamps flickered on and dusk had appeared. No doubt it was best to travel by night. His face was on the news and that would be his biggest hurdle to overcome. Bishop reached into a grocery bag and pulled out a bottle of hair dye and a hair trimmer. His dark roots had already begun to grow in, and the lighter brown color of Eli Parnell's passport photo needed to be touched up. Maybe something shorter would do as well. He'd already started growing the dark stubble on his chin.

As night settled in, Bishop, with his shorter, lighter hair and thick 5 o'clock shadow, threw his bag over his shoulder and walked out of the Super 8 to hail a cab.

"The bus depot on Cheltenham, please." He slipped onto the backseat.

Coverage of his story had been thankfully brief in the wake of a recent shooting that had taken place the night before in

Charlotte. The tragedy offered him a better chance of making it out.

The driver paid him no attention and it was less likely utilizing a cab would be traceable back to him. Ubers and Lyfts and those sorts of rideshares required online payments, names, and the online accounts. A cab meant he could pay with cash leaving no trail except that the driver had picked up a man with light brown hair at a Super 8 motel in Raleigh under the name of Parnell.

The bus depot was ahead, and the driver pulled to the curb where passengers disembarked. "That'll be $27.58, sir." He turned back to Bishop.

"Keep the change." Bishop handed him a 20 and a 10 and quickly stepped out so as not to let the driver get a better look at him. He hurried into the station and pulled on a ballcap and raised the collar of his jacket. He'd already done this once and got away clean. He could do it again.

Bishop approached the counter. "I'd like to purchase a ticket to Nuevo Laredo, please."

"You're traveling into Mexico?" the man asked.

"Yes."

"I'll need to see your passport, and you'll have to purchase a round-trip ticket unless you have a visa to remain in Mexico. Either the FM2 or FM3."

Bishop hadn't considered the legal requirements to stay in Mexico and he had neither of these visas. "I only intend on staying a few weeks."

"Then you'll only need to purchase a roundtrip ticket and provide your passport." The man waited for Bishop. "Sir? Do you need assistance?"

"No. Sorry." He set down his passport on the table. "How much for the roundtrip ticket?"

"$465, sir," the man replied.

He retrieved his wallet and counted the cash before pushing it toward the man behind the desk. "Here you are."

"Thank you." The man held the passport and examined it while studying Bishop. "Remove your baseball hat, please, sir."

He pulled off the hat. "I just got my hair cut." This was taking too long and Bishop's nerves stood on end.

The man finally turned back to his computer and scanned the passport. A few more clicks and a ticket printed. "Here you are, sir. Your passport and your tickets. The bus leaves in 90 minutes. You'll need to change buses twice. Have a nice trip."

Bishop felt the relief swell in his chest as he returned his passport to his bag and picked up the tickets. "Thank you."

It was Levi Walsh's job to reach out to the local authorities whenever they entered into a jurisdiction in search of a suspect. When the team, including Agent Palmero, arrived in Raleigh, they drove straight to the police department headquartered in downtown. The time was approaching 9pm and the call had been made of their impending arrival.

Lieutenant Jackson waited for them in the lobby. "I'll bet that's them." He said to the officer behind the desk. "They sure as shit look like Feds, anyway."

The doors parted and Palmero led the way. The lieutenant approached first, but Palmero made the introduction. "You must be Lieutenant Jackson. I'm Agent Palmero, FBI Houston office, and these are the good folks from the FBI in Quantico helping me track down a dangerous suspect." Palmero introduced the team and turned back to the lieutenant. "You have a man here who has already killed at least 6 that we know of, and we're pretty sure he's not finished."

"What can we do to help?" Jackson stood firmly and peered at the agents through narrow eyes with ham hands pressed against his thick waist.

"We'd like a team to help scour your city's CCTV footage. Right now, we have no idea where he is, but we know he's here."

"That'll take time and a lot of resources," the lieutenant replied.

"Yes, it will." Palmero looked back at the team. "We'll be right beside your people to help get it done. There's no time to waste. We know this man and we know he won't stay in one place for long."

"Fair enough. I'll put my best people on it."

The central headquarters of the police station in a big city like Raleigh had the equipment and the people to expedite the operation. The focus was to be on the bus depot to determine when Bishop, aka Parnell, had arrived and if he used a cab. The video surveillance footage would reveal that information.

The set-up had been quick, and the team was directed to the control center where most of the department's large-scale operations took place.

In the span of two hours, they had seven officers, three tech operators and the lieutenant directing the team inside.

"I understand that our window is closing," Lieutenant Jackson began as he walked inside. "But we worked as quickly as possible to get this up and running."

"It's better than any of us could've hoped for," Nick began. "Thank you." He checked the time. "We know that he arrived earlier this evening, which gives us a good shot that he'll stay in Raleigh through the night and leave first thing in the morning."

"Have we identified whether he used a cab when he left the bus terminal?" Palmero asked.

"Over here, sir." One of the officers waved him over.

While Palmero got an update, the others spread out among the officers to assist in their efforts.

"There's a lot of footage to scour," Kate said as Walsh stood near.

"Our best shot is tracking down Bishop's moves after he arrived. Hopefully, a drop off location from the cab company will be easy to narrow down. Palmero's running on that." Walsh peered at his phone as a call came in. "Excuse me for a minute." He continued toward the door and stepped into the hall. "Walsh here."

"I just got a hit on the Eli Parnell passport."

It was his NSA contact and Walsh wore a look of relief. "Your timing couldn't be better, my man. We're here in Raleigh now. Where is the son of a bitch? I got half the city police combing through video surveillance."

"You're not going to like this. The hit was from a bus depot in Raleigh. The Parnell passport was scanned. Your man bought a roundtrip ticket to Nuevo Laredo."

Walsh lowered his head. "Mexico?"

"I'm sorry, man."

Walsh inhaled a breath. "The good news is that it'll take him two days to get there. We'll just have to intercept the bus..."

"This is the part you aren't going to like, Walsh. The report I received is 48 hours old."

"That's impossible. You just said the passport was scanned. Are you telling me it was scanned two days ago and you're just now finding this out? Two days ago, this guy was in Charlotte working on an ambulance truck. What the hell is going on here?"

"I had the name flagged—both names. I should've received the details within minutes after it was scanned. I didn't. Call it a glitch, or whatever, but I just got the information and I viewed the report to confirm. I don't show he's arrived at the port of entry, so maybe there's still a chance you can reach him."

Walsh shook his head. "Shit. The guy killed someone just yesterday. No, man. You gotta double check this. Something's not right."

"All I can tell you is what I'm looking at right here. Eli Parnell bought a ticket to Mexico two days ago. I don't know what else to say. I wish it wasn't the case."

"Listen, I gotta go. I got manhours piling up on me here in Raleigh. I need to pull these guys off and figure this out."

"For whatever it's worth, I'm sorry."

"Yeah, man. I know. Thanks." Walsh returned his phone to his pocket and walked back inside. He spotted Nick and headed toward him. "We can stop looking."

Nick turned around. "Why is that?"

"I just got off the phone with my NSA contact. He got a hit on the Parnell passport. The guy bought a ticket to Mexico. It left two days ago."

Nick's face masked in confusion. "He's gone? What the hell? How is that even..."

"That's what we need to figure out. Something's way off here, and we'd better figure it out damn fast."

WALSH AND PALMERO borrowed a patrol car and with Walsh behind the wheel, he began, "Listen, I'm sorry I didn't say anything sooner. I couldn't risk a leak, but I'm telling you now. Eli Parnell is Theodore Bishop. A buddy at the NSA has been working with me on tracking down hits on the passport. He got one tonight, but it's all screwed up."

"I thought we were getting on pretty well, man. I thought we could trust each other," Palmero said. "This is all bullshit. Not only am I sitting here thinking you all kept me out of the loop, but now you're serving up some horseshit about Bishop leaving for Mexico before he killed his coworker? What the hell, man?"

"This is on me." Walsh turned into the bus depot. "I wanted to wait until I knew more. Now that I do, I don't like what I'm hearing. You can stay pissed off, or we can get to the bottom of whatever shit show this has turned into."

Palmero eyed him as Walsh pulled to a stop. "It's after midnight and my patience is out the door. We're getting to the bottom of this right now. I'll let this slide only because I think our problems have just begun and I'm going to need you all. But know this, you keep shit from me on my own investigation again and I'll have your head, you hear me?"

"Loud and clear." Walsh stepped out and hustled inside. He approached the ticket counter and flipped open his badge. "Agent Walsh, FBI. We need to know if a man named Eli Parnell purchased a ticket to Nuevo Laredo earlier tonight."

The cashier turned to his computer and typed in the details. "Eli Parnell." He peered at his screen. "Yeah, it looks like he bought a roundtrip ticket to Nuevo Laredo a couple of days ago."

Walsh shot a look to Palmero before returning to the cashier. "Do you remember seeing this man?" He held up a photo of Bishop.

"Man, I'm sorry, but I see hundreds of people every day. I gotta be honest with you, I hardly pay attention to them."

"Please. Just take a look. It's important we find him," Palmero added.

The cashier studied the picture for a moment longer. "I—I'm sorry. I don't recognize him."

"What about security tapes?" Palmero asked. "Can we take a look?"

"I'll have to get my supervisor."

"Please do that," Walsh said.

The cashier disappeared into the back and Walsh looked at Palmero. "How? How the hell does this guy kill someone yesterday and manage to be on a bus to Mexico at the same time?"

"If we knew that, we wouldn't be here," Palmero replied.

The cashier returned with his supervisor.

"I'm Ron Weise. Can I help you?"

"I certainly hope so," Walsh began. "We need access to your security footage for the past 48 hours."

It was 3am when Nick and Kate returned home. The flight on the Bureau's private jet was somber with hardly a word spoken among the team. Nick held open the door for Kate as she entered the condo. He locked it behind her and set down his bag. "It's probably best if we try to get in a few hours of sleep. Fisher wants a full briefing first thing in the morning."

Kate shed her coat and placed it on the hook next to the door. "I'm sure Eva will fill him in." She walked to the breakfast bar and dropped onto a stool. "I just can't believe it. We were so close. How could this have happened?"

"I wish I knew. Walsh said the video had been erased. An entire day, gone. And he couldn't identify Bishop on video from the prior day. That man didn't buy a ticket two days ago. That's all we know right now. It's a physical impossibility."

"I can't get my head around it," she replied.

"Look, we gave Border Patrol the information. All we can do is hope he hasn't crossed over yet." Nick stood in front of her and gently took hold of her shoulders. "It's late. We've been at this for the past 36 hours. We'll have clearer heads in the morning and can work through this."

"Sure. You're probably right."

He wrapped his arm around her waist and led her to the bedroom. "The work you did, though. Going to Providence and interviewing the girlfriend, it was good work. We wouldn't have known where he was going otherwise."

Kate stopped in her tracks and peered up at him. "Hang on. This morning, she said Bishop had contacted her the day before. And we tracked down the cell phone signal. So, how is it possible that he had left two days earlier? That doesn't make any sense. I mean, I know the guy's smart and knows how to hide, but..." Kate stopped dead. "He had help. That's the only answer. Bishop had help covering his tracks."

"Who could help him with something like that? He'd have to have friends in very high places with the means to manipulate national security data and private company surveillance. You can't just go in and change the date someone used their passport and bought a ticket. I mean, that could only be done by someone with access to State Department and Homeland Security data."

Kate pursed her lips. "I know... I just..."

"We aren't going to get answers tonight. You can stay up and fret through it, or you can try to clear your head and tackle this first thing in the morning. Whatever happened, it doesn't matter now anyway. Bishop's gone. If he isn't in Mexico yet, he will be soon. And if he did have the kind of help you're talking about, Border Patrol won't turn up anything either. Once he's inside Mexico, we won't get cooperation from them. I'm not sure I want to attempt it anyway."

"Why?" Kate asked.

"They don't even want us to designate their cartels as terrorists. They aren't serious about fighting crime and corruption. What makes you think they'll open up their country and say, 'hey, come on in FBI.' It won't happen. That's all I'm saying." Nick continued into the bedroom.

"It can't be worse than what we faced in Rio." Kate walked behind him. "I'll sleep on it tonight, but this isn't over. I won't stop looking for him."

WALSH WALKED into his apartment in Quantico and threw down his keys before dropping onto his sofa. He was a single man and his apartment was decorated to reflect that. He'd been married once but she left him before he finished a tour in Iraq years earlier. The only fortunate thing was that there were no kids involved. Only problem with that was that Walsh felt it had been his only opportunity to have children. He was 42 and time had run out, or so he believed.

However, in times like these, he appreciated the solitude. If he wanted to punch a hole in the living room wall, which was what he wanted to do right now, he could do so without someone yelling at him. It wouldn't solve anything, but it was his prerogative. The people he worked with were experts for a reason and that was because they got their man. It had been years since they let one slip by and that was because he had killed himself. Now, Bishop had outsmarted them. But there wasn't a chance in hell he did it alone.

Walsh walked into his kitchen and retrieved a bottle of whiskey and a glass. A two-fingered shot ought to do it. At least calm him down enough to sleep. All that he and Kate had worked toward was for nothing. The interviews, all of it, just to see Bishop slip through their fingers.

Agent Palmero had returned to his office in Houston and the

team was scheduled to meet at 7am tomorrow. Fisher would be pissed. He would blame himself for not being there and whatever flow they'd begun to have as a team with Fisher at the helm would vanish.

Walsh snatched his cell phone from the kitchen counter and pulled up Kate's contact. "No. Don't." He'd learned enough about Kate to know she would also be beating herself up right about now. Even with Scarborough there to vent to, Kate would take this personally. They all would.

Walsh set down the glass and walked to his bedroom.

20

It was 7am and the BAU team sat around the conference table. Some sipped on their mugs of coffee. Some picked at the bagels that had been brought in. All wore exhaustion and frustration. Fisher surveyed his people. "It doesn't look like any of you slept much last night," he said and pushed his hand through his thick hair. "It's no wonder considering how we left things in Raleigh."

"It wasn't the desired outcome," Nick began. "Our job was to root out the suspect, create a profile and assist the agent in Houston with predicting when and where we might find Theodore Bishop. We accomplished all of that."

"Except capturing him," Kate added. "Where do we go from here?"

"I believe we've reached the end of the road on this one, Reid," Fisher replied. "This isn't the same as what happened in Rio. There, we had a man, a wealthy man, who traveled back and forth and got sloppy."

"Why can't we contact the FBI's international office in Mexico

City and ask them to hunt down Bishop?" Duncan asked. "Assuming he did cross over the border or is about to."

"That is likely where we'll take this, and considering we know who the suspect is, there would be no need for our involvement. In Rio, we worked on profiling an unsub until we got a match. We know who we're after here," Fisher replied.

"Then we have to at least go through the process," Walsh said. "Duncan's right. If Bishop is headed there, and I have no reason to believe he isn't, let those guys in Mexico City know who they're dealing with. Leave it in their capable hands."

"There was something that I couldn't shake last night," Kate began. "When I spoke to the ex-girlfriend, Holly, she said she had talked to Bishop earlier the day before and we traced the call back to the bus depot in Charlotte."

"Which was how we discovered he was going to Raleigh," Walsh added.

"Right. But then we discover he'd been there a full two days earlier? I don't see how that was possible. Where was the disconnect and how can we figure out how this happened?"

Fisher nodded. "I'm not sure it's relevant at this point..."

"It's completely relevant," Kate interrupted. "I'm sorry. I don't mean to contradict you, but someone went through a lot of trouble to help Bishop evade us. Frankly, I'm surprised all the evidence showing Bishop had purchased a ticket to Mexico wasn't erased. Why leave that detail? Why tell us *where* he was going, but erase the *when*?"

"All I can say to that is, erasing the entire record of his purchase, deleting the scan; that might've been too difficult for whoever could've pulled off something like that," Walsh replied. "Maybe the best they could do was to throw us off his scent. Give Bishop enough time to make his move."

"For the sake of argument, say Reid is right. Someone intervened and helped Bishop get into Mexico. Reid and Walsh did the legwork. You both talked to his former classmates, co-workers. Was there anyone you came across who you believe helped him escape?" Nick asked.

Kate looked at Walsh. "Not that I could tell. You?"

"It was odd that most of the people in a position of authority over Bishop swept his wrongdoings under the rug," Walsh added. "But from what we discovered, no one wanted to face lawsuits. Pretty typical behavior, I'd say."

"Where does that leave us, then?" Duncan added. "Who helped him and where do we start to figure that out?"

"We have stacks of consult requests, we need to replace a team member, and I just don't think spending any more of our resources on something that can be handled by another office is what we should be doing." Fisher sighed. "I get it. I was a detective for a lot of years. I hated to walk away from an unsolved case. God knows I still do. But this isn't going cold. It's being transferred. You did your job. We all did our jobs. It's time to move on." Fisher stood. "With that, I'll get the ball rolling with the office in Mexico City. I'll ask that you all submit your relevant case files and any reports so that I can send them over, including the Oakview and Riverside ME reports on their victims. They'll need everything we have to build their own case file."

"Will we be able to assist them, should they ask?" Kate said.

"Of course." Fisher started to leave.

Nick stood up and turned to Kate. "I'm going to go talk to him." He followed Fisher into the hall. "Hey, can we sit down in your office for a minute?"

Fisher studied him before answering. "Sure."

They walked into Fisher's office and Nick closed the door.

"What is it you want to talk about? I've made the decision, Scarborough."

"I know you have." Nick pulled out a chair. "But I have to agree with Reid."

"Why am I not surprised?" Fisher looked away. "I'm sorry. I didn't mean that. Go on."

"No, you're right. I do tend to back her up because I believe she's right. Look, I've worked with Reid for enough years to know when she gets a wild hair, it's for a damn good reason."

"What do you want me to do? We can't just take over an investigation. You know that. If the Mexico City office needs our help, then great. I'm all for that. But let them do their jobs. It's what we would expect, isn't it?"

"What if we can run on some aspects here on our end? The case did start with us," Nick said.

"It started with Palmero in Houston," Fisher replied.

"And Palmero still has a suspect out there. There was a disconnect somewhere. Reid was right about that. I think you can see it too."

"You always come to her defense," Fisher said.

"I'll jump to the defense of anyone on this team if I think they're in the right, including you, despite what you might think."

Fisher shook his head. "I'm just not sure what direction to take and I feel like you're always so very sure. Maybe I'm doing something wrong. Maybe I'm not cut out for this job."

"You are, Fisher. I would never doubt that. I can't say I'm happy about what happened, but it sure as hell wasn't your fault. You know, maybe it should have been you all along. I think Cole turned to me because I had a few high-profile cases under my belt."

"Because of Reid."

"Yeah, because of Reid," Nick said. "But it's your show now. All I'm asking is that you don't dismiss what she's capable of. I know you've seen it yourself. She has a lot to learn, but damn if she doesn't pick up on the shit that we miss."

Fisher appeared to think on the matter. "I can't have her rattling cages. The guys in Mexico City answer to HQ, not us. If they get the sense that Reid is working on this without their consent, Cole will hear about it. There's a way to do this and make it look like it's all for those guys there, you understand?"

"I get it. I know she'll want Walsh in on it because of the groundwork they both did," Nick said.

Fisher nodded. "Yeah. Okay. I'll do what I can to help but nothing we currently have can fall through the cracks."

"Understood."

Kate was in her office with Walsh when Nick appeared. "Just the people I wanted to see." He walked inside.

"We were just discussing our options," Walsh said.

"I figured that might be the case. I just spoke to Fisher and he agreed that you both should move forward on the concern that Bishop might have help here in the US."

Kate glanced at Walsh with noted surprise and returned to Nick. "Well, I'm glad he listens to you."

"It didn't have anything to do with me. It had everything to do with the fact that he has faith in you. Both of you. As long as you don't start poking around in the Mexico City office without them asking for help, then you have the opening you need to find out what the hell happened and how we lost Bishop."

"What about Duncan? We'll need everyone on this," Walsh said. "We're still a team."

"We are. Like I said, do what you have to do. If Duncan needs to play a role, then so be it. Just keep this quiet. Do your jobs." Nick stood up to leave. "And find that son of a bitch."

Walsh waited for Nick to be out of earshot before he looked back at Kate. "Despite all the bullshit that has gone down since we got back from Rio, Scarborough's still a hell of a leader. Nothing against Fisher, but when it comes to listening to your team, he'll no doubt give you the rope you need."

Kate smiled. "So long as we don't hang ourselves with it. Where do you want to start?"

"You're the one with the hunch. You tell me," Walsh replied.

"Okay. I see where this is headed," Kate smiled. "The first thing I'd like to know is how the hell we lost two days? Your contact found a match to the fake passport Bishop used, but yet it was delayed."

"I can reach out to him and try to get clarification, but I would assume there was a lag in the reporting. I imagine it must happen on occasion. I can't say for sure, but it's something I can follow up on."

"Okay. Then we have Holly. She waited almost a full day before contacting us and that might have been only because we had talked to her now-boyfriend and then she saw something on the news. Which, by the way, I find incredibly interesting that she would be dating the same man who had reported Bishop's behavior to his higher-ups."

"Not to mention Holly insisted Bishop was trying to poison her," Walsh said. "I wonder if that means he'd discovered something about her. Something like she was cheating on him with this other doctor?"

"That's a possibility. More importantly, is that if she suspected he was trying to kill her, why not report it to the authorities?" Kate pressed on.

"I can't answer that. I would suggest it warrants another

conversation with Holly, though. Do you want to run on that while I follow up with my guy on the passport?"

"It's a good start, yes." She watched as Walsh stood up and prepared to leave. "Hey, Levi?"

"Yeah?"

"Thanks for believing in me."

"It would be the same if the shoe was on the other foot."

"You know it." She smiled as he left her office.

It should have come as no surprise to Kate that Nick had convinced Fisher to go along with her theory. It made all kinds of sense to her, but this morning's meeting confirmed she hadn't been able to convince Fisher, but Nick had. There was no denying he always believed in her and right from the very start. Walsh was right. Nick was a good leader. He listened to his team. Fisher seemed to shy away from going against the grain and perhaps that was because it was still early days. He was still finding his footing.

However, there was no mistaking that what Nick had done, he had done for her. If it helped the investigation, then all the better. But Kate knew he was making up for his past mistake. A mistake she'd begun to see as a lapse in judgment from an otherwise talented agent who could work a case like no one she had ever seen.

It had taken Kate years to learn to forgive. It started with a lie from desperate parents willing to do anything to keep their daughter from finding out who she was. She'd forgiven them for doing something far more egregious than Nick had ever or likely would ever do. Yet she had, thus far, been unwilling to forgive him for falling back on a vice that had become his disease. No one had been harmed by his actions. Maybe it was time Kate forgave him because as it stood right now, he might not be willing to wait much longer.

Now that Kate had been given a green light, it was time to

make a move. There had to be more to Dr. Theodore Bishop than what she already knew. Too many people had looked the other way where he had been concerned and she questioned whether it was due to a fear of lawsuits or a fear of something or someone else.

To know where to start, Kate would have to start at the beginning. Family. Somehow, in her experience, it always came down to family. Whether it be parents or siblings or a distant uncle, most of the killers she had profiled so far had violence or sociopathic behavior rooted in their family history. It was time to find Bishop's. They knew *who* he was. She needed to know *why* he was. From there, she could piece together where he might be now.

The work they had done to date on Bishop's family included a mother who lived in Providence and a father who passed away when Bishop was a teenager. She knew of no siblings but hadn't looked into the possibility of aunts or uncles or even cousins. It hadn't mattered to her at the time, but it mattered now. Nothing could be overlooked, including whatever role the ex-girlfriend, Holly, might have played.

"Hey." Duncan walked into Kate's office. "I heard you got the go-ahead to follow up on Bishop."

"It seems Fisher had a change of heart. In fact, I was just about to start looking into Bishop's family ties."

Duncan continued inside and sat down. "Didn't we already go down that road?"

"I think we made it about a quarter of the way. I want to finish the trip." She studied Duncan for a moment. "What do you have on your plate right now?"

"I'm cleaning up. Tying loose ends with the Riverside field office and gathering the witness statements to hand over to Mexico City. Why?"

"I could use an extra hand if you're interested," Kate replied.

"Interested? Nah," Duncan swatted away the notion. "Determined to find Bishop? Hell yes."

Kate smiled. "I thought so. Here's where I'd like to start."

Bishop pulled down his baseball hat and stepped off the bus. His bag was slung over his right shoulder and as he stepped down, it caught the arm of another. "Sorry about that." He looked at the man.

"It's okay." The man spoke with a heavy Central-Mexican accent and he seemed to let his eyes linger on Bishop for longer than necessary.

Bishop cast down his eyes and moved on.

It was time to find a place to put his head down. The long journey was over after spending two days on three buses to get here. Now it was almost midnight and he needed to find a room that was off the beaten path.

Bishop hailed a cab. "Habla Inglés? Cheap hotel?"

"Cheap, ah si; barato." The driver pulled onto the road and started into the city.

From what Bishop could tell so far, there weren't a lot of English-speakers here and this would present a problem for him as he spoke virtually no Spanish.

Several miles from the bus terminal, the driver stopped at what looked to be a cheap hotel. Maybe more rundown than Bishop had expected, but the upside was that it was probably very inexpensive. He had exchanged his money to Pesos and held some in his hand.

"265, señor."

Bishop counted the money carefully to ensure he didn't hand over more than required. He had no idea if he'd been screwed over or if the fare had been reasonable. There was no time to debate. He needed to get out of sight and the fewer people he made an impression with, the better. "Here you go. Gracias." Bishop stepped out of the cab and approached the entrance to the hotel. It was a 5-story building with a chipped peach-colored stucco exterior in need of a power wash.

He walked inside and approached a woman behind the desk. "Uno night, uh, Uno—uh, what's the word for night?"

"Noche," the woman responded. "I speak English. One night?"

"Yes, please. Thank you."

She typed on an old computer and turned to grab a key from the wall of keys behind her. "Room 358. Stairs are to your right. Check out is 11am."

"Gracias." Bishop made his way to the stairs and walked up to the third floor. The narrow corridor was lined with stained teal carpet and dingy orange walls. Florescent lights were mounted on the ceiling and cast down a sickly glow as he walked to room 358. Bishop had grown accustomed to living a lifestyle suited for the more downtrodden. However, on his own, after losing his medical license and trying to stay off the radar, he'd learned to adopt a meager way of life. It wasn't like EMTs made a fortune either. Some did all right, but in the grand scheme of things, it was nothing compared to that of a doctor. But there were more important things for Bishop than money.

He inserted the key and opened the door to a waft of stale air that smelled of smoke and booze. Something that never appealed to him. Drugs, alcohol, smoking. It all dulled his senses and Bishop needed to stay sharp at all times.

He tossed his bag onto the bed and pushed off his shoes. An old 19-inch television sat on top of a dresser that looked as though it could scarcely handle the weight. Bishop pushed a button on the TV to turn it on. There appeared to be no remote.

It flickered on and he switched over the channels. All the stations were in Spanish and none appeared to be news related. Bishop walked to the window and peered through the heavy green curtains at the street below. Several people walked by, some lay on the sidewalk, probably homeless and some were women, likely prostitutes. It was legal in Mexico City as well as in many states in the country.

He looked at one of the women leaning against a light post. From this distance, she appeared attractive enough. However, Theodore Bishop wasn't the type of man who enjoyed what other men enjoyed. His sexuality was never that important to him. And when Holly eventually figured that out, she called him on it. It was then Bishop realized she would never understand the type of man he was. It had been the source of many arguments.

Bishop let the curtain fall again and he returned to the bed and dropped down. As he closed his eyes, he recalled the exuberance he felt injecting the poison into his co-worker's neck. The shocked expression he revealed. The recognition that no one was going to save him. That was what brought Theodore Bishop the excitement he needed. It worked every time.

21

Theodore Bishop was born to Dr. Eugene and Carol Bishop in Harrisburg, Pennsylvania in 1988. A few years later, Dr. Eugene Bishop served overseas and upon returning home, the family pulled up roots and moved to Rhode Island. They resided in an upper-class neighborhood where the homes were miniature mansions hidden behind gated driveways.

Theodore Bishop was living a life in direct contrast to his upbringing. He'd lost his medical license, got certified as an EMT and continued to live essentially paycheck to paycheck.

So how was it that a man of little means managed to elude the NSA and the FBI? Not to mention that his entire career, which had been plagued by suspicious activity, he also came out unscathed? The question of how or why he lost his license still loomed.

There was only one answer for Kate. Someone was looking out for Bishop. It was unclear at this point if Bishop was aware of it, but there was no doubt in Kate's mind that someone continually cleared a path for Bishop to allow him to do the things he wanted to do and had done for his entire adult life.

She knew the father, Eugene Bishop, had been the Chief of Surgery at Our Lady of Mercy, the very same hospital where his son served his residency. She and Walsh had already spoken to the doctor who had worked with Bishop, who also happened to be in a relationship with Bishop's ex-girlfriend, Holly.

Kate searched the database records to discover that Eugene Bishop died when Theodore was 16 years old. An apparent heart attack at the age of 45 while he was heading up the surgical department at the hospital.

In her continued search, she discovered that Bishop's mother, Carol, remarried three years later to another doctor. "Robert Whitman." She peered at the monitor and searched the database for details on Dr. Whitman. "You gotta be kidding me?" Kate examined the information. "Chief of Surgery at Our Lady of Mercy from 2004 through 2010. She married the man who replaced her husband." Kate peered around and quickly realized she was talking to herself again.

It turned out that Carol Bishop also took Dr. Whitman's name when they married. She was now going by Carol Whitman and was still married to the doctor, who was now retired.

Kate got up from her desk and headed into Fisher's office, walking in without an invitation. Her mind clinging to a single theory, she could often forget about polite society. "I need to go back to Providence."

"Why?" Fisher asked.

"I want to talk to Bishop's mother, Carol Whitman. These people have money. Bishop's father was a prominent doctor and died from a heart attack at the age of 45. His mother remarried a few years later to the man who replaced Dr. Eugene Bishop as Chief of Surgery. They're still married."

"Why didn't we look into the mother at the beginning?" Fisher asked.

"There wasn't much point. We knew who we were looking for. We had our suspect."

"And now?" He pressed on. "What's your endgame, Reid?"

"I suspect Bishop's family has a great deal of influence in the community. Money and influence could explain how Bishop was able to slip away. If it was the mother who helped him, I might be able to convince her to tell us where he is."

"If you're right about this, the odds his mother would give him up after helping him are slim, at best," Fisher said. "What could you possibly say to convince her otherwise? This is assuming you're right and she's been clearing a path for her son, which I'm not yet convinced of."

Kate pressed down on the back of the guest chair with her arms. "You said I could pursue this if I could justify my reasoning and it didn't interfere with anything else that I'm working on. I'm not working on anything else right now. I just need a day to go back to Providence and talk to the mother. You said when I came to you that I needed to be certain. I am certain. She may not know where her son is, but there's a good chance she knows *who* he is and what he's capable of doing. I need this woman on our side, and I know I can get her to help."

Fisher folded his arms on top of the desk and leaned in. "I'll give you this one. But you aren't going alone. Take with you whoever has the time to spare."

"It's just a conversation with the mother. I can handle this on my own. Just like before. Will you trust me on this one?"

"It's a matter of safety, Reid."

"Do you think this woman will come after me? We know Bishop's in Mexico somewhere living it up. There's no threat here."

"There are no lone wolves here on this team either. Here's

what I would like to propose, then. One of the candidates I've been talking to has expressed great interest in filling Quinn's position. Why don't we consider this a test run and you can take him?"

"Who is it?"

"Jonathan Surrey from the Denver office."

Kate considered the proposal. "Are you sure this isn't just you attempting to send along a babysitter?"

"Reid, you know me better than that. Come on. Give me some credit here. If I have to bring someone on, wouldn't you prefer it to be someone you can work with? Or do you want me to make this a crapshoot?"

"No," Kate resigned. "That's not what I want. Fine. Should I call him, or do you want to?"

Nick shoved his hands in his pockets as he watched Kate gather her things. "And you're sure this is the direction you want to go?"

She peered at him. "If it wasn't, I wouldn't be going. Fisher agreed this is a step in the right direction. I'm right about this, Nick. I can feel it." She zipped up her laptop bag and pulled on her coat. "It's a good thing—doing this. And if it helps me get insight into Surrey, then all the better. I want to know what I'll be up against."

"What we'll *all* be up against," Nick replied.

"Exactly." Kate stood on her toes and leaned in to kiss him. "I'll keep in touch. I promise."

"You'd better."

Kate walked out of Nick's office and headed into the hall. She looked back to see Nick standing in the doorway. "Have a good day." She waved a final time before leaving.

A cab ride later and Kate waited at the gate for the flight to leave. It was the first flight of the morning after hustling last night to get booked as soon as possible. Agent Jonathan Surrey was due to meet her at the gate but had not yet arrived.

She hadn't spent more than an hour with Surrey on her consult at his office. Her first impression of him was that he seemed knowledgeable and respectful. Then she went on about her duties and that was that, which was why she had been taken aback when Fisher suggested him as a candidate for Quinn's job.

"Agent Reid?"

Kate spun around at the sound of her name. "Agent Surrey. It's nice to see you again." She offered a greeting. "I'm sure this must feel a little strange jumping into unfamiliar territory."

"Not at all. I had a chance last night to look over what's been done on the investigation to date. It's intriguing," Surrey replied.

Score one for the new guy. Kate was mildly impressed that he'd done his homework. Although, any self-respecting agent being thrown into a new case would have.

Jonathan Surrey appeared to be in his mid-thirties. She'd wondered how long he'd been with the Bureau. He still appeared fresh and eager, meaning he'd probably been on the job fewer than ten years. In Kate's experience, agents who had served longer tended to look that much more jaded. She, herself, had only been on the job for five years and she wondered if she had that haggard look.

He was well put-together. Stylish black hair that wasn't too short. Fit, but not overly built. Something along the lines of average. Smart dresser. He wore a fitted white button-down beneath a casual jacket and tapered dress pants. The black wool overcoat was a nice touch. It was approaching late-October and the weather in D.C. had turned cool. *Eh, he's all right,* she thought. What kind of person he would be to work for? That remained to be seen.

"I think our flight's boarding," he said.

"Well, I guess we'd better go, then."

T.F. GREEN AIRPORT was a few miles from the state capital of Providence and the flight had just arrived. The short duration allowed for more small talk between Kate and the man who might become her boss but hadn't revealed any great insight into him. Opening up to new people wasn't something Kate was known for. Walls still surrounded her and only a select few had made it past the guard gates. Surrey was not on that list.

She headed to the car rental kiosk and filled out the paperwork. Within minutes, the agents were on the road.

Surrey peered at her from the passenger seat of the rented 4-door sedan. "How did you get the mother to agree to the interview?"

"I asked." Kate glanced at him as she turned out of the airport. "She didn't seem reluctant at all, actually, which struck me as odd."

"In what way?"

"She has to have heard the rumors. The news reports. I'm sure she doesn't live under a rock. And yet when I spoke to her, she seemed to be casual about the matter." Kate glanced at him. "What made you interested in throwing your name into the hat for this job?"

"A move to BAU? Isn't that what we all want?" he asked.

"Not everyone. Have you worked on these types of investigations before?"

"Multiple murders? Not really. Just plain 'ol run-of-the-mill murders." Surrey grinned. "Honestly, I was impressed with the work you did for my field office. Agent Brighton couldn't stop talking you up."

"Somehow, I'm not surprised to hear that," Kate replied.

"Oh yeah, he's a talker. A hell of an agent, but given the chance, he'll talk your ear off and then some."

Kate laughed. "It took me about a minute to figure that out. But he's a great guy and a good agent. I'm glad his feelings for me were mutual. Fair warning, things are different when you get to HQ. Quantico is a different beast. There are a lot of politics involved."

"Like there aren't in any field office," Surrey replied.

"I suppose there are, but it just feels like it's more of a struggle to get your point across and to get approvals and things like that." She pulled alongside the curb that fronted the home. "This is it."

Surrey stepped out and waited for Kate. On her approach, they peered at the home. "Not a bad place to live."

The sprawling, elegant home was adorned with white columns that led the way to a double-door entrance.

"Not bad at all." Kate started ahead and reached the door, but before she could ring the bell, it opened. "Oh, hello. Mrs. Whitman?"

"Yes."

"I'm Special Agent Kate Reid and this is my partner, Special Agent Jonathan Surrey. I spoke with you yesterday about your son?"

She nodded and opened the door to allow them inside. "May I offer you something to drink? Coffee or a glass of water?"

Kate smiled warmly and noted the woman's appearance. In her late fifties, she had a Helen Mirren quality about her. A cream-colored blouse worn beneath a soft cream angora sweater. Tailored pants that hung perfectly on her slightly full waist. Cream shoes, closed-toed, with a kitten heel. There was no doubt she came from money. "I would love a glass of water," she replied.

"I could do with a glass, too, thank you." Surrey followed Kate's lead.

Mrs. Whitman summoned her housekeeper. "Would you mind bringing us some water, please? We'll take it in the den." She looked back at Kate. "It's a bit quieter in the den. I hope that's all right with you."

"Of course." Kate followed the woman through the foyer past the living room. She looked back at Surrey who stayed a few steps behind.

"Please, have a seat." Mrs. Whitman gestured to the seating area that boasted four oversized wing-backed chairs covered in a linen fabric and embellished with bronze studs. Two on one side and two on the other. In between was a small round wooden table.

The fireplace with white marble surrounds burned and crackled and was the focal point of the room. Kate felt the warmth envelop her. "Do you mind if I take off my coat?"

"Not at all. Please, let me take that for you." She took Kate's coat and looked at Surrey. "May I take yours as well?"

"Sure. Thanks." Surrey removed his long wool coat. He sat down next to Kate as they waited for Mrs. Whitman to return.

Instead, the housekeeper appeared carrying a tray with crystal-clear glasses of water, each adorned with a wedge of lemon and a full pitcher with ice. She set it on the table.

"Thank you." Kate reached for a glass and took a sip.

Mrs. Whitman returned and sat down in one of the other winged chairs. She folded her hands in her lap and crossed her legs at the ankles. "You had some questions regarding Theodore."

"Yes, ma'am," Kate began. "As I'm sure you're aware, he is wanted in connection with the murder of one of his coworkers, an EMT who worked with him in Charlotte up until a few days ago."

Mrs. Whitman cast away her gaze. "You'll forgive me, but it is difficult to hear of anyone speaking about my son doing something so horrendous." She inhaled a breath and returned her attention to them. "I am aware that he is a suspect."

"Are you also aware that he fled to Mexico as a result?" Kate waited for her to respond, but her expression hadn't shifted in the least with this news. "Ma'am?"

"Please, call me Carol. And no, I'm afraid I was unaware of that. I assume that, then, is why you are here? To uncover whether I know the location of my son? Rest assured, Agent Reid, I do not. We have been estranged for some time."

"I see. Can you tell me when you last spoke to him?" Kate pressed on.

"I don't recall, but it has been years." She revealed a smile laced with regret. "Our relationship changed dramatically after I remarried."

"Of course, you married Dr. Robert Whitman, who was once the Chief of Surgery at the hospital your husband and Theo worked."

"I see you do know a lot about my family, Agent Reid."

"I'm simply trying to get to the truth and find your son. I believe he's become desperate, which is why he fled the country. However, my concern is that he might've had help. If you know where he is, Mrs. Whitman—Carol—please help us find him. There have been other murders linked to Theo. Crimes that have not been made known to the public."

Mrs. Whitman turned serious and held Kate's gaze. "How many?"

"Five that we know of. Another case is pending."

A tear fell from Mrs. Whitman's eye. She blinked it away. "I wish I could help you, Agent Reid," she turned to Surrey. "Agent Surrey. But I simply can't. Whatever Theo has done he will have to answer for, but I have nothing to offer in your search." She stood. "Now, I don't mean to be rude, but I have an impending appointment that I need to prepare for."

Kate stood from the chair. "I understand. If there's anything you recall that might help us, please don't hesitate to reach out." She retrieved a business card and waited for Mrs. Whitman to take it.

"Of course. I'll show you out." With the card in her hand, Mrs. Whitman showed them to the door.

Kate heard the double doors close behind them and continued along the path to the car. She unlocked the door and slipped behind the wheel. Surrey stepped in and Kate keyed the ignition. "I had hoped that would go better."

"She's a mother," Surrey replied. "What else do you have up your sleeve, or are we done here?"

"Not nearly. I thought we'd drop in to see Dr. Whitman." She pulled away from the curb.

"You know where we can find him?" Surrey asked.

With a sly grin, Kate continued, "I might've had a peek at the photos on the bookcase. There were at least three that appeared fairly recent given Mrs. Whitman's appearance."

"And?" He pressed on.

"They were taken at the Greenley Golf and Country Club. Where else would you find a retired doctor but on a golf course?"

Surrey nodded. "Well, well, Agent Reid. It seems you are as observant as I've been told."

22

———————

While Autumn was in full swing, the daytime temperatures in Providence hovered in the high 50s to low 60s. Still great golfing weather. When Kate pulled onto the grounds of the Greenley Golf and Country Club on a sunny but cool Wednesday afternoon, she expected to see several golfers, likely retirees.

Agent Surrey peered at the parking lot. "Busy place."

"No guarantees, but I'd say we stand a respectable shot at finding Dr. Whitman here." She cut the engine and prepared to step out of the car when Surrey stopped her.

"Just so we're on the same page, you're hoping there might be some friction between the stepfather and the stepson that you'll exploit, is that right?"

"That is the goal. Unless you have another idea," Kate said.

"Nope. Just checking." He stepped out of the car and followed Kate to the clubhouse entrance.

The porte-cochere led to a set of heavy wooden doors with handles in the shape of golf clubs. The elaborate architecture was

Victorian styled as the building and grounds had been constructed in the 1890s.

Surrey opened one of the doors for Kate.

She approached a service desk. "Good afternoon. I was hoping I might find Dr. Whitman here today."

The man behind the counter looked to be middle-aged and wore a blazer over a polo shirt that was buttoned to the top. He narrowed his eyes. "Might I ask who is inquiring?"

Kate retrieved her credentials. "FBI Special Agent Reid." She nodded to Surrey.

"And I'm Special Agent Surrey."

The man glanced between them before turning to a desktop computer to type. "It does look like Dr. Whitman has checked in today. However, that was earlier this morning. I would imagine he has completed his round of golf." He looked at Kate. "You might find him in the dining area taking lunch."

Kate glanced around the man toward the rear of the building. "Is the dining area back there?"

"Yes, ma'am. Should I help you locate him?"

"No, thank you. We'll find him. I appreciate your help." Kate walked past the desk and glanced over her shoulder at Surrey, who had hurried to catch up.

"I think that might be him there." Surrey offered a subtle nod in the doctor's direction.

"Looks like the guy in the picture to me." Kate continued ahead and approached the man who sat alone with a plate of food that was almost empty. "Dr. Whitman?"

The older man with thinning grey hair and a long face peered up at Kate. "Yes?"

"My partner and I are federal agents. We'd like to speak to you about your stepson, Theodore Bishop." Kate pulled out a chair.

"We don't want to cause a scene for you, Dr. Whitman. It's just a few questions and we'll be on our way."

Whitman surveyed the restaurant and it appeared that no one had taken any notice. "Of course. Please, join me." He dabbed the corners of his mouth with a napkin and returned it to his lap. "If you're here then I should assume you've spoken to my wife, Carol? Theo's mother?"

"We have," she replied. "My name is Kate Reid. I work out of Quantico with the Behavioral Analysis Unit. This is Jonathan Surrey, my partner. Dr. Whitman, your stepson is accused of several serious crimes. Murder charges. My team and I have been assisting various FBI field offices in attempt to track down Theo. Unfortunately, he managed to slip out of the country and we now have a solid reason to believe he is currently in Mexico, though his location is uncertain."

"You think *I* know where he is?" Whitman asked. "I haven't seen, nor have I spoken to Theodore in quite a number of years. Carol must've mentioned this to you."

"She mentioned that she hadn't spoken to him. We don't mean to waste your time, Doctor, but we believe Theo had help getting into Mexico. We'd like to know if you're aware of anyone who might offer help to him."

"Myself included? Is that what you're driving at?" Whitman shook his head. "Under no circumstances would I help that young man. I gave it my best shot when he was younger, after he lost his father, but there was something in him that frightened me. It frightened his mother was well."

Kate glanced at Surrey. "Can I ask what made you leery of him?"

"I'll start by saying that he idolized his father. You may already know this, but Dr. Eugene Bishop was the Chief of Surgery at Our Lady of Mercy until he died."

"Where you then took over," Surrey interrupted.

"Yes. I was, in fact, promoted to the position. I could see Theo had wished to follow in his father's footsteps, which I supported. The boy had a brilliant mind. It simply needed to be molded; guided by a respected authority figure in the medical field. I had hoped I would be that figure. But when we saw..." He turned away.

"Saw what, Dr. Whitman?" Kate leaned in.

"His mother insisted it was nothing and that it was important for Theo to have a clean slate upon entering medical school. So we overlooked it."

"Dr. Whitman, please. What did you and Mrs. Whitman see?" Kate pressed on.

The doctor nervously glanced around the restaurant. "Shortly after his father died, Carol and Theo had been living in the home she had shared with Dr. Bishop. We started to see each other more regularly and it wasn't uncommon for me to stay the night.

Theo had gone out for an evening with friends, or so he told us. As Carol and I prepared for bed, we heard a noise, a screeching almost. Something that, well, the sound was just horrendous. It came from the basement. Theo's father had received various grants over the course of his career which allowed him to conduct experimental procedures in the field of surgery. Things that are today used quite regularly. So the basement was generally off-limits to Theo unless he wished to observe his father, which he had done on several occasions."

"What was in the basement?" Kate asked, hoping to jump to the conclusion of this story.

Whitman closed his eyes and shook his head before continuing. "A dog, a neighbor's dog, in fact, had been secured to one of the tables. He—he had been sliced lengthwise, his insides..." Whitman choked up. "Theo tortured the poor animal and had injected it, I assume, to put it out of its misery. However, the injection proved ineffective and the animal had survived. Until we found it. I then put the poor creature out of its misery."

Kate and Surrey traded knowing glances. She turned back to Whitman. "Theo is under investigation for the murder of 6 people that we know of. Some of the victims had existing conditions that were exacerbated by an injection that ultimately caused their deaths. Others had been denied oxygen or given something that induced a serious medical reaction. Dr. Whitman, why was something so clearly troubling not reported to the authorities at the time?"

"I am ashamed to say that I respected Carol's wishes. She had insisted it was merely Theo acting out as his father had only recently passed at that point. We didn't see any sort of similar behavior from him after that. I suppose we thought it had gone away. So when you say that someone is helping Theo escape justice, I can say with certainty that it is not Carol nor me."

Kate stood up. "Thank you for your time, Dr. Whitman. If you or your wife do hear from Theo, please, it's imperative that you reach out to us." She handed him a business card. "Sorry to have interrupted your meal." Kate pushed in her chair and headed toward the entrance.

Surrey followed and neither said a word until they reached the car when Surrey began, "What the hell was that about?" He opened the car door. "Torture? The kid tortures a dog and no one says a goddam thing?"

Kate stepped inside and turned the engine. "Dr. Bishop died from a heart attack at the age of 45. Seems a little young, doesn't it?"

"What are you saying?" Surrey asked.

"I'm saying, maybe these rescued victims weren't his first kills.

Given what we know now, don't you think it's possible he could've killed his own father?"

"You heard what Whitman said back there. Theodore Bishop idolized his father," Surrey replied.

"Okay. Say he put his dad on a pedestal. None of us is perfect. What if Dr. Eugene Bishop did something to make Theo reconsider who his father was?"

Surrey peered through the passenger window. "If that's the case, then we're dealing with a man far more dangerous than you might've originally thought."

Kate and her shadow-partner arrived at the Vital Records Department in Providence.

"We know the father died from a heart attack, Reid. What are you hoping to gain by pulling his death certificate?" Surrey asked.

"I want to see the name of the doctor who called it. The physician who completed the death certificate. Then I want to find him."

"Fair enough." Surrey followed her inside the building.

"Hello, I'm FBI Special Agent Reid." Kate approached the information desk. "I'm looking to pull a death certificate from 2004."

The hefty, older woman behind the desk appeared boorish and rolled her eyes after noting Kate's badge. "Name?" She pulled toward her monitor.

"Dr. Eugene Bishop. Died in September of 2004."

"One moment." Her fingers sped across the keyboard as if she'd done this a thousand times. She probably had. "Dr. Eugene Bishop." She looked at Kate. "You want me to print this up for you? I'll have to charge you $5 for a copy."

"That's fine. Yes, I would like a printed copy. Thank you." Kate pulled out a five from the wallet inside her coat pocket. When the woman returned with the copy, she looked at the money Kate had placed on the counter.

"Sorry, no cash. Apparently, they don't trust us with cash. Credit or debit only. Swipe your card right here." She pointed at the card reader.

"Okay." Kate again pulled out her wallet, returned the cash, and inserted her card.

A receipt printed from below the desk and the woman ripped it away. "Here you go, ma'am."

"Thank you so much for your help. Have a nice day." Kate walked toward the double doors. "Nice lady." She whispered to Surrey.

"Yeah. A real gem," he replied.

As they made their way outside, they stopped beneath the overhang of the building.

"So? Who was the doctor?" he asked.

Kate held the copy of the death certificate so they could both see it. "Um, oh, here it is. Dr. Phillip Hilgard. Our Lady of Mercy." She looked at Surrey. "There sure are a lot of connections to this hospital."

"Well, Dr. Bishop had been the Chief of Surgery. It shouldn't be too surprising he was brought there. Or maybe he had gone there when he experienced chest pains."

"It's something I'll bet Dr. Hilgard can help us out with."

"There's something else to consider, here, Reid. Like the fact he may no longer work for the hospital. The father died in 2004."

"You know what? You're exactly right." Kate retrieved her phone. "Let's find out if he still works there." She peered at him. "I guess there was a reason for you to be here."

The line answered. "Our Lady of Mercy Hospital. How may I direct your call?"

"I'd like to speak to Dr. Phillip Hilgard. I'm with the FBI and it's important I speak to him."

"One moment please."

The operator placed Kate on hold. "He must still work there. They put me on hold." The line answered again. "Hello?"

"Yes, this is Dr. Hilgard. How can I help you?"

"Doctor, I'm Agent Reid and my partner and I would like to talk to you about Dr. Eugene Bishop. He passed away from a heart attack in..."

"I know who he was," Hilgard replied. "What do you need to know?"

"Well, I'd like to review his medical records with you and discuss the circumstances surrounding his death."

"I'm sorry. Do you have a warrant, Agent Reid? Permission from the family? I'm sure you understand that medical records are confidential, even in the event of a patient's death."

"I do not have a warrant." Kate shot a look to Surrey. "It wouldn't be difficult for me to get one, but I thought you might be able to share some insight into Dr. Bishop's medical condition."

"What is this about, anyway?" Hilgard asked. "He died more than 15 years ago. What could possibly be relevant to you today?"

"His son, Dr. Theodore Bishop, is wanted in connection to multiple homicides, Dr. Hilgard. That is why I'm looking into the death of his father."

"I'm sorry. I can't help you."

The line went dead and Kate pulled the phone from her ear. "He just hung up on me."

"That sounds like an invitation to pay him a visit," Surrey replied.

THE SUN DIPPED below the horizon and only the fiery glow remained. Kate peered at it through the window of the restaurant while sipping on a glass of iced tea. "I thought we'd be on our way home by now."

Surrey nodded. "Getting a warrant takes time, but I think you made the right call. The doctor's behavior is suspicious. Who hangs up on a fed?" He grabbed his glass of water and swallowed a large gulp. "The more we come up against, the more inclined I am to believe you were right."

"What do you mean?" Kate turned back to him.

"I mean about the hunch that someone is helping Theodore Bishop. None of this is adding up. It's as though everyone in that man's life has shielded him."

"But why? How could they do that?" she asked.

"The only answer to that is whoever is helping him must wield a fair bit of power. The power to make or break careers, ambitions." Surrey nodded. "Yeah, it smells pretty bad."

"I need to know how far Fisher will go to back me. I thought this would be a quick one-off, get back and piece together what happened."

"Did you really think it would be that easy?" Surrey asked. "You've been doing this long enough to know better. You've been after this guy for what, two, three weeks? Now he's weaseled his way out of the country. Reid, I don't think any of this is going to be easy, which is why I'm glad it's you on the job."

A half-cocked smiled played on her lips. "Kissing up to me won't guarantee you this job, Surrey. I'm not the one who will make the call."

"First of all, I wasn't kissing up to you. What I said, I said based on my experiences. Secondly, I haven't decided if this is the right move for me in any case. Between the relationship you and Scarborough have, the fact that the Senior Unit Agent is also dating another agent; it all feels very swampy to me. I'm not sure I want to step into that muck."

Kate chuckled. "I can't argue your point. But what I can say is that Fisher is objective almost to a fault. Yes, he is in a relationship with Eva Duncan, but you know how hard it is to meet people outside of our line of work? Are you married?"

Surrey shook his head. "Divorced. And you might be right about meeting people. Still, I do my best to keep away from the political bullshit. As much as I admire what you did for our office and what you're doing on this investigation, I'm not sure I'm convinced this is the right move for me."

Kate nodded and reached for her phone. "Hang on." She peered at the caller ID. "Looks like we might've just gotten our warrant." She swiped to answer the call. "Reid here." Kate nodded. "Perfect. That's exactly what we need. Can you also send a copy to Agent Cameron Fisher at Quantico? Thank you so much. Goodbye, sir."

"You got it?" Surrey asked.

"Sure did. You don't mind if I step outside for a moment, do you? I need to call Fisher and get him up to speed. I'm sure no one in here wants to listen to me on my phone." Kate excused herself from the table. "I'll be right back."

"Take your time," Surrey replied.

Kate pushed through the door and walked outside with the phone at her ear. "Hey Fisher, it's me. Listen, I just got the warrant we discussed. They're sending you a copy as well."

"It's getting a little late to serve it tonight though, don't you think?" He asked.

Kate checked the time on her phone before continuing. "Looks like it'll have to wait until first thing in the morning. I know I promised we'd be back by tonight..."

"Don't sweat it. Do what you have to do. If you believe this is the right path, then keep at it, but let me know how things go in the morning. Oh, by the way, what do you think of Surrey?"

"He seems very capable," she replied.

"Capable? That's it? Doesn't sound like he's made much of an impression on you."

She sighed. "Don't get me wrong, he's a good agent. I can see that. And to be honest, he's offered helpful insight today. It just takes time to get to know people."

"But you're not ruling him out as a candidate for Quinn's replacement?" Fisher asked.

"I wouldn't rule him out. No."

"Good. Keep me up to speed on your progress. And Reid, try to get some sleep."

"I will. Good night." She pressed the end call button, but before going back inside, she wanted to update Nick. Call it a habit, or an obligation, it was just what she had to do. He quickly answered the line. "Hey, it's me."

"Hi, how's it going? Still there, I see," Nick replied.

"We hit a little bit of a snag but now that we got our warrant, we should be able to wrap this up tomorrow morning. I just wanted to give you a call before it got too late."

"It's never too late to get a call from you. Besides, it's what? 8 o'clock? What am I, 60?" Nick laughed.

"Sorry. You're right." Kate chuckled. "Anyway, it looks like we'll be staying here for the night. In the morning, we'll serve a warrant to the doctor who attended to Theo's father when he died."

"He doesn't want to cooperate, huh?"

"He hung up on me if that tells you anything." Kate peered

inside the restaurant. "Hey, um, we're getting ready to eat some dinner, but I wanted to touch base. I'll call you later?"

"Sure thing. Goodnight, babe," Nick said.

"Good night." Kate returned her phone to her pocket and walked back inside. As she returned to the table, their food had arrived, and Surrey had already tucked in.

"Everything good?" He said with a mouth full of food.

"It's all good."

23

K ate turned off the alarm on her phone and pulled up to the edge of the hotel bed. It was 5am and the pace of this investigation had caught up with her. Nevertheless, she was certain this was a means to an end. Understand the family dynamics of the Bishop's and she would figure out who had helped him slip into Mexico City. What she knew without a doubt was that it had been someone with money and influence. Manipulating national security data was no easy task. The risks alone would warrant a high price tag.

As she prepared to leave the room, Kate hoped it would be for the last time and staying another night wouldn't be necessary. That all depended on how cooperative Dr. Hilgard would be.

Downstairs, Surrey hovered over the vast buffet, snatching up every sugary carbohydrate in sight before tossing on a few sausage links and eggs on the plate for good measure.

Kate approached him. "I see you subscribe to the notion of a hearty breakfast."

He turned to her. "I eat what I want. I don't have anyone to impress. Morning."

She nodded and ladled a heaping serving of oatmeal into a bowl. "Morning. Did you sleep well?"

"Not really. I don't like traveling. Working in the Denver office means I don't usually have to."

"Well, that would change if you worked at BAU. Just saying." Kate filled a paper cup with coffee and took her tray to a nearby table. She emptied a couple of sugar packets into the coffee while Surrey sat across from her. "I don't know what time Dr. Hilgard will get in this morning, but I would suggest we arrive as soon as we can. I have no idea if we'll get pushback or if he'll just take off."

"If he does that, then we have ourselves a real problem. I don't think he'll be that stupid." Surrey sipped on his coffee. "Getting there early means we can get the hell out of here and I can get back to my office."

"So that'll be it? You don't want to see this through?" Kate asked.

"I was brought in to observe. I've done that. I have nothing to contribute to your ongoing investigation. I wasn't here at the beginning and the time it would take to get fully up to speed, you'd probably have found him by then."

Kate pursed her lips. "I see."

"You're disappointed?" He studied her. "Why? The whole purpose of my being here was to learn your style."

"Hey, I don't care what you do. My job is to find Theodore Bishop and I'll do that with our without your help." Kate shoved a spoonful of oatmeal into her mouth.

He grunted. "Look, Reid, no offense. I'm not one of those gung-ho agents who will stop at nothing to get his man, or woman. I've been at this for too long and I've learned that those guys? They burn out. They end up losing everything important in their lives for the sake of the one case they couldn't solve. I already lost a wife and a daughter because I neglected them. I learned the lesson, albeit, too late. I do the job and do my best, but I won't risk it all for a criminal or some psycho killer. Because I'll tell you one thing, Reid, there will always be another one right around the corner."

Maybe this wasn't going to be a good fit after all. Kate opened her phone and scrolled through it while she ate so she could end this topic of conversation. Every member of her team looked at investigations as she had. Get the unsub at all costs. At least, she thought they had. Wasn't it Fisher who initially suggested they leave this in the hands of the FBI international office in Mexico City? If she hadn't pursued this avenue, she would be sitting in her office working on some consult and reading resumes for Quinn's replacement.

Kate had subscribed to Nick's school of thought. Then again, Nick had chosen to make the move to Quantico to get out of the field, to slow down. That was what he told her. Things hadn't turned out that way, though. He'd been hands-on during every investigation they'd handled since her arrival. She began to wonder if that was because she was involved. Now Nick had paid the price for his management style. If he hadn't gone to Rio...

"You ready to go?" Surrey tilted back the paper cup to get the last drop of coffee inside.

"I'm ready." Kate gathered her dishes and returned her tray to the counter. She pulled her coat off the back of the chair and reached for her bags.

Surrey returned with a to-go cup. "For the road. You sure you don't want to take a coffee or something? Who knows when we'll get the chance to stop for food or drink again?"

"I'm fine." She started toward the lobby doors.

Surrey followed. "Well, I can see I plucked at a nerve. Hey, I didn't mean to piss you off, Reid."

"You didn't. I just want to get this over with. Same as you." Kate pushed through the doors and made her way to the rental car. "I'll drive."

"All righty." Surrey raised his brows and stepped inside the passenger seat. "This should be a fun day."

KATE PULLED the car to a stop in the visitor parking lot of the hospital. "I don't know if he's here yet, but I say we go in and wait."

"Whatever you say," Surrey stepped out of the car.

Kate retrieved the warrant from her bag and headed toward the hospital's main entrance. It would now be the third time she had visited this hospital and it was starting to feel like everything relating to Theodore Bishop originated here. "What is it about this place?" She said under her breath.

"What's that?" Surrey asked.

"Nothing. It's just déjà vu. But as they say, third time's a charm." She pushed inside and approached the information desk.

"Agent Reid. You're back," said the man behind the desk. "And with someone new."

"This is Agent Surrey. We're here to see Dr. Hilgard."

"I believe he's in his office. Should I call up to him?" He reached for the phone.

"No. Thank you. Do you mind telling me where I can find his office?" Kate replied.

"Sure thing." He pointed to the right. "Head over there to the elevators. Go up to the 8th floor. His office is the big one at the end of the hall. Can't miss it. "Says Administrative Director in big bold letters."

"Director?" She replied.

"Yes, ma'am. Dr. Hilgard practically runs this place. Well, the admin side of it anyway."

"Thanks for your help." Kate started toward the elevators. "He's up there on the food chain. Same as Whitman was."

"What do you suppose that means?" Surrey asked.

"I don't know yet, but maybe we'll find out." She stepped onto the elevator. Kate stared at the numbers, not wanting to engage Surrey. Although, it seemed unfair to hold his beliefs against him. What did she know of what he'd been through as an agent? Just because he didn't put his job before his life—anymore—didn't mean that was a bad quality, did it? "I'm sorry. I don't mean to be, well, kind of a bitch."

Surrey laughed. "You're not. And I would never use that word to describe any woman, regardless of what she might have done. Asshole, maybe. Anyone can be an asshole. But again, that's not what I think of you. I think you're passionate, and that's great. It would be a shame to see that light go out in you, but it will some-day, and you should be prepared for that."

The doors opened to the 8th floor and the two headed down the long corridor lined with offices. When they reached the end, it turned out the man behind the desk had been right.

"This must be the place," Kate said. "That guy wasn't kidding when he said it couldn't be missed."

"No. I like the big bold letters." Surrey turned to her with a smile. "He must be some kind of really important man."

Kate chuckled and pushed inside where a desk was positioned near the entrance and two chairs rested alongside the wall.

"Can I help you?" A young woman with short red hair peered at them with a furrowed brow.

"FBI. We're here to see Dr. Hilgard. Is he in?" Kate said.

The woman's face masked in concern. She glanced over her shoulder to the closed door. "I'll have to call him."

"So, he's in his office?" Kate walked around the desk.

"Ma'am. You can't just go in there."

"I have a warrant that says differently." She opened the door.

Surrey turned up his palms and shrugged at the woman before hurrying to Kate's side.

"Dr. Hilgard? I'm Agent Reid and this is Agent Surrey. We spoke on the phone late yesterday before you hung up on me."

The doctor removed his glasses and pushed away from his desk. "What are you doing here?"

Kate unfolded the warrant and slapped it onto his desk. "It would've been easier if you had just answered my questions. But since we're here now, we have a warrant to view Dr. Eugene Bishop's medical records."

Hilgard snatched the warrant and read it. "Well, I can see you'd prefer to go about this the hard way."

"The hard way?" Surrey asked. "I'm afraid you left us with no choice. We can go on back and grab those records on our own if you'd prefer."

Kate glanced at him with a wry smile.

"Fine." He typed on his computer. "I can retrieve them here. We put most of the archived files onto a database a few years ago. You might as well have a seat."

"Thank you." Kate pulled out a chair. "We aren't here to make your life difficult, Dr. Hilgard. We simply need to understand the circumstances that revolved around Dr. Bishop's death. He was young to have died from a heart attack."

Hilgard shifted his gaze. "It isn't as uncommon as you might think, Agent Reid." He peered at the screen and turned the monitor toward them. "Here you are. Cause of death, heart attack. I'm not sure what else you hoped to glean from this."

Kate looked at the monitor. "If you'd be so kind, we'd like to review the entire file. Autopsy..."

"There was no autopsy," Hilgard interrupted. "He died of natural causes and the family didn't request one."

"No?" Kate shot a glance at Surrey. "I think it would be best if you could get us a hard copy of the records. All of them. Including any and all medical history, not just the files surrounding his death."

Hilgard looked again at his monitor. "I'll have my assistant get those for you."

"And a place to take a look at them, too. That would be great," she added.

Hilgard stood from his desk. "Of course. It should only be a few moments. I'll take you to an available meeting room now."

X-RAYS, photocopied charts, lab results. All of it splayed out on the table while Kate and Surrey combed through each document.

"We've been at this for a while, Reid. I haven't seen anything that stands out, have you?"

Kate pushed aside the documents she reviewed. "No, but doesn't it strike you as odd that a seemingly healthy 45-year-old just dies from a heart attack?"

"Well, not according to Dr. Hilgard. He seems to think it's a regular occurrence," Surrey replied.

"No underlying problems, diseases, disorders." Kate shook her head. "Damn. I thought we'd find something in here."

"I know you did. Hey, you had to give it a shot. It was the right move."

Kate sighed. "I hate to beat a dead horse, but I just don't buy it. No autopsy? The wife of a prominent physician doesn't ask for an autopsy. What if it had revealed some sort of hereditary condition?

What if he had had mini-strokes before and he never got checked out?"

"You can 'what if' this all day, but it won't do you any good. How do you want to move forward on this, Reid? We can't sit here forever."

"Right. You need to be getting back." She pulled up.

"That's not what I meant."

Kate pressed her hand against her forehead. "I know you didn't. I just, you know, when I get those inclinations…"

"I get it. You want to run on it," Surrey replied.

Kate peered at the documents once again. "I have to be missing something." With her fingertips, she pulled each document, one by one, for another look. She re-examined the initial intake questionnaire when Dr. Bishop had arrived on the day of his death. "This one here. It says Dr. Bishop had been sick for a couple of days. Vomiting." She peered at Surrey. "It was attributed to a stomach bug or flu."

"Okay." Surrey appeared to wait while Kate's wheels spun.

"And yet, I see no other notations regarding this. It was as if they dismissed it."

"The guy was having a heart attack," Surrey began. "They might've been more concerned with that problem than a flu virus."

Kate peered into the distance. "This sounds familiar to me. I— I can't place it." She retrieved her phone. "Hang on. I need to call Duncan and ask her a question." Kate pressed the contact button and held the phone to her ear. "Eva, it's Kate. Yeah, doing all right. Listen, you remember back, maybe earlier last year, we had that consult out of Detroit?"

"I think so. I'd have to pull the file. Why?" Duncan replied.

"Didn't it have to do with some sort of suspected poisoning of a victim who the doctors thought had had a heart attack?"

"It's starting to ring a bell. Hang on." Duncan typed on her computer. "Do you have a minute to stay on the line, or do you want me to call you back?"

"I have a minute. Thanks," Kate said.

"Okay, I've got the file. It was last year. Detroit field office. They had a couple of victims they thought were related."

"Right. That's right. I remember now," Kate said. "One of the victims had a heart attack and the autopsy revealed it was due to his obesity."

"Yep. Hang on, I'm still reading this," Duncan said. "Turned out that only after the fact, after someone had bragged about killing this person in prison did the original ME go back for additional testing on his samples."

Kate might as well have had a light bulb glowing over her head as she sat upright and set her sights on Surrey. "The samples were tested again for poison. They hadn't been originally."

"You got it. How does this help?" Duncan asked.

"It does, trust me. I need to get my head around this. I'll call you back, though, okay? Thank you so much, Eva. I needed this." She ended the call.

"You want to tell me what that was about?" Surrey asked.

"I think Dr. Bishop might've been poisoned. And I think his son did it."

24

The winds kicked up with ferocity as it reached midday with the flag outside the hospital whipping and rattling the metal pole. Kate hurried through the doors and buttoned her coat on her way to the car. Agent Surrey seemed to catch onto the notion that when Kate's intuition struck, he'd better keep pace. And this had been one hell of a hunch.

"There's no way you'll be able to prove this, Reid." Surrey walked beside her. "They would need tissue samples, and not only would they no longer have samples since it's been 16 years, but there was no autopsy to begin with."

"I don't need to prove it." Kate unlocked the door and stepped behind the wheel. She waited for Surrey to get in. "I just need Mrs. Whitman to know that we know what her son did. We have enough on Bishop to put him away, but we need to find him first. Mrs. Whitman needs to be confronted on this because I think she'll crack." Kate fired up the engine. "We're going back to talk to her."

"You still believe she's been helping Bishop?" Surrey asked.

"I sure do. I think Theo killed his father to either protect his mother or defend her in some way." Kate noticed Surrey turn away and peer through the windshield. "You know I'm right."

He was silent for a moment and kept his eyes forward. "Maybe."

Kate smiled. "Uh-huh."

"That case you were talking about with your co-worker, the one in Detroit," Surrey added. "How had the victim been poisoned to make it look like a heart attack?"

She glanced at him. "It was a flower. Oleanders. They're incredibly poisonous and also extremely difficult to detect unless you were looking for it."

Surrey shook his head. "But how would a kid of that age— what was he then, 15 or 16? How would he have known about any of that stuff? Sure, his dad was a doctor, but he wasn't a chemist."

"That might be a question for Mrs. Whitman," Kate replied. "And since we're here now." She parked alongside the curb that fronted the extravagant home. "We should go and ask her." Kate jumped out and headed straight to the front door. With Surrey approaching, she rang the bell.

The door opened to the same housekeeper she had seen yesterday. "Afternoon. I was here yesterday speaking to Mrs. Whitman." She turned to Surrey for a moment. "We had a couple of quick questions for her if she has a moment."

"I'll go get her. Would you like to come in?" The housekeeper asked.

"Yes, we would. Thank you." Kate walked inside and when the woman left, she turned to Surrey. "It'll be tougher for Mrs. Whitman to ignore us if we're standing in her foyer."

"Yes, it will. I would've expected a door slammed in our faces had she answered herself."

Voices erupted from somewhere beyond the foyer. Kate turned to Surrey. "Here we go."

It took several more minutes before Mrs. Whitman appeared. "Hello, Agent Reid, Agent Surrey. I apologize for making you wait here. My housekeeper knew I was in an appointment. Please forgive the delay." She smoothed down her silk blouse. "Now, I am quite busy, so how may I assist you today?"

"Mrs. Whitman, you should know that we were able to obtain a search warrant to view your husband's medical records, including and up to the issuance of his death certificate."

"Why would you need to see that? I don't understand. You had asked about my son." She appeared flustered and pressed lightly on her styled hair as if to ensure nothing had fallen out of place.

"Would you like to sit down?" Kate placed her hand on the woman's arm.

Mrs. Whitman pulled away. "I certainly would not. Now, what is it that you wanted to ask, Agent Reid, or are you intent on continuing to waste my time?"

"I'll get to the point then. There is sufficient evidence to suggest your first husband, Theo's father, was poisoned. He was given something that induced his heart attack." Kate may have stretched the truth just a little, but it was the only way to ensure a reaction.

"What? What are you saying? That's not true. You know that's not true." Her face reddened. "I think it's time for you two to leave."

Kate held up a hand. "Mrs. Whitman, we just want to know where he is. We need to find your son before anyone else is killed at his hand. I'm sure this must be incredibly difficult for you to hear, but you know it in your heart what your son has done and what he is capable of continuing to do."

"You know nothing." Whitman's eyes darkened. "You have no idea about my son."

"We know he's in Mexico," Surrey began. "If the Mexican authorities capture him, and he has committed a crime there, he will not be extradited. He will spend the rest of his life in a Mexican prison. Is that what you want for your son?"

Mrs. Whitman eyed him and then Kate for what seemed like an eternity. "You don't know what his father was like. Theo tried to protect me."

"I'm sure he did, ma'am," Kate said. "Where is he?"

"He was such a quiet boy. And oh, how he admired his father. Until he saw what kind of man he truly was. A great doctor, yes, but a horrible husband. Theo found out his father cheated on me, and not just once. The deceit went on for years. When we thought he was out of town, helping other doctors. Well, he might've been doing just that, but he was also sleeping with anything in a skirt."

"How did Theo know anything about poisons?" Surrey asked as he caught a sideways glance from Kate. "He was very young to possess that type of knowledge."

Mrs. Whitman inhaled a deep breath. "He learned it from a movie. Around the time of all—this. A movie had come out. Something to the effect of using oleander to poison someone."

"I think I know the film," Kate said. "Theo was acting in your best interest at the time. Just as you are for him now. Please, Carol, we have to find Theo before he hurts anyone else. At least if he is returned, you'll be able to see him again. If he stays in Mexico..."

"He's in the capital," Mrs. Whitman blurted out. "He's in Mexico City."

"Where?" Kate pressed on.

"Please don't hurt him," she pleaded.

"Ma'am, the sooner you tell us, the sooner we can bring him back," Surrey replied.

"He's in a studio apartment. I'll give you the address."

"Did you arrange for him to leave the country?" Kate asked.

"I've been wiring him money. He needed me. I'm his mother."

"Thank you, Carol. You're doing the right thing," Kate said.

"You don't have children, do you, Agent Reid?" Her tone was harsh and deep. "Because if you did, you'd know this isn't the right thing at all."

THE AIRPORT WAS JUST AHEAD. Kate dropped off the rental car and she and Surrey headed toward the terminal.

"Fisher wants me back ASAP," Kate began. "I'll be taking a chartered flight."

"Then I guess this is where we part ways." Surrey offered his hand. "It's been a pleasure working with you, Kate Reid. I mean that."

Kate glanced at his hand before taking it. "The pleasure was all mine, Jonathan Surrey. You're very good at what you do."

"Back at ya." He smiled. "By the way, why didn't you press Carol Whitman on who she asked to alter the passport details? Someone did something."

"I didn't want to take the chance that she would alert whoever did it. I'm still not entirely sure she handled it on her own. But I need to find Theo first. The rest will be figured out later."

He nodded. "Take care, Reid. And good luck." Surrey walked through the double doors and disappeared.

As much as she hadn't wanted to admit it, Kate had learned a lot from Jonathan Surrey. She learned the type of agent she really was and the kind she ought to be. Whether the two would cross paths was unclear.

Kate walked through the private charter terminal and eventually boarded the plane for Quantico. As she sat in the window seat, she realized how much she had changed since her early days as an agent. Now here she was, hardly 5 years later, and she faced a censure hearing. That would leave quite a black mark on her record and could prevent her from achieving her goals. It was something she didn't reveal to Surrey. If he was to be hired, he would find out anyway and he could judge for himself the circumstances surrounding it.

But more importantly, Surrey had shown her that the job wasn't just about the hunt. If she hoped to have a long career, acceptance that the outcome won't always be what she desired, then she just might get one.

The plane touched down after a turbulent flight. She spotted Nick on the private airstrip standing in front of his car. He smiled at her approach.

"Boy, am I glad to see you." He offered a tender embrace.

"I'm glad to see you too. So what's the plan?"

He smiled. "Leave it to you to jump right in. Let's go. I'll get you up to speed."

KATE AND NICK walked into the conference room where the team waited.

Fisher smiled as they entered. "And there's the woman of the hour. Congratulations, Agent Reid."

"Thank you, but let's hold off on the accolades until we actually catch him." She sat down. "Scarborough filled me in. So we have the office in Mexico City on board?"

"They're coordinating with the local authorities now," Walsh replied. "Good job, by the way."

"Thank you." Kate turned back to Fisher. "When do we head out?"

"We don't," he replied. "The international office will take him into custody and work on getting him back here and transferred to the Houston office. Scarborough has already coordinated with Palmero."

"Oh. So that's it for us? Nothing left but the paperwork?" Kate asked.

"Dr. and Mrs. Whitman will be brought in for questioning by the Providence Police," Duncan began. "It's probable that Mrs. Whitman will be charged with aiding and abetting. Not sure if any charges will be brought against Dr. Whitman."

"I'm not sure why I had to hurry back. It sounds like everything is under control," Kate replied with irritation in her voice.

"I wanted you here to help answer questions and to assist the team in Mexico. I hope that's okay with you?" Fisher asked.

"Yes, of course. Is there anything else? It's been a long day and I'm sure I have a ton of emails to get through before I go home."

"No. There's nothing else," Fisher added. "When something breaks, I'll let you all know. Everyone did a great job on this investigation. Well above and beyond. Thank you."

Kate nodded and stood up to leave.

Nick caught up to her in the hall. "Look, Kate, I know you're disappointed, but you know where the jurisdictional lines are drawn."

"I do. I just thought...It doesn't matter." She switched on her office lights and walked inside. "I'm glad to be back either way."

"I'm glad you're back, too." He followed her inside. "Why don't you get caught up and then we'll sneak out a little early and grab some dinner?"

"Sure. I'd like that. Thanks." Kate sat down at her desk.

"Okay then." Nick smiled and walked out.

Kate began scrolling through her emails when she spotted Fisher at the door. "Hey. What can I do for you?"

Fisher took a seat. "I know you're pissed, Reid. I get it, okay? I came in to say thank you. Getting the mother to come clean...it was no easy task."

"Thank you," Kate said.

"I know it's difficult for you to relinquish control, but those guys in Mexico, they do know what they're doing. They'll bring Bishop back to Houston to face justice."

"I'm sure they will." Kate studied him. "But there's still something I need to figure out."

"Such as?"

"We now know Mrs. Whitman has been helping her son, sending him money and all that. But that doesn't explain how Walsh's NSA contact got it wrong when he sent over the information regarding the ticket purchase. We're talking a good two days of delayed details. How does that happen?"

"The only possible scenario I can think of seems far-fetched," Fisher replied.

"Let's hear it."

"Well, these people have money. We know that. With money comes influence and power. I don't think it would be too far out in left field to suggest the Whitmans have influence, which in turn could result in selective information being buried."

Kate raised a brow. "Yeah. That's what I thought. How do I go about finding the link? How does a doctor, even a Chief of Surgery, and his wife know anyone with that sort of capability?"

"A friend of a friend?" Fisher replied. "Isn't that how these things usually go? Somebody knows somebody else who can ensure things are diverted, overlooked. Even so, Reid, I'm not sure it matters now."

"It matters to me. Anyone involved in sweeping Bishop's

wrongdoings under the rug for years needs to be held accountable. The Whitmans and the Bishops may be wealthy and powerful people, but that doesn't mean they should escape justice in order to protect their names or their son."

Fisher stood. "How about we take that on after they bring in Bishop? I promise you, anyone involved in the murders, directly or indirectly, will pay the price. Can you give me that?"

Kate nodded. "I can. Thank you."

He started to leave but turned back. "One last thing. When we last talked, you didn't seem all that impressed with Surrey. Any final thoughts about that?"

Kate looked away and considered her answer. "I'm torn, to be honest. On the one hand, he's good at his job. No doubt. I knew that from my experience with him in Denver. But on the other, he has a different philosophy than we do."

"How so?" Fisher asked.

"He doesn't seem like the type of agent who takes home his work. I think he gives it his all, but at the end of the day, he's happy to set it aside."

Fisher chuckled. "And that's a bad thing? That's how you survive in this business, Reid. Take my word for it."

"You're not that way," she insisted.

"Are you sure about that?" He turned away again. "I'll get with you as soon as I know something."

Kate returned to her unanswered emails but couldn't get the idea out of her head that there was more to the families, particularly, Mrs. Whitman, than what she knew. Walsh had helped her at the beginning of this investigation, and it was his NSA contact who retrieved the vital information that ultimately led them to believe Bishop, who was now going by the name of Eli Parnell, was in Mexico. So maybe it was time to get his input once again.

She picked up her phone. "Levi, do you have a minute? I

wanted to talk about Carol Whitman," she nodded. "Great. No. I'll come to you. Thanks."

Kate noted the time and her promise to Nick that the two would leave early and have dinner together. The week had seen them jetting back and forth and getting little in the way of sleep, so the time together was needed. However, as she was prone to do, getting to the bottom of things, and not letting them go, was her way. It might not have been Surrey's way, but it was how she preferred to do things.

She wrapped her knuckles on the doorframe as she peered inside Walsh's office. "Hey."

"Kate. Come in." He set his attention to her. "You think there's more than meets the eye with Mrs. Whitman, huh? Good. Me too. Let's talk about that."

She sat down and wasted no time. "I want to know everything about the Whitmans and the Bishops. Their circle of friends, any political ambitions, whether related to the hospitals or government. I want to know who they know because, Levi, someone knew what we were up against and knew how to throw us off track."

"I couldn't agree more. And since we're no longer involved in this case, what's the harm in pushing forward?"

"See? This is why we get along so well. We're the same," Kate said.

Walsh revealed a crooked smile. "Maybe so. That said, where do you want to start?"

"We take a look at charitable organizations Mrs. Whitman is a member of. Dr. Whitman too. I'm also thinking medical boards, hospital administrative boards."

"Because the folks on those boards usually hold sway," Walsh replied.

"Exactly. I want to find a connection to someone either on the political side, who could influence law enforcement, or who might be a member of law enforcement…"

"Or possibly someone, a lobbyist maybe, who holds influence over someone in power. And any connection we can find to the intelligence community."

"Yep," Kate nodded. "So how do we go about doing that?"

Walsh eyed her. "I thought you knew?" He laughed. "Just kidding. There are a few places we can check. The hospital boards will have members listed in a public database. Charitable organizations might be a little tougher, but I think if we can pull the Whitman's taxes, we'll be able to find donations, which will give us a place to start."

"We'll need to go to the DOJ to sign off on the request for tax returns. But it's possible to do it without the Whitman's knowledge," Kate replied.

"Agreed. However, Fisher will need to be informed about this. If we go over his head to the DOJ, and considering you're already about to be censured, it's not worth the risk."

"Nor is it worth the risk of pissing him off. I won't go around him like that," she said.

"Good. But you'll need to consider the prospect he'll say no," Walsh added.

"I'll present the case. He won't say no. There's no way this family has been able to do what they've done without outside help."

"I'll be there to back you up, but this has to come from you. Trust me on this. It could change the outcome of your censure hearing if you put together a solid case against the family that allowed their son to commit atrocities."

Kate nodded. "Okay. Thank you, Levi. I'm glad to have you in my corner."

"Always."

25

The restaurant near the bayside condo in Woodbridge that Kate and Nick shared was where they had chosen for a late dinner. The quaint restaurant that oozed French flair was a nice change of pace from the fast food they had eaten over the past several days. Even better was that it had been just the two of them tonight after Kate kept her promise and left Walsh, setting aside their plans until tomorrow. What difference would it make in any case? The FBI international office in Mexico City was organizing the arrest of Theodore Bishop.

Kate was beginning to come to terms with the idea that the case was over, at least from a standpoint of bringing in Theodore Bishop. Fisher was right. They had done their jobs and led the authorities directly to him. It was all standard operating procedure now.

She raised the glass of wine to her lips, feeling guilty to be drinking in front of Nick, but he had insisted it was fine. Kate wondered if there would ever be a point where he could drink again or was it time for her to concede that he was, in fact, an alcoholic, no matter how she spun it. This would be their life now. Kate had never been a heavy drinker and had seen what booze had done to her father before he finally got help. This was familiar territory.

Nick sipped on his sparkling water and sliced off a piece of mouthwatering filet mignon. "I'm glad we're doing this. It's about time." He placed the steak in his mouth.

"Me too. This job doesn't leave a lot of room for us, does it?"

He shook his head and swallowed the bite. "Maybe it's time for us to make room."

Kate held his gaze. "There was something Jonathan Surrey said to me earlier this morning. He said that I didn't know how to leave behind the work and that it would cause me to grow resentful and eventually burnout."

"How long has he been with the Bureau?" Nick asked.

"About as long as you, I believe. Though he's a bit younger, more around my age."

"Burnout?" Nick appeared to consider the idea. "Well, you know that was why I wanted to transfer to BAU Headquarters. Then, of course, I started to feel like I was missing out. It's a strange thing, you know?"

Kate nodded. "I'm sure it must be. I just don't think I know how to be any other way. This work is my life. It's our life."

"Where will that leave us, then, when we're too old to do this job anymore? What will happen to us? Will we have anything in common?"

She was taken aback by the question. He'd never expressed concern in this way for their future. It was always just assumed they would be together. Maybe this was something she needed to hear. "I think it's getting past the time to consider a family, Nick. It's unlikely, given my history, that I would ever conceive anyway, but we aren't getting any younger either. And with this job?"

"I understand that. I wasn't speaking solely to the idea of a family. I'm talking about us."

Kate's phone buzzed and so did Nick's. They peered at each other before swiping open the screen.

She read the text message. "Oh no."

Nick shot a look at her. "He's gone."

THEY RETURNED to the office where the others had already gathered. It was after 11pm in Washington, and Mexico City was on Central Standard Time.

"As you know, Bishop wasn't at the apartment his mother had informed us about. The agents had their team in place alongside the Mexican authorities and when they approached the door, there was no answer," Fisher began. "Subsequently, they forced their way inside only to find his clothes gone. They also found this." He tossed a photo onto the conference table. "He kept a scrapbook of the disaster sites he not only visited, but all natural disasters that have taken place worldwide over the past ten years."

"What the hell is with this guy's obsession with disasters?" Walsh asked.

"It's where he feels he has the most power," Kate began. "Little oversight because of the chaotic nature of the scenes. Desperate people all looking to him for aid. What more could an angel of death ask for?"

"How long do they think he's been gone?" Duncan asked. "Any idea when he left? Surveillance video, anything like that?"

"If any exists, it's in the hands of the Mexican authorities," Fisher added. "That's something the office down there will have to deal with."

"Why are we here, then?" Nick asked. "If those guys are tasked with finding him, where do we fit in?"

"That's a good question. Here's what I'd like to do. Reid, get on the horn with Carol Whitman. There's a damn good chance she alerted her son out of guilt. If so, she might know where he fled to. Scarborough, you and I are going to Mexico City to assist the office there."

"When are we leaving?"

"As soon as we're done here," Fisher replied.

Walsh looked around the team with noted concern. "And the rest of us?"

"Wait!" Kate peered at her phone. "I know where he is."

"What? How?" Fisher asked.

She walked over to him with the phone open to a news article. "Look at this. The day before yesterday, a magnitude 6.7 earthquake struck Guadalajara." Kate looked at him. "He's there. I know he is. He wouldn't be able to resist the urge, even if his mother told him he was about to be captured, or in spite of that fact."

Fisher eyed the rest of the team. "Well? Given what we know about Bishop, do we agree he's likely to be there?"

Nick raised his hand. Walsh raised his and finally, Duncan raised hers.

"We should go there as a team," Kate said. "We know more about Bishop than any of those guys down there. I'm sorry, but it's true."

"Damn it." Fisher sighed. "I'll need to clear it with the Mexico City office, but I have to agree with you on this one. We can't afford to let him slip through our fingers this time. He won't give us a third opportunity."

$\sim$

THE CHARTERED FLIGHT arrived in Mexico City at midnight, local time. The team was greeted by a handful of Mexican National Guardsmen, a civilian police force created in 2019. Dressed in military gear, their presence was intimidating.

"I thought our people were coming?" Nick asked Fisher as they stepped onto the runway beneath a pitch-black sky.

"I was informed that the secretary of Security and Civilian Protection wanted to keep his people in the loop. They insisted their people escort us."

"And what about the Mexico City office?" Kate asked him.

"They'll take us there." Fisher turned to Walsh. "You might need to take point with these guys."

"You got it, Boss." Walsh headed the pack and met who appeared to be the officer in charge as they stood in front of the military-style vehicles and carried assault rifles across their chests. He held out his badge with one hand and raised the other as a precaution. "Hola, señor. Mi nombre es Walsh. FBI."

"I speak English, Agent Walsh, but I appreciate the gesture." He offered his hand. "I'm Alejandro Perez, Unit Coordinator. I've been instructed to escort your team to your FBI office in the city. If you and your people will step inside the car, we'll get started."

"Absolutely. Thank you." Walsh turned back as the others were fixed in place still several feet behind. "They're our escorts. It's time to move."

"You heard him, let's go." Fisher gestured for the team to move ahead toward the black Ford SUV. He stepped into the passenger seat of the large, bullet-proof vehicle.

The driver kept his eyes ahead while the rest of the team stepped into the car. It was Perez who walked over to the driver and leaned in the open window. He spoke in Spanish. "Take them to the FBI office. They're expected. I'll have Lopez driving the lead car and Castillo in the rear. Stick to the main roads and do not veer off course." He pulled upright and tapped the edge of the door twice. "Move out."

On their arrival into the large city, the U.S. Embassy that housed the Bureau's international office appeared in the distance.

The motorcade pulled alongside the front of the building. The passenger door of the car in front of the team opened and Perez stepped out, shifting his gaze as if there was a threat of an attack.

The driver of the SUV came to a complete stop and stepped out, making his way toward Perez. Words were exchanged unknown to the team, then Perez made his approach.

He opened the passenger door and looked at Fisher. "It's time to get your team inside, sir."

Fisher stepped out and turned to the rear. "I think they want us inside as quickly as possible."

Without delay, the rest of the team emerged and followed Perez through the double-doored entrance of the embassy. The 6-story building was surrounded by larger high-rises and was heavily secured.

Kate wondered why they were being rushed inside as though a mob might attack them. "What's going on?" she asked Nick.

"There have been several demonstrations around here lately, so I guess they want to take every precaution."

"It's the middle of the night," Kate replied.

"Since when would the time of day stop anyone from doing something stupid?" he added.

"Point taken."

Inside the embassy, a raised front desk stretched across several feet. Behind that desk were guards.

When a man approached with a smile, Kate assumed he was their contact.

Fisher spotted him and extended his hand. "Senior Unit Agent Cameron Fisher."

The man accepted his hand. "SSA Ruiz. Pleased to meet you. I understand you let a killer loose in our city." He turned away. "Follow me. There are a few people who would like to get a grasp on the situation we have here."

"Of course." Fisher pursed his lips and looked back at the team. He followed Ruiz down the hall toward the right rear side of the building.

"In here, if you'd be so kind." Ruiz opened the door to a large room lined with rectangular tables and computers. "My team is just ahead."

Fisher led the way again while the others followed.

Kate felt as though they were about to be scolded for letting Bishop slip through their fingers. Maybe they were, but these guys didn't get their shit together fast enough in her opinion. If Fisher had just let them offer help sooner, they might not be in this situation.

"Here they are, folks. Our friends from BAU Quantico." Ruiz gestured to the team as though they had been a consolation prize. "Senior Unit Agent Cameron Fisher is going to get everyone up to speed on things and see if we can't pinpoint where our man has gone to. Agent Fisher?"

"Thank you. I know it's very late and I'm sure most of you have been here since probably 6am this morning. The man we're looking for, Theodore Bishop, whose passport shows his name is Eli Parnell, has once again slipped from our crosshairs. We had the address his mother insisted was accurate. As you already know, he wasn't there. However, we have a very good sense, based on our profile of Bishop, of where he is now."

"Where might that be, sir?" An agent asked.

"We think he's headed to, or likely already arrived, at the epicenter of Guadalajara's earthquake that occurred roughly 48 hours ago."

"Why the hell would he be there?" Another agent with serious eyes and arms folded aimed his question at Fisher.

"I sent the profile to SSA Ruiz when we discovered Bishop made his way to Mexico. Since then, we've had some recent developments take place. We are very certain Bishop will be there because he feels he must be," Fisher replied.

"He must be?" Ruiz asked.

"Yes, sir." Fisher turned to Kate. "You want to field this one?"

"Sure. I'm Kate Reid, I put together the profile you all have. Now, I understand your team discovered a binder filled with pictures and news articles relating to several natural disasters over the past decade."

"That's right," another agent replied. "What's that got to do with anything?"

"There isn't much time to make my point clear, so I'll just say that the victims we know of were found to have been rescued from different disaster sites. Hurricane Edward, in Texas, the wildfire in Riverside, California, and most recently, the hurricane that hit the Bahamas."

Ruiz nodded. "That's why you believe he went to the site of the earthquake. Makes sense." He set his sights on Fisher. "Sounds like that's where we need to be. Let's go hash out the logistics in my office."

Fisher followed Ruiz. "With all due respect, I'm not sure it's a good idea to have your team alongside mine."

Ruiz sat down. "You know what, Fisher? It really bugs the shit out of me when people say that. 'With all due respect.' If you were being respectful, you wouldn't be standing here in my office, in my city, telling me my people aren't needed on your little operation." He leaned back in his chair. "You come here all the way from Quantico for a guy you let loose, what twice now?"

Fisher widened his stance and peered at Ruiz. "In all fairness, we gave you his address. I suppose we could've drawn you a map..."

Ruiz held up his hands. "Okay look, maybe we're getting off on the wrong foot here. Pissing on each other isn't going to help us capture this asshole."

"Agreed," Fisher replied. "And the longer we sit here, the better the odds he'll take off again. If he does, he'll be lost to us forever."

"That might be a bit of an exaggeration," Ruiz replied.

"I don't think so. There's still a chance Bishop's mother alerted him after she told us where he was. Guilt or whatever you want to call it. If she did, there are no guarantees he's even in Guadalajara. He might be in Guatemala for all we know."

"Then why come down here if you and your team aren't even sure where this dude is?"

Fisher gripped the back of the chair across from Ruiz's desk. "All I can tell you is that Agent Reid is right about Bishop. He's at the site of the earthquake. The draw for him is too much to resist. So, what I would propose is that you let us go there, maybe take one of your guys..."

"Oh, don't think the Guard won't want one of their own with you too. That, my friend, will be non-negotiable."

"Okay. A member of the National Guard, one of your team, whoever you want to send, and my people. We will find him. I promise you that."

Ruiz seemed to consider the proposal. "Well, I reckon if you'd rather put your team at risk than mine, no skin off my nose, right?"

"No, sir," Fisher replied.

Ruiz inhaled a deep breath. "I'll help you arrange it with the Mexicans, but you'll want to move fast, so I'll have my guy arrange for a car and communications. I'll expect you and your people to keep us informed. The secretary will also want briefings. You're talking a site where we have Red Cross and whoever else volunteering. And now you say there's a killer looking to finish off victims?" He shook his head. "That will be a top concern for the officials."

"Then we agree?" Fisher asked.

"We do, so let's roll."

26

Dawn had broken through the clouds and the sky was a watercolor painting in hues of orange and purple. The city was waking up and the team was about to begin their hunt for a killer.

SSA Ruiz had arranged for one of the Mexican Guardsmen, the man who had escorted the team from the airport, to assist in the effort. Alejandro Perez now waited in the room that had been dubbed the Ops Room inside the American Embassy.

Fisher and his team prepared to depart on the flight organized by Ruiz. Several charter jets were at the embassy's disposal and it would take an otherwise 6-hour drive and turn it into an hour's flight. Given the time constraints, it was the best plan.

"It's time," Fisher began. "We have communications set up. Perez and Brewer will be accompanying us. We need to get him, and we need to get him now." Fisher started out of the room and toward Ruiz's office. "We're ready."

Ruiz joined him. "I'll take you to the airstrip." He snatched his keys and waited for the others to meet up in the lobby. "You're riding with me, folks. Time's wasting." When everyone arrived at the meeting point, he started outside. "I would suggest you try to close your eyes for the duration of the flight. I know you all have been up the entire night. I'm sure your teammates would feel better knowing you weren't making life and death decisions going on no sleep."

Ruiz jumped in his SUV and fired up the engine. When the rest piled inside, he pulled away from the curb. "Aside from Agent Brewer, the rest of you should know that Guadalajara is a lot like Mexico City. You got your really rich folks and your really poor folks. The earthquake's epicenter was in El Centro. That, my friends, is where a lot of the poor folks live. And what I mean by that is, the surrounding structures will probably be in rough condition. The damage there, I haven't seen it myself, but I did get word from the Red Cross that it is substantial because the existing infrastructure was in bad shape to begin with. All's I'm saying is watch your back. You start tracking down your boy and find yourself in some abandoned building, you best count your blessings it don't collapse on you."

"What are the hospitals in the area like?" Kate asked. "Bishop is smart enough to get a name badge and a doctor's coat and make his rounds. If security is lax, we should be aware of that."

"Security?" Ruiz glanced at her through the rearview mirror. "You come across any security, you let me know."

Perez was in the far back row. "I'd like to say something, here, Agent Ruiz. The people in that neighborhood, they are good people. They don't have much, but that doesn't mean they aren't human."

"My apologies, Perez. I meant no disrespect. I'm just trying to give these people a sense for what awaits them. Hey, Mexico City is my home. It's a good, safe place to live." He turned right. "We're here."

The door flew open and Walsh jumped out. He waited until everyone stepped out and closed the door. "Where to now?" He asked Perez.

"Through this building and to the back. We'll board immediately." Perez looked to Ruiz. "I'll take care of them from here, sir."

Nick took Kate by the arm and fell behind the others. "I know how much you want Bishop, but it would be best that if he's spotted, you don't approach him. We don't know if he's armed. We don't know anything."

"Are you going to mention that to the rest of the team?" she asked.

"What do you mean?"

"I mean, I don't want you to single me out, Nick. I know how to approach a suspect. I risked my life in Rio with Quinn. I've risked my life plenty of times. We all have. I know you mean well, but I need you to give me some breathing room here."

"You're right. I just keep replaying the events in Rio. For God's sake, here we are again in another country."

The small 15-seater jet sat alone on the runway with a set of stairs pushed against the door. Perez was the first to board and summoned the captain's attention while the others walked onto the plane. Moments later, the engines started, and the staircase was pulled away from the aircraft. Perez returned to the front of the cabin. "We've received clearance. Prepare for takeoff."

THE FLIGHT WAS short and allowed for a few members of the team to get in a power nap, but Kate couldn't shut down her thoughts of Theo Bishop and the people with money and power who had protected him.

Perez had arranged for another member of the Guard to pick

them up from the airport in Guadalajara and drive them to the community of El Centro. The team was divided into two vehicles and as they neared the site of the earthquake's epicenter, the more severe the damage had been. The community clearly struggled but now appeared to be utterly devastated. It hadn't made major news in the US because it hadn't affected enough people. The collateral damage wasn't nearly enough to make the headlines.

But Kate knew that Bishop would be there. He had nowhere else to go that could feed his desire to be seen as a hero and a god. It would have taken him time to produce the type of documents he would've needed in order to get a job as a paramedic or EMT, or whatever the equivalent was in Mexico. Not only that, but it seemed highly likely Carol Whitman, Theo's mother, would've warned him they were coming.

She looked on with the others at the devastation. Rubble in the streets. Piles of broken concrete, bricks, wood framing scattered around. People in tears wandering aimlessly, presumably in search of their missing loved ones. First responders wearing masks and carrying shovels as they hand-dug specific locations such as the busy market they had just approached.

"Oh my God." Duncan placed her fingertips over her lips. "I didn't think it would be this bad. It looks like a war zone."

"It's not as bad as other quakes we've had in the region," Perez began. "It's just that the infrastructure here is incredibly poor."

"Where are we planning to stop?" Nick asked.

"A first-aid unit has been deployed about half a kilometer from here," Perez continued. "That's where we'll organize our resources and track down your killer."

The driver continued on with caution through the broken streets, maneuvering his way around victims, rescuers and the rest of the fallen community. A white tent with a red cross appeared ahead.

"This is it," Fisher said. "This is where we'll find Theodore Bishop." He looked at Perez. "We should stop here. Any closer and we'll have too many eyes on us. We don't exactly look like rescue workers. I don't want to tip him off if he's in close proximity."

"I agree." Perez turned to the driver. "Détente aquí." (*Pull over here.*)

He rolled to a stop and the second car followed his lead. The doors opened and the team, along with Perez and another member of the Guard stepped out into the bright sunlight as late morning had arrived.

Dust had settled except where digging had commenced. The tent was several feet away with doctors, nurses, and other aides flowing in and out.

"Are they still bringing in people?" Kate asked.

"I couldn't say, Agent Reid." Perez started ahead. "Please, this way." He led the team to a nearby alleyway where the buildings on either side revealed severe cracks, broken windows, but otherwise still had four walls standing. Perez pulled out a map and laid it on top of crates he had picked up and stacked for use as a table. "Officer Gutierrez will guide us through the map. He is native to this area and has assisted the cleanup crews. His knowledge will guide you in your efforts to divide and conquer, as you say."

Gutierrez pointed on the map and began to speak Spanish. Perez listened and translated. "He says the worst damage is across these streets here and here. The workers are digging out this area here where the marketplace was heavily occupied at the time of the quake. This means there could be substantial victims that have yet to be discovered."

Fisher nodded and glanced at Nick. "If Bishop is looking to take advantage of an injured victim, I'd say there is the most likely place."

"I'm not sure he would risk going inside the tent," Nick

replied. "It seemed heavily populated with volunteers. It's probably too risky."

"Then we split up and surround that area there?" Walsh asked. "Seems the most logical place to start."

"It is in my opinion," Fisher said. "There's one thing we don't know about Bishop and that is whether he's armed."

"We have no reason to believe he would be," Kate began. "Though I imagine we can't ignore the possibility."

"It is extremely difficult to obtain a weapon here—legally," Perez began. "Most certainly, he would not have been allowed to cross into the country with a firearm. And carrying a gun in public is a crime."

"What are the odds he's made friends with people who could provide him with a weapon?" Duncan asked.

"Hard to say. We should stay vigilant, as always, in the event we have him in our sights," Walsh replied. "If he gets spooked, who knows what sort of behavior he'll exhibit in the face of capture."

"Walsh, you and Reid will take this block." Fisher pointed to a street on the map. "Perez, can I ask you to assist Agent Duncan and search this block here? Scarborough and I will take Gutierrez and hit these two blocks here. Walsh speaks enough Spanish to get by if a civilian approaches but having you and Gutierrez will give the rest of us a way to communicate if necessary. We have radio communications ready to go, so use them. I want to know where everyone is at all times. You get eyes on Bishop, you call it in. Is that clear?"

"Crystal," Walsh replied.

"Yes, sir," Kate answered.

"Then it's time to move." Fisher checked his weapon and turned to Perez. "Bishop is still an American citizen. We will do our best to take him in peacefully, but if he resists, I am authorizing deadly force. Will that be a problem for you?"

"Not even a little bit."

The team headed in the direction of their respective quadrants. Kate caught up to Walsh who had a small lead on her. "If it was up to me, I think we should head toward the location where they're still searching for victims."

"It's outside our designated parameters," Walsh replied. "Then again, no one's watching. Lead the way, my friend."

Perez approached Agent Duncan. "Ma'am?"

"Ready when you are," she replied.

"Then please, follow me." He led the way to the east where they were to begin their search. "I admire you and your people."

"Thank you, but why is that?"

"Coming here to find your killer. Taking responsibility for your citizens and helping to protect mine from this madman," he replied. "If only our government cared as much for our citizens and protecting them against the cartels." They reached the block. "This is it. I'll monitor this side. You take the right. Check the windows above, check the fire escapes. Any place you think he might take refuge." He peered at her for a moment. "I apologize. It isn't my place to issue orders."

"No need for that. But just so you know, I do know what I'm doing."

"THERE's a lot of activity here. It's too easy for Bishop to hide among these people," Nick said. "If he makes an appearance, things could get messy."

"We'll have to take it as it comes, Scarborough. I just hope Reid's on the right track. If not..."

"She's not wrong."

Gutierrez said something in Spanish and pointed ahead.

"I think he wants us to go this way," Fisher added.

"Why don't I take this street ahead and you and he can take this one," Nick replied.

"You aren't going alone. Not a chance in hell. That wasn't part of the plan," Fisher replied.

"Being here wasn't part of the plan either. Look, we don't have time to stroll around this neighborhood while Bishop could be out there finding his next victim. I can handle myself. You know that, and you know I'm right. I've got the radio if I need help." He started in the opposite direction.

Fisher shook his head but didn't object to the last-minute change in plans. He continued to trail the guard and surveyed the rest of the area.

HALF A DOZEN AID workers were huddled atop a mound of debris, shouting in Spanish and pointing below their feet.

"Levi, look over there." Kate glanced at the scene ahead. "They're looking for people. This is where we want to be."

"Let's widen our perimeter and check out the surrounding areas. I see a few ambulance trucks, a first aid station...." He continued to assess the area. "National Guard stationed right over there." He looked over his shoulder at Kate. "Bishop would be crazy to get this close."

"We aren't dealing with a sane man. He thinks he's untouchable. We're about to prove him wrong." Kate started ahead, giving a wide berth around the rescue area. She needed to be right on this one. Money, resources, and international favors had all been granted. If it turned out she missed the mark, there would be consequences and probably consequences much greater than a Letter of Censure.

⌁

"Perdóneme." (*Excuse me.*) Bishop tapped a man on the shoulder.

The rescue worker spun around and eyed him. "Agarra una pala," (*Grab a shovel*). He wore a beige jumpsuit with a safety vest, a hard hat, and a mask.

Bishop had arrived late yesterday evening and gathered the gear he would need along with a badge he stole from a nearby worker. After spending the night on a park bench a few miles away, he made the trek on foot early this morning and was ready to get to work. Except the work he was looking for didn't involve the use of a shovel. An ambulance had been left unattended long enough for him to slip inside and take whatever they had that would do the job. Although, he wasn't overly concerned about disguising the end result. No one would bother going through the effort of performing an autopsy on victims around here. It would prove difficult enough to ID the bodies. Given the state of the surrounding area, most people had been crushed beyond recognition.

"Red Cross." Bishop held up his badge to show the man. "Medicine."

"Por ahí." (*Over there*). The worker pointed to the nearby medical station.

"Gracias." Bishop had no intention of being seen with other doctors or medical aid workers. He needed to find where the bodies were. But if they were buried, what chance would there be to find anyone alive?

Bishop combed the area, moving away from the huddle of

workers who focused on one main area. Farther up the street, more buildings appeared in tatters with concrete fragments resting in the middle of the road. He walked inside what appeared to have been a TV repair shop. Merchandise lay on the floor, shattered. Shelves collapsed. He scoured the area but found no one inside.

Back out into the rising sun and heat. The smell of dust and death permeated the region. He returned his mask to his face and continued to traverse the devastated area, away from the people, away from anyone who might wonder what he was doing. The bag he carried over his shoulder looked like a medical bag and if anyone had questioned him, he had a prop to aid in his cover story.

Another building that remained standing, though just barely, appeared ahead. A cell phone store. Bishop walked inside. "Hello? Uh, Doctor en Medicina?" He walked inside and listened.

"Ayuda."

Bishop leaned in as he'd heard something faint. "Medicina?"

"Ayuda."

The voice cried again, and Bishop started in the direction of the sound. He stepped over displays and crushed iPhones under his feet until he made his way to the rear of the building. Bishop squatted and peered below what looked like a cashier desk.

A young woman, possibly still in her teens, peered at him. Her eyes were swollen from tears and the salty trails they left cut through the grime that had landed on her skin when the dust settled. Her left arm had been impaled by a piece of rebar protruding from the foundation. She was stuck and blood pooled around her. "Ayuda," she cried.

Bishop stroked her long black hair. "It's okay. I'm here. You're safe now."

27

Radio contact between the team had, so far, indicated a giant goose egg. No one had seen Bishop or had spoken to anyone who had seen him. Bishop was either not there and had never been there, or he was making one hell of a good ghost, slipping in and around people unseen.

The grim reality had set in. Kate's neck was on the line and she had yet to find the murderer. "We've been at this for an hour. What if I was wrong?" Her eyes pleaded.

"Give it time," Walsh replied. "Did you think he would just turn up with his hands in the air for us? This isn't over yet."

"What are we missing? Where else could he have gone?" She gazed around the street they had already searched twice. "The team has been inside every building. Spoken to everyone they've come across and shown them Bishop's picture."

"I'm not ready to throw in the towel just yet," Walsh began. "Let's keep going and trust in the process. We'll reassess with the team in an hour."

"If you say so."

NICK WAS ON HIS OWN. There had been no sign of Bishop and he'd scoured his designated area twice. The entire team had done the same and still no sign of the killer. Concern that Kate had been wrong was paramount in his mind. The extent of an operation like this could spell the end of her career if they struck out again. Although he was pretty sure Fisher would defend her until the end. It wouldn't matter, though, because she would fall on the sword, regardless.

He maintained certainty that she was not wrong; that Bishop was here; it was simply a matter of finding him. He would be somewhere away from others and that was where Nick needed to look. He pressed the button on his radio. "Still no luck here. I'm expanding my search."

"Scarborough, where are you going?" Fisher asked.

"I'll head north and take the next few blocks ahead of Walsh and Reid." Nick turned back and walked along the main thorough-fare that had grown busier with rescue workers and medical aid stations. The rainy season was over, and the temperature soared into the high 80s. Now the air was dry and dust from the transfer of people and vehicles kicked up into the air.

He pushed through the growing chaos as National Guard Humvees arrived in greater numbers. Concern that if one of them encountered Bishop, the surrounding Guardsmen might not know what was happening, drew to the front of Nick's mind. It could make a bad situation even worse.

Nick pressed again on the radio button. "Walsh, Reid, you copy?"

"Copy, Scarborough. Walsh here. You near us yet?"

"Approaching roughly 300 yards behind the start of your quadrant. There are a lot more Guardsmen here now."

"Roger that."

"Duncan here. Gutierrez left to find whoever's in charge and get them up to speed so we don't run into any problems."

"You're on your own?" Fisher interrupted.

"He's in my sights. Just waiting on him to return," she replied.

"Copy," Fisher said.

Nick pressed on. His intention wasn't to join Kate and Walsh's efforts, but to move the search ahead and enter into a new area where he might still find Bishop. He held the radio up again. "I'm walking past Walsh and Reid now."

The market where the bulk of the damage had occurred was behind him. He moved ahead into a less populated area where there was still damage but no obvious collapse of any of the structures.

Nick walked into the TV repair shop and called out, "Anyone here? Hola?" No reply. He moved through the building but saw no evidence anyone had been inside when the quake struck. "Damn it." He walked out again and carried on north until he reached a café. "Hola?"

Tables were overturned, pictures were on the ground, their glass frames shattered, but there appeared to be no sign of anyone inside.

"Hola?" He tried again. Still there was no answer. Nick walked out and picked up the radio. "I'm checking north of the marketplace. Still no sign."

Ahead was another small building, which looked like a cell phone store. Nick walked inside. "Hola?" He moved in and noticed slightly more damage, but no one answered. "Hola? Policia." Nick spotted blood near what looked like a register desk. He carefully stepped toward it. "Anyone here?" He peered around the desk before leaning over the top and that was when he spotted her. "Oh my God." He pressed on the button. "I need help in here.

There's a woman. She's injured." He hurried around the desk and squatted below. "Miss? Miss?" He placed his fingers on her wrist and felt a faint pulse. "She's still alive."

"Scarborough, where are you?" Fisher yelled through the radio.

Nick looked around for the name of the business. "It's a cell phone store. Just n..." He cringed and dropped the radio to reach for the back of his neck. With his hand clamped down, he turned to see a man running through a rear exit. Nick immediately felt light-headed. His vision blurred as he tried to reach for the radio again.

"Scarborough?" Fisher asked.

"Reid and I are headed north to the cell phone store. Someone get help now!" Walsh was out of breath and sounded like he was running.

Hurried steps and quick breaths sounded when Fisher got on the line again. "Perez is getting help. Everyone needs to get to Scarborough's location."

KATE RAN THROUGH THE STREETS, nearly stumbling twice on the rubble. "Oh, God. Oh, God. Please." She huffed and coughed and pumped her legs as fast as she could.

"Reid! Hang on." Walsh did his best to catch up, but he was slower and heavier than Kate. "Be careful! Jesus!"

"I'm coming. I'm coming, Nick. Hang on." Kate pushed harder and faster. "I see the building!" She glanced over her shoulder at Walsh. "It's just ahead. Hurry!" Kate slowed and glanced up. "This is the place." She rushed inside. "Nick? Nick, where are you?" Her eyes scanned the damage. "Where are you?" Her heart raced and her eyes reddened.

"Nick!" With no response, she searched for him, lifting every-thing in her path and calling out for him. It wasn't until she saw the blood, that her own blood turned cold.

Walsh slowed as he made his way inside. "Kate." His weapon was drawn, and he made his way toward her on the right of the building. "Scarborough?"

"Levi, over here." She looked down at the blood and walked around the desk where she finally spotted him. "He's here! Nick? Nick are you okay?"

He was slumped against the side of the desk while the young woman, rebar still protruding from her arm lay next to him.

"Oh God. Come on, baby." Kate tapped on his cheek. "Nick? Wake up. Come on now. Wake up." She tapped his cheek again when she spotted his eyes flutter.

Levi hurried around the desk. "Buddy, are you okay?" He noticed the girl. "Jesus. Where's the help? We need some goddam help in here!" He screamed.

Fisher and Perez pulled up in one of the guard's Humvees and rushed inside.

"Reid? Walsh? Where are you?" Fisher scanned the store.

"Over here." Walsh appeared from behind the desk. "He's over here. He's alive and there's a girl here too. Where's the medic?"

"Right behind us." Perez leaned out of the doorway. "Aqui. Aqui." (*In here.*) "La prisa!" (*Hurry*).

Two medics rushed inside.

Walsh pointed down behind the desk. "Here. Come quick." He looked at Kate who held Nick in her arms. "Come on, Kate. Let them help." He tried to help her up, but she wasn't budging. "Kate, let them do their jobs. You have to move."

She carefully pulled out her arm from under Nick's head and

took Walsh's hand. "Okay. It was him. Bishop. He was here and he did this. I know he did."

Walsh nodded. "Let's worry about Nick and this girl here first, okay."

"No. He'll get away. Levi, we have to find him. If we don't go now, he'll vanish. I won't let that happen."

Walsh turned to Fisher with pleading eyes.

Fisher nodded. "Go. Find the son of a bitch."

"I'll go with them," Perez said.

"I need you here. Please. I need someone to translate." Fisher picked up the radio. "Duncan, what's your location?"

"We're passing the marketplace now. Did you find him?"

"We did. He's hurt. Just get here as fast as you can." Fisher turned back to Walsh, but he and Kate were already out the door.

KATE ANGRILY WIPED away her tears as she hurried north. "He has to be going this direction. If he turned back, he'd run into too many people. He's going this way."

"Kate, just take it easy, okay? I know you're pissed. So am I, but we need to have cool heads. We need to be smart and understand Bishop's endgame."

"His endgame is to kill as many people as he can before we catch him. *That's* his endgame. Now he knows we're here and that we're coming for him."

"Then let's try to think logically about this. Where would he go? Much farther and we'll be out of the worst of the quake zone. He won't find anyone who needs help."

Kate began to think of Agent Surrey and how he approached situations. Walsh was right in that she needed to think clearly. Bishop was running out of options. He could opt for self-preservation and hitch a ride and they would never find him again. Or, he would do as she believed, and try to prove he was smarter than they were. He always believed he was smarter than everyone else because he was allowed to get away with anything, including murder.

She considered Surrey. He would be methodical and study every angle. There wasn't time for that approach, but maybe she could use his process to a degree. "Patterns." Just as she so often found, there were patterns to every killer's operation.

"What do you mean?" Walsh asked.

"The one thing I always try to find is patterns. Surrey did the same thing in Denver, but he was better; more precise."

"What are you saying, Kate? What do you want to do here?"

"Bishop has had help since the beginning."

"We know that," Walsh replied.

"Right, but what if he was on his own? Like he is right now. His mommy won't be able to get him out of this one. He's looked to her to bail him out of every problem he's had. What will he do without her help?"

"Run for the hills? I mean, I'm not sure where you're going with this and we're running out of time."

"I know. I just—I'm just trying to figure this out in my head," Kate replied. "Bishop doesn't know anything else besides acting on his impulses. And I think his impulses are telling him he might as well do what he can because there's no turning back. His pattern of behavior suggests finding victims who are hurt or dying and need his help."

"Gotcha so far. Go on," Walsh replied.

Her eyes sparked with an idea. "The homeless. I saw several encampments on our way here. That's where he'll go. It's the only place left where he'll find desperate and defenseless people. Those are the ones he thrives on. That is his pattern of behavior."

Walsh smiled and picked up his radio. "Fisher, tell me Scarborough's been taken to a hospital?"

"He's on his way now. He was alert enough to tell us where Bishop injected him. We don't know what he was given, but they have managed to stabilize him and on arrival, they'll run tests for every substance they can."

"Tell them to look for something Bishop could've stolen from one of the medical stations," Kate said to Walsh.

"Hey, have them check what the med stations have. Reid is certain Bishop would've lifted something from there."

"Got it. What's the plan? Where are you two?"

"We need a car. We feel confident Bishop will take refuge inside a homeless encampment. He'll have plenty of victims to choose from and no one will give a damn."

"I'd say she's on the money. We'll head your way," Fisher replied.

Walsh looked around. "We're standing in front of a small grocer's market."

"Be there as fast as we can."

PEREZ WAS behind the wheel of the SUV as he traversed the streets, careful to avoid raising alarms. The National Guard didn't take well to cars speeding around areas where people still searched for their loved ones.

Fisher was in the front passenger seat and turned back to Kate. "There's still time. We won't let him leave this city, Reid. I'll be damned if I let that happen."

"Who's with Nick right now?" she asked.

Perez peered through the rearview window. "I trust Gutierrez with my life. He will ensure your agent's safety. And he is in the care of one of the best doctors in the country."

"Are you sure you don't want to be there with him?" Duncan placed her hand on Kate's shoulder.

"No. I can't. I have to be here to help find him. I know Bishop. I know this is where he'll be."

"You seem to have been right the first time, Agent Reid," Perez began. "I will not doubt your word this time."

Perez pointed to the right. "This one here. This is the largest encampment near the epicenter. Close enough that Bishop could have fled on foot but far enough that no rescue workers would need to venture this way."

"Reid, you and Walsh take this one here." Fisher looked at Perez. "I think it's best if we split up to cover more ground. Is there another area close by?"

"Yes, two kilometers ahead. It's possible he might've chosen to move deeper into the city since he knows you're looking for him."

"We're on it." Kate jumped out of the back seat and Walsh followed.

Fisher leaned through his window. "Hey, keep close radio contact and do not, under any circumstances, leave each other's side. I'll be damned if we let him get the drop on one of us again."

"Roger that." Walsh turned to Kate. "Let's go."

Perez pulled away with Duncan and Fisher while Kate started ahead. "I'm not feeling as confident as I was earlier that we'll find him here."

"You gotta keep the faith, Reid. If you don't, then he wins for sure. We have to try."

She nodded. "Where should we start?" Kate peered ahead at the rows of makeshift tents. Poles with blankets thrown over them for cover. Blue tarps over pallets and crates. "My God. There could be a thousand people in here."

Walsh placed his hands on his hips. "At least. We have no choice but to get moving." He stepped ahead and turned back. "Kate, we'll find him."

She followed close behind and traversed through the tent city. A man clawed at her leg and she drew her gun in surprise.

The man's eyes widened as he held up his hands. "No dispares! No dispares!" (*Don't shoot. Don't shoot.*)

Kate exhaled a breath and holstered her weapon.

Walsh quickly turned back to her. "Jesus. Are you okay?"

"I'm fine. I almost blew that guy's head off, but other than that, I'm fine."

"I need you to keep a clear head. If we cause a panic in here, and Bishop just happens to be hiding out, we'll lose him. Not to mention we might get caught in the middle of something we don't want to be in. It's just us out here."

Kate nodded. "I'm sorry."

"I know you're worried about Scarborough, but I need you here 100 percent. Got it?"

"I got it." She pressed on. "It's a needle in a haystack." Walsh didn't respond and only pushed forward leaving Kate with no choice but to see this through. It was her idea and she'd put everyone's life on the line insisting they would find Bishop in one of these places.

She had to think. Where would he go in a vast tent city like this? Where could he get away with hiding? She doubted he spoke the language, making it even tougher for him to find shelter. "He won't be in one of the tents. No one will trust him. He has nothing to offer these people."

Walsh turned back. "What do you suggest?"

"Look for a natural shelter. Trees, dense shrubbery. Someplace where he could be alone until dark. That's when I think he'll find his next victim, but not in the light of day. Not when he knows we're looking for him."

"It's midday now. That gives us a lot of time to find him." Walsh pressed on the radio. "Fisher, what's your 20?"

"We've reached the next encampment and are beginning the search."

"Reid thinks he'll find a place to hide among the trees and greenery until after dark. Then he'll hunt for his next victim." Walsh listened as Fisher spoke to Duncan and Perez.

"Copy that. That's where we'll start. Fisher out."

Kate looked toward the east. "Hey, over there. That looks to be a fairly dense area."

"And several folks are using it for shade too. Let's check it out." Walsh started ahead.

They reached the edge of the tree-lined area where the homeless used the trees to string shelter between them. Kate moved in, stepping carefully between the shelters, peering down for any sign Bishop was there. She stopped dead in her tracks. "Oh shit. Do you see that?"

Walsh looked ahead roughly 10 feet from where they stood. "Is that a medical bag?" He started forward with hurried, but cautious steps.

They reached the spot, and both drew their guns. Kate scanned the area to the left. Walsh looked to his right.

"I don't see him. I don't see him." Kate's pulse quickened. "He's here, goddamn it. Bishop! FBI!" she yelled.

"Kate, don't." Walsh grabbed her arm.

"He's here, Levi." She continued ahead. "Bishop! It's over. Show yourself!"

A young woman emerged from beneath a blue tarp strung between two trees. The black medical bag lay feet from her. "Ido. El hombre se fue."

"What?" Kate squatted down. "Habla inglés?"

The woman shook her head. She couldn't have been older than her early 20s.

"Don't be afraid." Kate searched for a word she might understand. "FBI." She picked up the bag. "Man?"

"Si. Uh, man." The woman made a gesture with two fingers as if to indicate the man had run away. "Escapar."

"Escape?" Kate asked.

"The woman nodded."

The radios they held buzzed to life. "Here! He's here! In pursuit." Fisher huffed as though he was running.

Walsh jumped up and held the radio. "Copy." He turned to Kate. "Grab the bag and let's go. They're in pursuit. We need to move."

Kate pushed up and both ran through the rest of the encampment until reaching an open area.

"What now? We can't get there. It's a mile away." Her breath was labored as she pushed her hand through her hair and shot her gaze back and forth. "Levi. What the hell can we do?"

He shook his head. "Nothing. They got this, Kate. They'll catch him." Walsh placed his hands on his face and rubbed hard. "Damn it. Damn it!" With the radio in his hand, he waited for an update. "Come on, man, give me something here."

Kate looked at the radio and then to Walsh. "What the hell is happening, Levi?"

"Just hold tight. There's nothing we can do for them right now. It's on them."

Kate paced a small area of the sidewalk where they stood and looked like lost tourists. Finally, the radio came to life again.

"We got him. Bishop's in custody."

"Fisher?" Walsh answered. "What the hell happened?"

"It was Duncan. She spotted him. He fled and she was in

pursuit. Perez and I followed. She caught up to him. Duncan opened fire."

"Is he dead?" Kate asked Walsh.

He shrugged when Fisher came through again.

"Bishop took one in the leg. Perez is arranging for him to be transported to the nearest hospital."

Kate peered up at the sky in relief.

Walsh smiled before pressing the button. "You mind giving us a lift out of here, then?"

"On our way."

28

The dust had settled and within a few days, the team was back at Quantico. Fisher and Unit Chief Cole walked into the conference room while the team awaited an update.

"We just finished a conference call with the State Department," Cole began. "They are working with Mexico on an agreement to have Bishop returned to us, where he'll be remanded into the custody of the Houston office for prosecution."

"What about the murder of the woman in Guadalajara?" Scarborough asked.

"I don't claim to understand the political maneuvering of the State Department, but suffice it to say, it was the outcome we had hoped for." He studied Scarborough. "Are you feeling 100 percent again?"

"Yes, sir. Doing just fine."

"We got lucky that the only thing Bishop got his hands on from the medical station was a sedative," Kate said.

"And that you got there in time before he had a chance to pump enough of it into Scarborough to kill him, like he did that girl," Walsh replied.

"I'd like to recognize Duncan for the work she did as well," Cole continued. "You acted swiftly and without hesitation. Well done."

"Thank you, but like you said, it was a team effort," Duncan replied.

Cole nodded. "With that, I'll turn this over to your Senior Unit Agent to finish the briefing. Congratulations, everyone."

After Cole left the room, Fisher began. "I just want to say that I am honored to be heading up a team of agents like you." He turned to Scarborough. "You took decisive action when it appeared that we were losing ground. It almost cost you your life. Reid, your hunches were dead on with Bishop and the work you and Walsh did, along with the additional legwork you and Surrey did, it made all the difference." He looked at Duncan. "And you took your shot when you realized it was going to be the only solution. You did it without putting anyone else in harm's way." He gazed again at the team. "That said, we got our man and I know Agent Palmero and the rest of the Houston office is damn happy we did. It also means we'll be working closely with him to help him compile his case. Duncan, you and Scarborough will also be working with the Riverside field office again. They'll supply evidence to build on Palmero's case. So, we aren't finished yet, but at least we're home. That's all I've got. Thanks, guys."

The team gathered their files and started to disburse. Kate turned to Nick. "I need to talk to Levi. I'll check in with you later."

"Sure."

"Hey, Levi, you have a minute?" Kate turned to him as he pushed in his chair to leave.

"Yeah. What's up?"

She pulled him aside. "I'm sure you can probably guess what I'm about to say, but there's still the question of who was helping Carol Whitman and her son. I've had a chance to look into a few things since we got back."

"You don't waste any time, do you?" Walsh replied.

"Nope. So here's what I know. Carol Whitman's father, Theo's grandfather, served with the Bureau."

"What? Walk with me. Let's talk in your office."

Kate followed him as he headed out of the conference room. "I was just as surprised to find that out as you are." She entered her office and perched on the edge of her desk while Walsh sat down.

"How the hell did you find that out?"

"It wasn't that hard, actually. I ran a background check and discovered her maiden name was Gustafson. She was born in Alexandria, Virginia."

"Okay." Walsh appeared to wait for the big reveal.

"I discovered where she went to school and then onto college."

"You covered all the bases," Walsh said.

"I had to know the people she knew, the ones in her circle. People tend to stay in contact with college friends. They get letters of recommendation from professors, etcetera."

"Sure," he said. "Go on."

"And here's where it gets interesting." Kate pushed off the desk and returned to her chair. "She attended Georgetown."

"Wow. Good school. Gotta be pretty rich to go there too."

"Yes, sir. Her father just so happens to have a building at the school named after him. He made a sizeable donation."

"That doesn't tell me how you came to discover he was a fed," Walsh replied.

"Bear with me. When I realized he had a building named after him, I started looking into why. I found half a dozen old news articles on his FBI career. Turned out, he was integral to several high-profile investigations. Think James Ingram."

"The agent who helped with the investigation into JFK's assassination, the KKK, and just about every major investigation the Bureau came across in the 1960s?"

"Yep. Apparently, Gustafson wasn't all that dissimilar. His contributions to the Bureau were well documented," Kate added. "I have to assume the money must've come from speaking engagements, books, whatever, after he retired."

"Carol Whitman, formerly Carol Bishop, formerly Carol Gustafson, had connections at the Bureau?" Walsh asked.

"Can you imagine the people she must've been introduced to when she was growing up? You can't tell me some of those people would turn her away, given who her father was, if she asked for help."

"It would be unlikely, no doubt," Walsh replied. "Who was it then? Who manipulated the data? Who changed the logs and altered timelines to give Theo Bishop enough time to escape? We're talking serious crimes here. If it was someone inside the Bureau..."

"If it wasn't someone inside, then it was someone inside who knew someone else." Kate shook her head. "I don't know where that trail leads. In fact, I'm not sure I'm ever going to know. Carol Whitman has been arrested for helping her son. Given what her father has done, I'd be surprised if she served any time at all. They'll figure out a way to make it disappear, just as Carol did for Theo."

"You're right. They won't touch her." Walsh held her gaze. "Will you be okay with not knowing?"

"I'd be crazy to flesh this one out. Going after one of our own?

I might as well submit a letter of resignation now. Forget censure."
Kate stared off into the distance for a moment. "On the one hand, I
feel like I got my answer. There wasn't a chance in hell Carol
Whitman could do what she did for Theo and not have an expert
or two in her corner. Then I remembered something Jonathan
Surrey said to me about being okay with not getting your man."

"But we did get him," Walsh added. "We got Theo Bishop."

"Yeah. We did. That's what I'm trying to remain focused on.
Bishop can't hurt anyone else. I have to be okay with that. I don't
like not knowing the full story, but even if I did, what good would
it do me?"

"You're finally taking someone's advice, huh?" Walsh smiled.
"No, I hear what you're saying and it's the right call."

"Is it the call you would've made?" She asked.

He raised the corner of his mouth in a crooked smile. "Does it
matter what I would do?"

Kate held his gaze and saw something in his eyes. The silence
between them was enough for her to know his answer. "Well, I
need to stop by Fisher's office and talk to him about the hearing
tomorrow."

Walsh got up from the chair. "You'll get through it just fine.
We're all in your corner, Kate."

"Thanks." She followed him into the hall where he continued
to his office and she headed to see Fisher. Outside his door, Kate
began, "Hey? Can I take up a little more of your time?"

Fisher still stood at his desk and prepared to sit. "Of course. I
have a feeling I know what this is about. You go before the Board
tomorrow."

Kate sat down. "Partly, but I'm ready for that and I'll accept
whatever they decide to do. To be honest, I fully expect to be
censured."

"Just to be clear, whatever the result, it will not end in your dismissal from this post. And if I have anything to say about it, you won't receive the written reprimand at all."

"I appreciate that, but I know what I did, and I know it was wrong."

"Regardless, we've all made mistakes, Reid. In the grand scheme of things, yours pales in comparison to some I've seen go before the Board. Ruby Ridge, Waco. A lot of those guys were issued Letters of Censure and forgive me for saying so, but the shit that went down there? Way worse than tailing a colleague because he was trying to get dirt. Even Scarborough's hearing was BS if you ask me." He raised his hands. "Aside from that, what else did you want to talk about?"

"You asked me what I thought about Surrey," Kate replied.

"And you said that you didn't feel one way or the other."

"That's not entirely true. I get that he's very good at his job. He's an excellent profiler. But more than that, I learned something about myself during this investigation." She paused for just a moment. "We almost didn't get him. Bishop, I mean. And I'm not sure I would've been okay with that."

"I'm not sure any of us would've been okay with that," Fisher replied.

She nodded. "No, but Surrey said a few things to me, particularly about my personality. My work ethic."

"What are you getting at, Reid?" Fisher reached for a toothpick and placed it between his lips.

"I think I was wrong about suggesting Surrey was just okay. To be honest, I could absolutely stand to learn a thing or two from him. And not just as it relates to profiling. He seems to have learned how to compartmentalize. To keep his personal life separate. I don't think I've figured that out just yet." She inhaled a breath. "But I'd like to. If you want my opinion on whether I think

Surrey would be a good addition to this team, I'd like to say that, yes, I wholeheartedly believe he would be a great addition to our team."

Fisher smiled. "That's very good to hear." He pulled up in his chair. "Then I assume you've spoken to Scarborough about your feelings?"

"Well, no not yet."

"Oh."

Kate noticed the look on his face as though he'd revealed something he shouldn't have. "What is it?"

Fisher shook his head. "Nothing. I'm sorry...I...you should talk to him."

"Yeah. Okay." She stood up and looked more confused than ever. "Thanks." Kate headed straight for Nick's office and walked inside. "What the hell is going on?"

Nick peered up from his computer. "I'm sorry?"

"I just came out of Fisher's office. I told him what I thought about Surrey and he said I should come talk to you. What the hell is going on, Nick?"

"Christ." He walked to his door to close it.

"You're scaring me. What's this about?" she added.

"Sit down." Nick perched on the edge of his desk while Kate took a seat. "I've been kicking around an idea and I mentioned it to Fisher when we got back from Mexico to get his thoughts."

"What idea? And I'm sorry, but we live together. You didn't think to come to me first?" Kate gripped the arms of the chair with white knuckles.

"It's just an idea and I needed to ask him if it was even possible. There was no point in mentioning anything to you until I had all the facts and could speak to you with some certainty."

"Just say whatever you're going to say, Nick. Please."

"I wasn't prepared to do this here. Not here."

She waited with a stone face.

"First of all, I love you and nothing will ever change that."

She shifted uncomfortably in her seat.

"Now I can see that I've made you more nervous. Okay, here's the deal. I've been thinking about this for some time. Pretty much since we got back from Rio." He held her gaze. "Kate, I'm going to ask for a transfer." He raised his hands. "It's not for the reason you think. It has nothing to do with Fisher taking the lead role. He deserved it and I do not hold it against him."

"A transfer? You've been thinking about this for months and have said nothing to me?"

"Only because I wasn't sure. I'm still not, frankly, but the more I think about it, the more I think that maybe it would be best."

"For who?" Her tone was harsh and louder than she had intended.

"Kate, you are an incredibly talented agent. You've proven that again on the Bishop case. Noah Quinn was paranoid about you because your talent far exceeded his. I think if we're both being honest, we both can see that you would absolutely thrive if I gave you the room to do so. And I haven't."

Her shoulders dropped and she lowered her gaze.

"You know I'm right. The last thing I ever wanted to do was to stand in your way. I wanted you to join the Bureau because I saw it in you then. I still see it only it's much stronger now." He pushed off the desk and squatted in front of her. "But here's the takeaway. If a transfer was to happen, I would want it to be close. I know I can't go back to the Washington Field office. Jameson is in charge there now. But other offices would make it possible for me to stay here—with you."

Kate's eyes reddened as she held his gaze.

"Given the fact that I was recently demoted, I'm not sure what, if any other office, would want me on board, let alone as their senior agent. But Fisher thinks that given my record with the Bureau and a good recommendation from Cole, it could be possible."

"I don't want you to leave, Nick." She reached for his hands. "I can't do this without you."

"Oh, yes you can. You've proven that time and time again. But I don't want to leave you, Kate. And I know we can make this work. Somehow. It wouldn't be easy, but people do it all the time."

She nodded and wiped away a rogue tear.

Nick raised his index finger and stood up. He walked around his desk and reached for his laptop bag. Inside the bag, he retrieved a box.

Kate looked at the box and her lips parted slightly with a small gasp of breath.

Nick returned to her side and bent down on one knee. "I've had my problems with alcohol and I'm working on that every day. I've also had my problems with stepping back so you could do what you needed to do to learn and grow as an agent. I'm trying to fix that too." He opened the box to reveal the stunning solitaire inside. "I am a flawed human being. But I am also so in love with you. Kate, will you be my wife?"

Tears ran down her cheeks with reckless abandon. She looked at the ring and turned her sights to Nick. He was the third man who had wanted to marry her. Kate had agreed to the first one, but it had ended before it began. The second man was murdered before he could ask, and it was only later she discovered his intentions. Now there was Nick. A man she loved in a way she didn't think was possible. Here he was asking to spend the rest of his life with her yet he was also abandoning her for reasons she knew were right but struggled to accept.

His face shifted anxiously in the wake of her delay.

She held his gaze and her eyes smiled. "Yes."

Nick exhaled. "Oh, thank God. You had me worried for a second." He laughed and wrapped his arms around her. "I love you, Kate."

"I love you, too."

THE END

ABOUT THE AUTHOR

Robin Mahle has published more than 30 novels in the mystery/thriller genre. She also writes historical fiction as <u>Christine Chase.</u>

It is Robin's fast-paced style of storytelling combined with tense action and thrilling twists that bring her readers back for more. So be sure sure to subscribe to her newsletter to keep up on all the latest releases, sales, and giveaways. Go to <u>robinmahle.com</u> and sign up today!

If you enjoyed Ms. Mahle's work, please share your experience by leaving a review on <u>Amazon.</u>

ALSO BY ROBIN MAHLE

The Kate Reid FBI Thriller Series (17 books)

The Chef (stand-alone psych thriller)

The Man in My Attic (stand-alone psych thriller)

The Compound (standalone psych thriller)

The Remy Fontaine Fugitive Hunter Thrillers (4 books)

The Det. Rebecca Ellis Thrillers (5 books)

The Allison Hart PI Thrillers (5 Books)

The Lacy Merrick Thrillers (4 books)

**Visit robinmahle.com and sign up to receive Robin's Newsletter so you can stay up to date on her new releases, events, contests and even exclusive new material!